HOPE OF REDEMPTION

by

Steve Graziani

Grazarts Publishing

Printed in the United States of America
First Printing, 2017

ISBN 978-0-9961375-6-0

Grazarts Publishing
1839 Blake Ave, Loft 12
Los Angeles, CA, 90039

www.grazarts.com

Cover Art by Steve Graziani

To:
Kim & Risa

CHAPTER ONE

A blanket of trees gently waves on the hillside. The Ozark Mountains are in late summer, slowly inching towards fall, and the forest has just started to dance with colors. The yellows and oranges of the sugar maples compete with the bright reds of the silver maples, all cushioned on a thousand shades of green.

The number of colors in the trees is matched by the variety of lifestyles of those that live among them, pockets of worlds living out of sync with time... with little care for what the land below thinks.

Hope McCoy lives in one of these pockets... or just on the edge of one. This angelic-looking woman of nineteen sits in a homemade rattan chair on the porch of her small isolated cabin. The soft golden locks that frame her face only seem to be missing a halo, though a hint in her smile suggests the contrary.

Hope sees something different in the lush scenery, as if she were viewing the world through her own private kaleidoscope. She has always walked a bit of a different path... and has never been that interested in hiding it.

An easel holding a blank canvas rests on the porch in front of Hope. She sits staring at it and carefully studies the nature that lies beyond. Then she closes her eyes while a light breeze ruffles her sundress. When she opens them, there is an intense resolve in her glare.

Hope picks up a brush and almost viciously attacks the canvas with bold strokes of blood red crimson and jet-black paint. Arching stroke after stroke, she builds her dark vision. The canvas shudders on its easel. As it begins to fall, Hope's left hand grabs the top to steady it while her right hand continues the inspired attack. In her creative frenzy, a blob of red paint splatters back onto Hope's cheek. She swiftly smears most of it away with the back of her hand, and then continues assaulting the canvas.

Exhausting her primal urge, Hope collapses back in her chair. The canvas is completed, a dark abstract that would have psychiatrists drooling with theories... but they'd all be wrong. Hope notices a smear of blood red paint still on her finger. She licks it off and smiles.

On the far side of the canyon, a road skirts the waist of the mountain, semi-obscured by trees. Tiny flashes of light moving between openings in the foliage catch Hope's attention. She leans forward and brushes a delicate mobile of bird skeletons aside to take her binoculars from the porch post. Hope thinks... *a girl's got to keep an eye on the neighborhood.*

Fleeting glimpses of a minivan reveal a full luggage rack. Hope lowers the glasses, shakes her head and lets out a sigh, "More visitors... it's gettin' rightly overworked."

This is Hope McCoy... and perhaps what's missing is not a halo... but horns.

CHAPTER TWO

Robert fumbles with a map while trying to steer with his elbows. His wife, Mary, is busy taking photos out the window... doing her best to ignore Robert.

A sudden gust of wind whips through the window of the minivan and slaps the map into Robert's face. He quickly pulls it away, but not before a squeaking swerve on the road. Mary stopped counting how often Robert does something foolish years ago, but he still senses her silent snicker. He snaps, "I could use some help here... We already have enough damn pictures of trees... Where the hell are we?"

"Coming into the town of Redemption... and I wanted a picture of the one you're going to crash us into," she replies.

Robert tries glancing again at the crumpled map while he drives. "How the hell do you know that?"

Mary Goodridge slyly points at a road sign up ahead: "*WELCOME TO THE FRIENDLY TOWN OF REDEMPTION - POPULATION 258*"

Robert grumbles under his breath as Mary grins. The Goodridges have been married for twenty-two long years.

Robert's a little apprehensive as they slowly drive down Main Street of Redemption. The small town is pristine... too pristine. Not a piece of trash can be seen anywhere. The spotless store windows frame their displays. It's like a town straight out of a Norman Rockwell painting, frozen in time... with nothing that could be considered even slightly offensive.

But what has their full attention is that the streets are empty... not just lightly active, but absolutely desolate... not a man, woman, child or dog. Robert slows the car down to almost a crawl.

"Where is everyone?" he asks, not necessarily expecting an answer... though he knows he'll get one.

"Do you think I've got a swami's turban on my head?" Mary snaps in her perky style.

Robert grumbles under his breath again, knowing she will never let him have the last word.

He pulls the minivan into a parking space in front of the Holy Cross Hardware and quietly scans the length of the street, distrustful of the stillness. Nothing. No one.

Mary breaks the silence, "We just going to sit here and bake in the car?"

The unknown has more appeal than her chiding, so Robert opens the door and gets out. He glances over, disappointed that Mary gets out as well.

With a slight sigh, Robert steps onto the sidewalk and directly up to the hardware store's front door. A hand-printed sign hangs on it: *BACK IN AN HOUR – IF YOU HAVE NEEDS LEAVE MONEY ON COUNTER.*

Bewildered, Robert twists the door's knob and it opens. He sticks his head in... nobody. "Hello... anyone here?" he calls... no response. Closing the door, he shakes his head and glances up and down the street... still no one.

"Where is everybody?" Mary asks, stating the question as if for the very first time. "This must be the emptiest town around."

Robert doesn't waste time pointing out that it's the only town they've seen in fifty miles. With a wave back at the hardware store sign, he says, "And apparently the most trusting one."

Voicing more concern, she asks again, "Rob, where are they?"

"How the hell should I know?"

GONG... sounds a bell in the distance, trailed by hollow echoes.

They both turn to see a church at the end of the street. It's clearly the most prominent building in town. Another gong comes from the church steeple.

"There's your answer... satisfied?" says Robert.

"But it's Tuesday," she responds, clearly not satisfied.

"Maybe it's a wedding, or a funeral ... how should I know?"

The church is prominent not only because of its size, but because it's placed at the far end of town in the dead center of Main Street. For a town the size of Redemption, the far end is not all that far. High above it, on the hill behind the church, is a fifty-foot tall white cross, as if the church didn't make enough of a statement on its own.

The double doors of the church swing wide open and towns-folk stream out in their Sunday best, though it's Tuesday. When they see Robert and Mary standing down the street, all their smiles broaden, as if someone had set out a Sunday feast for them... on a Tuesday.

As a group, the townsfolk start walking towards the Goodridges. As they continue forward many peel off into different buildings. Even those who split away never take their eyes from the town's new visitors. It seems like the whole movement is choreographed... a dance that has been performed before.

Robert wonders if it's his imagination, but he can still feel the burn from the eyes of all those who have gone indoors, even as the smaller delegation in the street continues towards them. He leans over and whispers to Mary, "Think we oughta get back in the car."

"Nonsense, Rob... They look like friendly people to me."

"Too friendly, if you ask me," he replies. Before he can object any further the group is upon them. Robert puts on the best fake smile he can muster.

The leader of the vanguard, a robust man, shoves his hand out well before reaching Robert and Mary. With a booming, "Well, hain't this great, we were a-hankerin' fer some visitors, and here ya'll are... My name's Marcus, Marcus McCoy. I'm the mayor of Redemption." Marcus grabs Robert's hand in both of his and shakes it with vigor. "Who you folks be?"

Caught off guard by this unabashed enthusiasm, Robert can't help glancing down to count fingers when Marcus finally lets go. Looking up, he says hesitantly, "Robert and Mary... Goodridge."

Meanwhile, a willowy lean man sleazes over, peeks into the windows of their minivan, and rejoins the group. "And I'm Pastor Cain," he says, turning back toward the new arrivals. "No young'uns with ya'll?"

Mary shows none of the guarded nature of her husband. With a laugh, she says, "Off to college... thank goodness. You know what raising kids can be like... you want them forever but you're happy when their gone."

Glancing around at the sparsely populated street, Robert comments, "I guess you don't get a lot of visitors."

"Don'tcha fret, we gits our few... I can git ya'll a dern good price at the bed n' breakfast up yonder, if ya'll wanna settle in apiece... We got lively doin's tonight at the Last Chance Saloon," says Marcus, with a politician's smile.

Gabriel, the last of the three in the welcoming party, nods his silent agreement.

It's all way too friendly to Robert's liking. He replies, "We're actually planning on racking up a few more miles tonight."

Mary elbows him... with *that* look. "You said your back was hurting," she says and turns to Marcus. "We'd be happy to join in on the festivities."

Marcus grins and gives Robert an all too friendly nudge, "Bob, gotcha yourself snared good that time, didn't ya?" He adds, with a wave of his hand, "Jes' park on down next to the B&B and we'll help ya'll with yer pokes."

Mary's the only one that hears Robert's silent growl.

"Well... guess it would be nice to have a shower and a bit of rest," Robert says, with a defeated tone.

"That's jes' fine... we'ez don't kick up our heels till later," says Marcus with too much satisfaction. Pastor Cain seems very pleased as well.

Gabriel appears a little less enthusiastic. He's met new visitors many times... maybe too many.

As Robert and Mary start to get back in their minivan, he pauses a second, and gives a glance back at the trio of smiling men. There's something that's nagging at him, but he just can't put his finger on it. Robert's concerns are interrupted by...

"Are you getting in the car... or not?"

It's late afternoon and Main Street is back to its normal buzz, if it can be called a buzz in a town so small. A few stores are open and people meander on sidewalks. Not far from the Holy Cross Hardware is Abigail's Renewal General Store. Fronted by a large deck, it has a makeshift sign nailed up: *THE CRACKERBARREL*. A few folk sit around on the deck jawing. Life is good now that there are visitors.

Gabriel, from the earlier meeting, is the town's handyman, and the best shine brewer around. He casually wanders down the street alongside of Marcus. From some distance behind them, they hear the familiar sound of a skateboard. Both grimace, knowing what's coming.

Marcus peels off with, "Whatever it is, I hain't a-hankerin to hear her crazy ideas today. Run interference fer me, Gabe."

Though he has absolutely no interest in notions, Marcus quickly disappears into a notions store,

Hope skateboards down the street, appearing oblivious to the townsfolk who turn away as she passes. When she reaches Gabriel, she says, "Hey, old man... My pa's gittin' right quick, hain't he?"

"Might be you jes' take a passel of patience and he hain't in the mood," Gabriel says. Though sounding grumpy, his tone can't hide the kindred spirit he shares with Hope.

With a friendly poke at Gabriel's side, Hope says, "You didn't skedaddle."

"Someone has to talk to you... or you jes' won't go away." He stops and turn to her, "What's on your mind, Hope?"

"See you got visitors... it settled?" she asks.

"Girl, you know right well we'ez hain't done the formals yet." Gabriel takes the official line, regardless of his personal views. This can be heard in his voice.

"Don't rightly matter anymore, does it? Thought you would be one to understand that," she says, as if looking for a fight.

It's clear where this is heading, and Gabriel has gone down this path too often. "If you's gonna go on 'bouts your brush strokes... might be you shouldn't have stopped feedin' the town."

"I'm jes' sayin' it's gittin' stale," she counters.

"Not my contraptions... jes' your artsy eyeballin'," Gabriel says as he turns to leave.

"But I... " Hope starts to say.

He cuts her off with, "'Nuff said, girl... I got chores." Gabriel heads down the street before Hope can say anymore. Though he's not going to admit it, he knows exactly what she means.

CHAPTER THREE

The Goodridges have had their rest, and Robert would love nothing more than to hit the road. Unfortunately, he knows Mary is not about to let him get away with it. This is borne out by her busily getting dressed for the evening's festivities. Robert tries to ignore this by obsessively trying to find a channel on a television with zero reception.

"Leave that box alone and get dressed... I think we're the guests of honor," says Mary with energetic enthusiasm.

Robert slaps the uncooperative television on the side, jiggling the snow. He figures the longer he drags his feet, the less time they'll have to spend at this backwoods shindig. He makes one last attempt at a reprieve.

"We really need to go to this thing? They're going to... what did they say... kick up their heels, whether we're there or not. Let's get a good night's rest and take off early in the morning." Even as he says this, he knows there's a snowball's chance in hell of changing her mind.

Mary pushes past Robert and snaps off the snowy television. "Nonsense. How many times are we the guests of honor... anywhere? We're going! Now get your jacket."

A loud knock sounds sharply at the door.

"Who could that be?" Mary asks.

Robert shakes his head at the question, and then heads for the door, "Maybe someone that can fix the damn television."

He opens the door to find a nineteen-year old, freckle-faced young man standing there.

"Hi... I'm Ethan. They sent me to fetch ya'll to the festivities," the young man says. Robert simply stares at him. The boy adds, "I run errands for the town council." He tries to make his duty sound important, as all young men do.

Feeling pushed, Robert puffs up loudly, "We will... "

Mary is quick to cut him off, "We will... be there in a few minutes. Thank you for stopping by... Ethan."

Before anything else can be said, Robert slams the door on the freckle-faced boy. Mary gives him *that* glare.

Fifteen minutes later, the Goodridges approach the door of the Last Chance Saloon. Loud merrymaking can be heard from inside. As they cover the last few feet, Robert keeps glancing over his shoulder.

"What are you looking for?" Mary asks. She's too busy brushing herself off for their entrance to really care.

"That kid has been following us in the shadows, all the way. I feel like I'm being herded."

"That's nice, dear... Now you're going to be nice in here... understand?" With one last brush at her skirt, she reaches out and opens the door.

A few strong drinks, in a short window of time, have an amazing effect on Robert's temperament. It doesn't hurt that a very attractive barmaid named Prudence is serving them up. Aaron, the owner and bartender, and a member of the town council, makes sure those drinks are especially strong. With his way of mixing, the drinks taste deceptively benign. Everyone has a job... this is one of his.

The locals are partying, but with an air of improvisation, as if it's being put on for show. Far too many of the partyers keep sneaking glances at the Goodridges throughout the evening. And there are far too few arguments for this many people drinking in a bar.

This doesn't seem to bother Robert because he's already two sheets to the wind, and having far too much fun poking jibes at the locals' dialect. No one seems to mind... or, at least, they're not showing it.

In the background of the celebration, Pastor Cain wanders about stealthily with a small notebook in hand. He seems to be meticulously scribing all that's going on... especially with the visitors. His skulking around and trying to be unnoticed, is almost comic, but he's oblivious to it.

Over the course of the evening, it doesn't take much for the townsfolk to separate Robert from Mary and positioning them at opposite ends of the bar. And by now they each enjoy being their own focus of attention.

Mary is just about as buzzed as her husband, but far less aggressively. She is beaming from the flirtation lavished upon her by a virile local farmer named Clarence. Flirting is something of an ancient memory to her, having been married so long. The Goodridges' constant banter and bickering are what pass for flirting between them now. Mary likes the touch of warmer attention Clarence shows her, even if he's a ridiculously younger man.

"So... how long ya'll been hitched?" Clarence asks.

It's not exactly the question she wanted to hear, but the young man is still focused on her.

"Twenty-two long years now, but it's not my first rodeo. I was married once before... a *long time* ago." She punctuates it with a laugh, and then wonders why she mentioned that at all... maybe to sound more worldly.

"What happened to that one?" Clarence asks, while leaning in a bit closer.

"He drank too much, so I got rid of him... You know how that goes," she says with a slightly guilty grin.

Clarence gives a slight glance over at Pastor Cain, who seems to be inching closer, but trying not to look like it. Clarence asks, "What's you mean by... got rid of him?"

Slapping Clarence on the knee, Mary giggles, "Well, he's still kicking around... if that's what you're getting at."

She almost topples from her barstool. Clarence catches her. Mary likes that as well.

Pastor Cain, like an unsavory little rat, creeps close and quickly scribbles a note in his pad.

While Mary carries on her little flirtation, Robert gets truly sloshed at the other end of the bar. He cops a little feel of Prudence, the barmaid, and quickly pulls his hand back as if were an innocent accident... after all, as he excuses himself, she *was* cozying up beside him.

He slurs, "Can't believe I just did that."

Prudence gives him a big smile, "Jes' men bein' men... no fret to me." After which she glances over her shoulder at Pastor Cain, who is busy scribbling another note in his pad.

Marcus and four members of the town council sit at a small, country version of a medieval roundtable tucked into the far end of the room. Instead of bar drinks, they all have sodas... all but Gabriel.

While the rest pretend not to notice, Gabriel pulls a small jug out from under the table and pours a bit of moonshine in his soda. Hanna, Marcus' wife, is the only one to shake her head at his well-known and regular deception. Gabriel is too important to the group to challenge him on this.

After all, life is picture perfect in Redemption... no use smudging the illusion. Aaron puts his bartender's apron aside and joins the council.

"Isn't the pastor finished?" asks Naomi. She's the town's librarian and looks the part, all prim and proper.

Aaron points over his shoulder, "He's on his way."

Pastor Cain, the seventh member of the council, finally comes over and takes a seat.

"Well, how's it fixin' out?" asks Marcus.

The pastor smiles, which is rare, and shakes his little notebook, "They's earned a place amongst us."

"With right slim pickin's, can't believe we'ez still goin' through this dance," grumbles Gabriel.

Sounding righteous, Hanna says, "We go through it 'cause that's what we do here in Redemption... And it's the right way of a doin' things."

Looking at Marcus, Naomi starts, "If that daughter of yourn hadn't stopped... "

Marcus' harsh glare cuts her off.

"Like I done said, these formals don't rightly make sense," Gabriel repeats. "But done is done... I got fixin's to be gittin' to." Without waiting for a response, Gabriel gets up, takes his jug and leaves.

"'Bouts time to git to wrappin' things up," Aaron says as he gets up.

Marcus holds up two fingers and the bar owner gives him a nod of understanding. Before he heads for the bar, Aaron waves for Daniel to join him. "Think I'll be needin' a hand to give our good visitors a ride back to the manger."

Daniel, only twenty, is unofficially part of the council. Like Ethan, he carries out errands for the decision makers. He nods without comment and heads to converge with Aaron.

A half-hour later, Daniel arrives at the B&B with a drunken Robert and an equally toasted Mary. A couple folks from the B&B are waiting to help the Goodridges out of the truck. Once the Goodridges are inside, Daniel waves at the darkness across the street.

Taillights switch on in the blackness of the alley. A tow truck backs up across the road and quietly two men jump out and hook the rig up to the Goodridges' minivan. They do this with practiced precision. They jump back into the truck and drive away with the Goodridges' means of transportation... cleanly and quickly.

CHAPTER FOUR

Robert sits up on a metal bunk, but his eyes remain shut. He holds his head against what is coming... a massive hangover. He tries but he cannot remember how they left the bar. Nothing registers yet, except that the bed is hard and cold.

Mary screeches: "Where the hell are we?"

That registers! He opens his eyes and glances around... when the world comes into focus; it is not the B&B. The room is a harsh, barren stone cell with no windows and a metal grated floor. There's a closed steel door at one end of the room and open metal double-doors at the other. They lead into darkness. Light flickers down from neon above like Morse code... every dash echoes through Robert's aching head.

Still wobbly, he staggers to the closed door and tries to open it. It won't budge. He bangs on it with his fist. Big mistake... he grabs his head. When the echo clears, he peers back towards the open doors at the other end and the dark throat beyond them. They're too open to risk just yet.

Mary yells again, "Robert... I said, where are we?"

He waves at her to back off and snaps, "I'm... trying... to... find... out." He adds, "Could you *please* keep your voice below a bullhorn?"

"But... "

"But nothing! Shut up! There must be an explanation... a quiet one." His voice reverberates off the walls, causing him to grimace yet again.

A sharp crackle comes from a speaker mounted high on the wall. Then come repetitive, and way too loud, hollow thumping sounds as if someone were tapping on a microphone. Thump... thump.

"I hain't teched, I can see the light... I'm a fixin' to git to it." It's the voice of Marcus.

Mary, as though whispering will hide them, "Who's he talking to?"

"Like I should know?" responds Robert, without taking his eyes off the speakers.

The speakers crackle once again. This time it's clear the Goodridges are being addressed. "Mornin', mightin' ya'll join us... we'ez jest yonder down the tunnel."

Despite his hangover, Robert yells at the speaker, "We're not going anywhere ... What the fuck is going on here?"

Marcus' comes back, "Hain't no call fer such wordin'. Jes' might be I can help ya'll out in gittin' goin'."

Robert peers back and forth between the two doors, anxious to see where this help is going to come from. He also looks for something that can be used as a weapon. Nothing stands out that's not bolted down in the barren room. Waiting for an assault always distorts time... a few seconds feel like minutes to Robert.

Whoosh! ... A blast of flames shoots up from the floor grate nearest the closed door.

Mary screams and jumps on one of the metal bunks.

"Better be gittin'," blares from the speakers. A second blast of flames comes from the floor, one grid closer. Robert doesn't want to be pushed into that dark tunnel, but his options are limited... if any. He grabs Mary's arm. Despite her wailing panic, he pulls her from the bunk and pushes her towards the open doorway. A third blast shoots up where they had been.

"Now we'ez movin'," cracks the speaker.

As soon as Robert and Mary barge into the throat of black-ness, the doors swing closed behind them with a loud clang!

The Goodridges are swallowed.

In the darkness Mary loudly whispers, "You grabbed me... that hurt!"

Robert laughs, happy she's out of her crying, screaming mode.

Neon lights flicker to life above them. They find themselves sitting in a tunnel carved out of rock, as was their stone cell, but narrower. Down the center are rail tracks... where they lead, other than into darkness, is unclear. Speakers are carved into the rock walls, just as in the cell.

They crackle, "'Nuff rest time... we'ez need to keep workin' together."

With a jolt that shakes the floor, the closed metal doors start creaking forward on the rails. They stretch from wall to wall, so there's no escaping them.

Mary screams at the speaker, "What do you want from us?"

Robert struggles to his feet and helps Mary up. "I guess they want us to move on down the tunnel."

"But why?" Mary whimpers.

"Mary! I don't know," says an exhausted Robert. He glares up at the speaker and musters as much defiance as he can. "When my wife and I get a hold of you... "

The speakers don't care. The metal barricade continues for-ward. So do Robert and Mary.

The Goodridges emerge from the tunnel into a sun-drenched pit. The brightness strains their eyes at first. When they are able to focus, they see twelve-foot high spiked log walls surrounding the pit.

The pit is not a pit... it's an arena.

A round of applause from above greets them. High up, behind the spiked logs, are bleachers filled with townsfolk. All are dressed in casual picnic attire. The arena is about ninety feet in diameter. Bleachers circle the entire area, except for one section. Resting in that divide is a grandstand where the town council sits.

If the arena isn't ominous enough, there's an apparatus within it that has Robert more concerned. A very thick four-foot high mechanical post extends up from the center of the circle. It's fitted with a collar that supports two long blades that extend from log wall to log wall.

Robert doesn't immediately see any motor or mechanism attached to this bizarre apparatus. On second look, though, he sees a massive sprocket chain that comes out of a pipe near the wall. It leads to gears that are engaged by another chain that extends through the wall. None of this makes sense to him.

Even less makes sense to Mary, who now has shifted back into panic mode. Uncontrollably, her feet seem to be running in place. Robert takes her by the shoulders and forces her to look in his eyes.

"Calm down ... this is all some kind of sick joke," he tries to assure her. He doesn't believe his own words, but her panic doesn't serve either of them.

The applause swells again.

Robert looks up to see Marcus step up to a podium on the grandstand.

Marcus taps on the mic mounted on the podium. "Robert and Mary, fine of ya'll to join our doin's... 'Specially, with you bein' the guests of honor."

"What the hell are you talking... " Robert yells.

He's cut off by Marcus, "Done told ya'll afore, hain't no use fer such wordin'."

"What are you going to do for bad words?" yells Robert.

Mary grips his hand tighter, as if politeness would make any difference now. He brushes her hand away. Robert stands in braced defiance. He turns 360 degrees around, glaring at the crowd.

When his gaze returns to Marcus, Robert says, "If you're going to kill us, can't you do it in good English!"

"What do you mean... kill us?" Mary whimpers.

Robert pats her shoulder and quietly says, "Sorry... I didn't mean kill us."

"Ya'll thought our wordin' prit' near funny last night. Hain't said nothin' 'bouts killin'... yet," says Marcus.

This comment gets a muffled laugh from the townsfolk, which in turn get a harsh glare from Marcus... after all, things have to be done with appropriate decorum. Marcus gestures for Pastor Cain to come to the podium.

The pastor steps to the mic and clears his throat. "I hain't goin' thru the whole accountin'... Jes' a few spec's."

Robert yells up, making a point of not using any profanity, "What's this about? ... What did we do to you people?"

Marcus leans in next to Pastor Cain, "Rest yer heels till the good pastor finishes... Git on with it, pastor."

Pastor Cain dryly looks back to his pad and reads, "Blas-phemin'... Bein' downright uppity... shuckin' kin... That 'bouts a nuff."

Mary, petrified of the crowd, just stares at Robert. She meekly asks, "What are they talking about? I don't get it."

Robert, without even looking at her, gestures for Mary to be quiet. He yells back to the grandstand, "So what the fuck do you want from us... an apology?"

"Tsk tsk, such language again... All I is askin' is if ya'll want to be redeemed for your sins?" Pastor Cain calmly says.

"If it gets us the 'F' out of here... then fine, we'll do it... whatever you want." By now Robert is sure nothing he can say will stop this. He's just going through the motions for Mary... and perhaps to stall while he looks for another out.

Marcus steps up and gently pushes Pastor Cain aside. "That's settled... 'nuff jawin'." He addresses the crowd now, "We'ez gonna have a lawful redeemin' that keeps us all in a right peaceful state... A quick reminder, don't ya'll forget the picnic directly followin' today's redeemin' ceremony."

He starts to gesture toward Gabriel, but Pastor Cain quickly steps up and sticks a slip of paper in front of him. Marcus takes a second to read the note.

Though he looks a bit put out by the interruption, he nods to the Pastor. "I've been reminded that Charity has a new berry cobbler recipe she's achin' to share with ya'll after the doin's." Marcus shakes his head at the timing.

Charity waves with a smile from her seat in the bleachers. Charity uses her pies to gather gossip on folks. Even in a picture perfect town, gossip thrives.

With an irritated glance all around, making sure there are no more announcements, Marcus nods over to Gabriel. Gabriel comes to a mechanical box on the grandstand. The crowd cheers.

It's clear he has somewhat of an honored role in this tradition. He makes a slight bow to the audience, but shows little enthusiasm. After one last glance down into the arena to make sure everything is as it's supposed to be, he pulls one of four large levers on the box.

With a sharp mechanical clank from the thick pole in the center of the arena, the blade it supports shudders. The blade begins to rotate, slowly at first... and then gradually picks up speed. The leading edge glistens with recent sharpening.

Mary is vapor-locked, glancing all about for a door that doesn't exist. Robert grabs her by the shoulders and shakes her. He needs her to focus.

"Mary, when I yell, you do what I say... no arguments." After a glance at the approaching blade, he adds, "I love you."

Those rare words from Robert are just enough to catch her attention. She vigorously nods her head in understanding. Mary even manages to muster a broken smile... for a fragment of a second.

As the blade approaches, Robert pulls Mary to the ground with a loud, "Stay down till I say!" The first blade swishes over them. Mary, in panic, starts to get up but Robert tugs her back down until the second half of the blade passes.

There's applause from the gallery. They want a dark redemption, but they want a drawn out show in getting there.

Watching the event with a discerning eye, Gabriel pulls another lever on the grandstand. With a grinding sound, the collar holding the blade lowers.

Robert drags Mary to her feet, all the while timing the blade's advance. "When I yell jump... you jump!" She glances in panic between Robert and the approaching blade. "Jump now!" Robert yells.

In unison they jump over the swishing blade. Both clear it but Mary trips as she lands. There's no time to wrestle her to her feet so Robert yells, "Stay flat!"

He easily jumps over the next pass. The blade clears Mary.

Up on the grandstand, Marcus gives Gabriel a puzzled shrug. Gabriel just smiles as he takes hold of two levers. The first, he pulls just a little, and then he shifts both hands on the second, in preparation to pull at the right moment.

The blade picks up speed. Robert doesn't have time to get to Mary and lift her up before the next impending pass. He can only hope it doesn't lower much farther. Robert counts to himself, trying to time the new speed. When it's about four feet away, Robert jumps again. To his surprise, and at Gabriel's command, so does the blade! It slices Robert mid-section, spewing a trail of flying blood as it goes. Both halves of Robert fall to the ground.

Mary lies frozen, staring at the two halves of her husband. His mouth still gasps for useless air... his eyes flicker, not yet accepting what has happened. She curls into a fetal position. She's not even aware of the spinning blade. So caught up in the light drifting from Robert's eyes, she doesn't hear the next loud clank. The blade drops to within eight inches of the dirt. It redeems her... horizontally.

The crowd roars at the spectacle.

On a cliff high above the west side of the arena is Hope's Perch, a vantage point where she watches the games. It's been some time since Hope's been invited to the actual event... something that doesn't fret her. Hope's little landing is all decked out with a lawn chair, an ice chest and a little side table with an umbrella.

She watches the spectacle through her binoculars. Once Mary's ordeal is concluded, Hope takes a drag from a joint and stands up. With a lackluster smile, she holds one thumb up and one thumb down.

She mumbles to herself, "This screams fer change."

Down in the arena, few are interested in Hope's opinion. Few even look up in her direction. The only one that bothers to do so is Gabriel, and he seems to get her ambiguous thumb signals. Gabriel takes a breath and releases a reluctant smile and nods to the odd girl on the perch.

Hope gives a slight wave and retreats.

With a showman's timing, Marcus gestures Gabriel to the podium. The gallery's applause grows as he approaches the mic. When he steps up, and he tips his hat then, "Ya'll makin' me as red-faced as a summer rose... Jus' wait fer my next idea... Ya'll gonna love it."

After playing his part in the show, Gabriel steps back. Actually, this was one of his oldies. He sees things as getting a bit stale as well, but he disregards it as just being moody. When he gets to coming up with a new creation, Gabriel's sure he'll snap out of it.

CHAPTER FIVE

It's midday services in the town of Redemption. The day of the week doesn't matter, since there are midday services every day of the week. At the pulpit is Pastor Cain, while the town council fills the front pew. Not that services are obligatory, but very few would dare to not show up... that is, excepting Hope.

"We want to thank you, Lord, for the prit' near steady stream of sinners... For the chance to set 'em on the right path to salvation." If Pastor Cain knows nothing else, he knows where to place pauses in a good sermon.

He gets a rousing 'Amen' from the congregation.

"And... fer doin' our duty we gets to live in peace and harmony." He gives the room another well-timed pause.

"Amen!" rings out from the pews.

Cain continues, "And we pray one of your instruments fer providin' sees the error of her ways."

Many in the congregation involuntarily glance at Marcus... the wise ones don't do so for long. Gabriel leans into Marcus. "That man hain't never gonna let up on Hope."

"At least she's off-limits... That's the best I can do for her," replies Marcus.

With life rolling on smoothly in town, no one will challenge his authority over that. He still holds onto the hope that his daughter's thinking will come back around... not a lot of hope.

With her legs straddling the chapel roof's ridge, Hope sits near its steeple. She occasionally gets a kick out of listening stealthily in on the self-righteous sermons. Something about the mixture of their absurd and hypocritical nature appeals to her artistic nature. Once she's had enough, she lets out a soft laugh and takes another hit of a joint.

Another sunny afternoon in the Ozark Mountains finds Hope lazing again on the front porch of her cabin. She's kicked back with her feet propped up on the rail. Hiking boots and sundress... the contradiction that is Hope.

The cabin is well isolated from the town by road, but is only a fifteen-minute walk from her cliff perch that overlooks the town and its gruesome arena.

Sipping ice tea, Hope occasionally picks up her binoculars to check out the hillside. On one of her passes, she sees three young backpackers on a hilly meadow well above the tree line. They seem to be hiking directly towards Redemption, but they probably don't realize it. Normally Hope would stay out of it. The town needs to feed. But more and more she's become conflicted. She tries to ignore them.

Finally she slams down the binoculars. "Dang!" Hope grabs a small bag and heads off in that direction.

Tom Klein kicks at dandelions as he walks through the meadow. The floating seeds that drift in the light breeze fascinate him. It doesn't take much to fascinate Tom. He's a young man of eighteen, and is blessed with the feeling that the world is still new. His imagination constantly interrupts his reality.

Rick, an athletic looking young man, walks alongside his girlfriend, Lisa. She's just plain *hot*. They both follow Tom by a few yards. All wear backpacks... exploring an America that's not on the beaten path.

Tom mumbles to himself, while energetically scribbling in a note pad. He bursts with energy, "I got it... aliens fly over and drop dust that impregnates all the flowers."

"What drivel are you going on about now?" asks Lisa. It's clear from her tone that Tom's not her favorite person.

Tom continues, ignoring Lisa, "And... and the flowers develop the ability to shoot little barbs... that turn humans into slaves... yeah." As he scribbles more, "Gotta get that down."

Not liking being ignored, Lisa flips Tom the bird. Rick shakes his head as he reaches up and tries to bring her finger down. Tom is Rick's friend. For Lisa, unfortunately, that means he comes with the relationship package.

"Tom, I think they already did a movie like that... something about triffids back in the sixties," Rick says. Rick's a true jock but he still has a kinship for his childhood friend and his crazy imagination. Sometimes it's a friendship that's strained.

Tom, without turning, "I know... I know... but this is different... it's much bigger."

An irritated Lisa snaps, "Who cares? You and that damn note pad... All you do is take your infernal notes... you never finish writing anything!" She punctuates this by making a nasty face at Tom's back.

Tom spins around just in time to catch Lisa in mid-face-making. "I refuse to let you stifle my creativity."

As Lisa tries to come up with a mean snappy response, Tom stares off past her. He points at something over her shoulder. Both Rick and Lisa turn. An angelic looking girl in a fetching, translucent sundress emerges from the tree line into the meadow.

Hope heads straight towards them.

Even with Hope at a distance, Lisa's streak of jealousy emerges. "Who's she... and what the hell's she doing out here?"

"Maybe... it's her mountains," says Rick. He loves Lisa, but sometimes she can be a royal pain in the ass.

"She looks like an angel," is all Tom says, though the glow in his eyes says much more.

Hope strides across the meadow, without the slightest hint of caution in her movement. Tom can't take his eyes off her and he has no desire to write in his note pad... only to watch.

Once Hope reaches the trio she remains quiet as she takes a good look at each of the new arrivals. Her perusing skips over Lisa quickly, but she gives both guys their due.

Lisa, uncomfortable with this, grouses, "Something you want, girl?"

Hope ignores her. She reaches into her sundress pocket and, with a smile, pulls out a joint, "Ya'll gotta a light?"

If Rick and Tom went for their lighters any quicker they would have both sprained their wrists. Sparked flames emerge from each lighter in a tie. Lisa elbows Rick.

Hope grins. She places a hand on Tom's hand to steady the flame. Not taking her eyes off of him, she leans in to light the joint. Since Tom hasn't stopped staring, after she takes a drag she leans back in and blows out the lighter. Then to give balanced attention, she passes the joint to Rick.

Lisa grinds her teeth at this trollop.

Hope casually points off in the distance towards the unseen town, "If ya'll a fixin' to go down yonder, I'd be shed of that idee," she warns.

"How cute... I mean, your version of English," Lisa says.

Hope just gives her a smile, along with a stare. "Though I'm sure ya'll would be right welcomed down yonder."

Rick's not interested in a growing catfight so he waves a hand between the two girls to break the stare. He asks Hope, "Who are you... and why don't we want to go there?"

Hope doesn't answer the 'who' part. After another up and down look at all three, she turns. Walking away, she says, "Best, ya'll jes' follow me." She doesn't bother looking back to see if they do.

There's something so intriguing and odd about this gal that Rick and Tom just shrug and start to move out after her. Reluctantly, Lisa follows, but her attitude shows in her body language.

Hope keeps up a pretty steady pace, neither burdened by a backpack nor bothering to glance back. The three newcomers struggle to keep up with her, leaving little time for conversation. This is just fine with Hope, at least till she gets to her destination.

The threesome has fallen well behind. The last view of Hope was when she disappeared through a dense stand of trees.

"OK... the wood fairy's gone. We should go on our way," Lisa says, happy to use it as an excuse to forget about Hope.

"No, no... she went right through there." Tom gives a determined point at the stand.

Trying not to sound too enthusiastic... and not to get in trouble, Rick says, "Look, whoever she is, she wouldn't have gone through the trouble of finding us just to lose us. I vote we keep going... a little farther."

Lisa can see this is not a battle she's going to win. Exhausted, they all trudge the way Tom pointed. As they emerge from the other side of the stand of trees, they see Hope plopped down casually on the steps of her cabin.

As they approach, a bit out of wind from the trek, Hope waves at some log stumps, "Upright a log and rest your heels. I'll tell you... "

Lisa cuts her off with a sharp, "Who are you?"

"Done forgot my upbringin's... I'm Hope McCoy and that there town is Redemption... literally."

Hope's not quite sure why she is attempting to make an exception with this trio. Maybe it's because the boys are cute, regardless of the girl they dragged along. She knows that's not enough reason. There's some kind of new brush stroke in her mind... she just hasn't put her finger on it yet. As long as they don't become too obnoxious, she'll play with them for a while... at least till she figures it out.

"Now that the formals are done, let me tell ya'll a right interestin' story 'bouts that town yonder."

All take a seat. They're not sure why or how, but now their appetites have been whetted, even Lisa's.

CHAPTER SIX

Marcus saunters up Main Street this lazy afternoon, on his way towards the Crackerbarrel in front of Abigail's. When he gets there, he sees Pastor Cain, Samuel, Charity and Caleb sitting around gabbing... they tend to do that a lot. Walking up on the deck, Marcus smiles at the lot.

"What ya'll jawin' 'bouts today?" He's not sure he really cares but, as mayor, that's the kind of question he asks.

"Just ramblin' 'bouts this and that's. Talkin' 'bouts the fine redeemin' we had yesterday," says Caleb.

Caleb's the town's undertaker. He has a lot of free time in a town of only 258. The folks that get redeemed don't actually require formal internment, so that doesn't take much effort on his part. On occasions when the redeeming simply leaves parts, a number of large trash bags will do just fine.

Before anything else is said, Charity, the town's busybody, energetically points down Main Street.

All turn to see an unfamiliar station wagon driving into town... it has a luggage rack. With a lecherous smile, Charity perks up. "Looks to be a purely dern good week fer us."

"Don't go a hatchin' your eggs afore they's ready," warns Marcus.

This only gets a frown from Charity. It's quickly replaced by a grin as the car gets closer... nothing's going to dampen Charity's appetite.

The car pulls up directly in front of the store. Suddenly the left rear passenger door bursts open and two kids jump out. They rush past the group at the Crackerbarrel and into the store... with an overwhelming sense of urgency. The locals lose their broad smiles.

A middle-aged man gets out and yells after the kids, "Mind your manners in there." Then, seeing the few townsfolk watching intently, he says, "You know kids... when they have to go... they have to go."

Samuel asks, "Where 'bouts ya'll headin'?"

"Tennessee, but we've been driving for a while. We were hoping your town had a campground nearby," the man answers.

Having already seen the kids, and before Charity tries to sug-gest otherwise, Marcus says, "I'm a feared you're outta luck. The only campground in these parts is some 40 miles yonder." He points the way out of town.

The kids rush out of the store and directly back into the car, almost knocking Charity over on their way. She glares at them.

The man yells at his kids, "What do you say?"

"Sorry, ma'am," comes meekly from inside the car.

The man nods to the folks, "Looks like we have a bit further to go. Thanks for the directions."

"But... " Charity starts to say.

"But nothin'... As the man said, they have a fair piece to go." Marcus nods good day to the visitor.

The stranger gets in the station wagon and drives away.

Still glaring at the departing car, Charity snaps, "Those there kids looked like hellin's to me."

Pastor Cain shakes his head. "Charity, you know the rules. No young'uns, no one teched and no kin... At times I think you're prit' near too good a church go'er."

"And the first to throw stones," quietly grumbles Samuel.

Appearing to speak to the pastor, but eying Marcus, Charity curtly says, "Yeah, I know 'bouts the no kin part, all well nuff."

Before Marcus can put the glare in his eyes into words, Pastor Cain intervenes, "Girl, we'd gone thru that afore. Hope's both kin and a speck teched."

Marcus is not willing to leave it at that. "She's *my kin!* If you have more to say on the matter, I'd truly think twice 'bouts it."

The skirmish of words is broken as Gabriel drives up in his old truck and leans out the window. "Ya'll see'd Daniel an' Ethan 'bouts?"

Finally, taking his glare off Charity, Marcus responds, "Not recent... what fer?"

"Needs 'em up at the pit."

Everyone's focus on Charity quickly dissipates. She's more a person of irritation, than one of consequence in Redemption. Samuel, a paunchy man, is happy to go on to another subject. He asks, "Gabe... What'cha you buildin' fer us this time?"

"You know I hain't gonna tell." Then Gabriel adds, "If you'd see 'em, push 'em up yonder."

Samuel knows it was a redundant question. Gabriel always keeps his contraptions guarded, like they were protected children. In his mind, asking is common and traditional courtesy... to Gabriel, it's simply tiresome.

CHAPTER SEVEN

Tom, Rick and Lisa are on the edge of their log stumps... each entranced and somewhat drop-jawed by Hope's story. Hope wraps it up with, "And... That's why I see it as favorin' performance art."

There's dead silence for the longest few seconds.

Finally Rick breaks out laughing, "You can tell a hell of a story... You had me going there."

"All I can say is... Brava!" Tom says this with less doubt and much more admiration. Even Lisa nods her admission of being entertained.

"Ya'll think I'm shuckin'?"

Lisa shakes her head. "You have to be... there's no such place like that. But with a good stone on, I totally loved the story... Even if it is all bullshit." From anyone else, this might not sound that bad, but from Lisa it's catty.

Hope puts forth a fake smile, determined not to take the bait. She glances over at Tom... at least, he has promise.

Rick doesn't help by asking, "Where did you come up with a high-end term like performance art up here in the hills?"

This strikes a nerve and Hope stands. "It's a fool that sees us all as teched up here."

Tom wants to stay on the story. "Never mind them... How about showing us this arena of yours?"

"Naw... Gabriel is right peculiar 'bouts his surprises," responds Hope.

"Of course," mumbles Lisa rather loudly.

Hope gives her a quick cat's eye and heads for the cabin door. As she goes inside, Hope looks back at them, "Ya'll welcome to stay for vittles... Looks like a storms a brewin'." There's no sign of the brewing storm in the sky... yet.

"You're kidding, aren't you," says Lisa. It's not clear if she's referring to the idea of a storm, or the idea of staying.

With a flip of her hand, Hope says, "Stay or go... as suits you. Cool your heels out here and figure out yer mind. Ya'll safe here." In a quiet tone as she goes in, "Fer now."

Hope wonders why she's being so generous with these three. She wonders how long it will last.

Patches of red sand spot the arena pit. Ethan rakes the patches to blend them into the surrounding dirt. Not that the image is distasteful, but Gabriel feels large clumps of dried blood are distracting. Gabriel has always told him, *'Every new piece in my pit deserves a new canvas'*... at least somewhat new.

Ethan and Daniel, in addition to handling chores for the town council, help with Gabriel's creations. Both enjoy the creativity... it's more rewarding than the simple errands the council has them do. More important to Gabriel than their help, though, is that they can be trusted to keep his little toys a secret until their debuts.

Ethan scrapes away at the dirt, while Daniel helps Gabriel work on a large frame resting on two sawhorses. Meticulously they strap sharp wooden spikes to the frame. Occasionally Gabriel corrects Daniel's positioning... even the smallest detail is important.

At one point Gabriel glances up towards Hope's perch. He can't hide a slight hint of disappointment that she's not up there taking a peek. Officially his work is off limits to her, as it is to the rest of the town… but he doesn't mind her getting a little look now and then… as long as it's not the finished piece.

Tom and Rick sit quietly on stumps in front of Hope's cabin, occasionally glancing at each other, conflicted over this truly bizarre situation. If true, it's both scary and exciting enough to reach down to their core.

Lisa paces back and forth between them. Her look says, *Can't believe you two are considering this.* Her dramatics don't seem to be getting her point across, so she finally snaps, "Why aren't we getting the hell out of here… right now?"

In a very short while, clouds have started to form in the sky above and they're gradually darkening. It looks as if Hope knows her skies and this is a perfect excuse for the guys.

"If she's right, we wouldn't want to get caught out in a storm." Rick is trying to appeal to Lisa's logic… sometimes a hard task.

"If she's right… I don't want to miss it," Tom quietly says, more for Rick than trying to sway Lisa.

Lisa stares at the two of them for a second. It's even clear to her that she's going to be overruled so she lets out a pouty sigh of surrender.

The creak of the cabin's screen door interrupts the trio.

Hope comes out, paying little attention to her guests. Something far off has sparked her vigilance. Like a fox on high alert, she smells the air. She listens to sounds floating on the breeze.

Tom watches her intently, trusting that she's truly sensing something. Rick and Lisa observe her as an oddity.

Now, sure of her senses, Hope reaches out and takes the binoculars from the porch post. She peers at the far hillside. As she does, a faint echo of rumbling bounces through the canyons.

Tom steps up onto the porch to Hope's side. He whispers, "What is it?"

Hope gives him a light laugh. "Bikers... and they're too fer away to be hearin' you."

She hands the binoculars to him and points to a section of the hillside. He takes the glasses and looks towards where she pointed. There are hopscotch glimpses of Harleys on the road between open patches of trees. He lowers the glasses and turns back to Hope with a look of curiosity.

"Ya'll might get a gander at the arena after all." She turns to head back into the cabin and says, "Ya'll comin' in... or not?"

Rick and Lisa give a hesitant look at each other.

"I know it's a fair amount to be take in... and, I'm a piece, too. But it's a speck late to try and get out of these hills today... that is without ya'll goin' down through town."

"I could use a breather... and a bite to eat," perks Tom. He's already hooked. A breather and bite to eat is just a good excuse. He'd stay if they were offered no more than a shed and a drop of water.

Rick is already heading for the door, so Lisa gives a less than enthusiastic shrug and joins him. Hope holds the door open as they enter.

As Lisa passes Hope, she says, "You're right about one thing... you are a piece to take in."

Tom holds back, more captivated by Hope than the events. He gestures for her to lead the way, but before she goes he asks, "Is what you told us really true?" This comes off with a tone more of fascination than accusation.

"Hell... hain't rightly sure why I told you... only told one other," and she heads in.

Tom happily follows.

CHAPTER EIGHT

As Hope predicted, the storm has seriously rolled in. Rain pounds the street, mixed with cracks of thunder and flashes of glowing sky. The lightning reflects off the three Harleys parked outside the Last Chance Saloon.

One of the townsfolk scurries down the sidewalk, holding a piece of cardboard over his head to deflect the drenching downpour. He glances at the row of bikes with a brief smile and rushes into the bar... hoping he's in time.

Three bikers, all sporting outlaw cuts, stand at the bar.

The crossed swords patch of the 10th Mountain Division sewn on below their colors dispels any doubt about the toughness of these three characters.

Again, the locals populate the bar, creating an impromptu party. They enjoy the game of watching their prey unaware of their covert attention. Despite the abrasiveness of the bikers, all the townsfolk are on their best behavior.

Maybe if the drinks were not so strong and so fast coming, these boys might not be so belligerent... they might even be good guys. Maybe not... being drunk probably just brings out their nature more quickly. Either way, their drinking serves the town's purpose.

Sarge is not the largest biker but, judging by his stance, he's clearly the leader. He yells at Aaron, "Another fuckin' round over here, barkeep!"

Rootbeer, the biggest one, is already slurring his words: "That's the way to tell 'em, man... gotta keep these yokels on their toes."

Marcus and Gabriel sit at the town council's table. They observe the event from a distance. Gabriel notes, "Hain't much ponderin' due with these here boys."

"Everyone's due the rituals... even no accounts like them," responds Marcus. He's well aware of the outcome but, for him, the art is in the set up... and he knows, for Gabriel, the art is in the execution.

Marcus waves for Aaron to keep the ritual, and the drinks, flowing. Aaron nods and brings over another round to the bikers. "This round is on us... the town of Redemption."

The third biker, Shaker, takes his drink and turns to the crowd. He holds it up in toast, "To Redemption... mighty fine of you." He adds, in a slightly less loud voice, "Even if you are a bunch of inbred hillbillies."

He's half playing the drunk... and half yearning for a good brawl. All this gets is laughter from the crowd. The drunken bikers continue to dig their hole deeper and deeper... one offensive action after another.

Rootbeer leans into Sarge, "Anything get to these folks?"

"Who cares?" is Sarge's only answer.

What they don't know is that the locals know who will have the last laugh.

Pastor Cain attempts to do his usual hovering in the background with a notepad, but this is such a slam-dunk that he finally puts the pad away. With a shake of his head, he goes over and plops down at the council table.

While the thunder cracks, Hope is busy rustling up some supper. Her three new visitors are taking in the unique nature of Hope's mind, as displayed within the cabin. There's little doubt that it's dark. Abstract paintings of deep harsh colors adorn most of the walls. Flashes of light through the windows propel the images into greater depth. The only warmth in the cabin comes from the soft glow of candles and lanterns.

Lisa is repelled, and yet captivated, by a dried up Christmas tree in the corner. The decorations hanging from the stark limbs are small dead animals: lizards, sickly birds and emaciated fish. She figures there must be some art thing to it, but it completely escapes her. She reaches out to touch what look like sweaty candlesticks hanging from the branches.

"I'd be a careful with handlin' those, if I were you," Hope yells in from the kitchen area.

The remark catches Tom's attention. After taking a closer look at the tree, he says, "Those aren't what they appear to be... are they?"

Not looking up, in a nonchalant manner while cutting greens, Hope replies, "'Course they are... art hain't art without a real edge."

Incensed by Hope's casual air, Lisa starts to storm towards the kitchen area of the cabin, but Rick cuts her off. As he shoves her towards the front door, "We'll be back in a second." Lisa puts up a bit of struggle, but finally allows her boyfriend to hustle her out.

After they've left, "A might high-strung... hain't she?"

"She can be... but she's Rick's choice, not mine."

Outside, the thunderstorm matches Lisa's temperament. Once out on the front porch, she twists away from Rick's grasp. She doesn't like his wanting her to wind down before she says more biting things to that girl inside. More than that, she's really upset that he's taking control. Lisa likes to be in charge, and ever since they met Hope, that's slipping away... or, at least, so she thinks.

Waving at the cabin, she rants, "That bitch has sticks of dynamite hanging from that tree! You don't find that more than a little crazy?"

"I'm sure it's just for shock effect... like the crazy story she told us." In truth, he does find Hope a little crazy... maybe that's her appeal. "It really doesn't matter, we can't go anywhere in this storm." With perfect timing, his words are punctuated by a loud clap of thunder.

Not to leave Rick with the last word... and to make one of her other concerns perfectly clear, Lisa grumbles, "The only effect I see is you and that no account friend of yours drooling over her round bottom!"

If it's true or not, she knows it's a necessary preemptive stroke. Hope has hers... Lisa needs hers.

Rick chuckles as he shakes his head at the accusation. He knows it's not completely false... he's a healthy young male, and Hope is attractive. But saying anything would be adding fuel to the fire and he says nothing.

After staring at him a second, waiting for a wrong word, Lisa adds, "Come morning I want us out of here... I'm not going to get all *Deliverance'd* by some blond hillbilly with perky tits."

To Rick's relief, the sound of pans clanging loudly together emerges from inside the cabin.

Hope's yell, "Supper time ya'll!"

Marcus and Gabriel have wasted enough time watching the inevitable outcome in the bar. They pass by the three bikers on their way out. As they go, Marcus holds up three fingers to Aaron. This gets a nod of understanding from behind the bar.

Before they're out the door, Rootbeer staggers over to them and slaps Marcus on the back, "You sure do know how to welcome visitors."

Marcus gives the biker a smile, "You hain't seen nothin' yet." After another look at Rootbeer's bulk, he glances back at Aaron and holds up four fingers.

Aaron is a bit concerned, but he shrugs his acknowledgement of the change... they are big'uns. And he figures Marcus didn't take well to being slapped on the back. No matter... with a smile, he gets to the task of preparing the mickey, as ordered.

At dinner Lisa can't seem to help the occasional glance back into the living room at Hope's dynamite tree. With such a quirky, maybe dangerous, host she figures it's wise to keep her concerns to herself.

With dinner wrapping up, Lisa attempts to be cordial in her snippy way. "That dinner was a surprise... better than I expected."

"What did ya'll expect... road kill stew?" Hope smiles.

"Sorry, I didn't mean it to sound like that," says Lisa, though that's exactly how she meant it. Tom shakes his head, while Rick tries to stay out of hot water by remaining neutral.

"'Course you did," says Hope, getting up from the table.

Trying to change directions, Tom asks, "Hope, how about telling us more about your town?"

Hope glances over her shoulder and says, "Ya either experience art... or you don't... 'nuff jawin' 'bouts it. I got chores to git to."

She heads for the front door, grabs a small, empty backpack hanging on a coat rack by the entrance, and goes over to her bizarre dead tree. With her back to the dining room, Hope stealthily gathers a few of her *candlesticks* and stuffs them into the pack. Without another word, she promptly exits through the front door.

The abruptness of her exit catches all off guard.

Lisa snaps, "What was that all about? Where's she off to in this storm?"

"Beats me... but it's clear we're not invited," Tom says, relishing things that irritate Lisa.

"Have a heart, Lisa... she's been nothing but nice to us so far," says Rick cautiously.

Of course, Lisa has to have the last word, "So far!" She shoves her plate brusquely away with a pout.

CHAPTER NINE

Late morning and two bikers lay on metal bunks in the rock holding cell. The third is sprawled out on the grated floor. All rumble the room with their snores. They dream biker's dreams, completely unaware of anything beyond the bar last night. The large metal door at one end of the cell clanks open with no effect on their slumber.

Marcus, Aaron and Gabriel step in. Gabriel shakes his head. "You certain they's gonna wake up from four drops?"

"Prit' near certain they will ... they's truly big'uns," Aaron says. There's a bit of uncertainty in his voice. He's not sure since he's never used four drops before. They're still breathing... that's a good sign.

"Timin's the important thing... townsfolk are gatherin'," says Marcus. Being a politician, he's always about keeping the crowd entertained... and that is about timing. He can't imagine the unruly mobs of Rome had much patience for sleeping lions.

A glint comes across Gabriel's face. "Why don't we'ez jes' hose them down and run... They's bound to find the pit."

"Dern shine of an idee," responds Marcus. He's happy for such a simple solution. He also knows if it doesn't work, Gabriel will find another quick solution since he's not about to have his new contraption go unseen.

The three kids sit close together on the steps of Hope's porch... between them a mixture of feelings, ranging from uneasiness to anticipation. Will Hope truly show them this strange event? Can it even be true?

They had not seen Hope since the night before. When they awoke she was snoring away in the loft bedroom. Lisa found it distasteful that a young lady would snore so loud, while Tom found it refreshing and unpretentious. Hope would have found it neither, since it was what it was.

Finally Lisa says, "She's nuts... We should get the hell out of here while we can."

A sudden creak of the screen door behind them startles the three. Hope comes out.

"She might be right... But if ya'll is leavin', I'd do it quiet like."

It's clear from Rick and Tom's faces that Hope's hint the night before whetted their appetite. It's not so clear from Lisa's. Hope knows how to work people. She'll let them make the first move... and she knows they will, regardless of Lisa.

Rick nudges Tom, figuring that it would be better if he said something... better, at least, for Rick's relationship.

Tom takes the hint, "But... what if we really do want to see? I mean... if it's real."

Hope was sure he has the appetite for the unusual. She gives him a knowing wink. With just the right amount of hesitation, Hope finally says, "It's hard to come back from. But if ya'll truly do, you's best make certain of your minds now 'cause I'm headin' out to the perch presently."

With this, Hope grabs her binoculars from the porch post and heads towards a path. She's baited the hook enough... they'll follow, or not. What she doesn't let on is that it might be unhealthy for them if they don't choose to follow.

Tom's the first to his feet. "I have to see this."

With a slight glance at Lisa, and trying to show less enthusiasm, Rick stands up. "I don't believe it... I have to take a look too."

His eyes are almost pleading Lisa to join in. He'd prefer it to be willingly so he doesn't have to argue with her about it... but either way, he's going.

After a strategic pause silently expressing her objection, Lisa shakes her head, gets up and starts to follow Tom. Pleased not to have a battle, Rick doesn't think that Lisa possibly has a hunger as well... one she's able to mask behind their enthusiasm.

Three very wet bikers stagger back from the rolling doors. Despite their hangover from drink and a seriously heavy mickey, they make one more try at stopping the doors. They throw their shoulders at the advancing metal. Their dug-in heels scrape against the stone floor as the barrier grinds forward.

"It's no use!" yells Rootbeer.

"Then let's go kick some ass!" yells Shaker.

"Damn straight!" Rootbeer adds, just as keyed up as Shaker.

"Settle down... We did get a little drunk last night... and I ain't sure what we did," says Sarge, trying to get some perspective on what is happening to them.

He knows that if they're going into fight, it's best to pull the anger out of it. Cold means focused... anger means mistakes.

"Ain't no reason to throw us in a cell," Rootbeer declares.

Shaker adds, "Or douse us with cold water!"

"We've had both done before. All I'm saying is we ain't angels... Let's figure out what the hell this is all about before we rush in." Not wanting to lose the edge, Sarge adds, "If need be, then we kick ass!"

Hope comes down a path flanked by dense bushes. Tom is at her side. Rick and Lisa are not far behind. As she approaches her perch, Hope takes a second to gesture for the three to stay low. She points to some loose bushes off to the side of her perch, where they can see without being seen.

With a touch more dramatics than necessary, the three hunker down close to the ground and crawl to where Hope indicates. Lisa silently grumbles, probably because the guys are more into what they're doing than paying any attention to her. They inch along the last couple of feet to the edge of the ridge, sweeping the bushes aside as they move. A branch snaps back hitting Lisa. She glares over at Hope whom she blames for all of this. Hope is not paying her any attention either.

Hope stands on the precipice of her perch looking down on a packed arena for a couple seconds, as if to let all below know she is there. Perhaps it's more to rub salt in old wounds... either way, she fully enjoys the ritual.

She can see a few of the folks below sneaking peeks up at her and averting their eyes when her eyes meet theirs. In Hope's head, her perch is the grandstand... not that platform down in the arena. From here she oversees what they all think is their creation.

The only exceptions are Gabriel and Marcus on the grandstand. For Gabriel, no arena event would be complete without Hope. Though Marcus wishes she wasn't there, he always knows his daughter will be up there and he can't help looking.

After the appropriate amount of time, Hope takes a seat in her lawn chair. She glances over at her three guests, who have just reached the edge from where they can get the full view below.

She whispers loudly, "We hain't missed any of the doin's."

It's as if they can't hear her; their eyes are glued to the arena... in half disbelief. Lisa, the skeptic, has inched forward... far enough that Rick pulls her back.

They stomp down a stone hallway towards the light at the end. There's no illusion of compliance, just one of hard deter-mination. In the darkness behind them sounds the hollow grind of the doors.

Rootbeer snorts, "When I get my hands on the son-of-a-bitch behind this!"

"But let's figure out who we're fighting first." Sarge still tries to keep them focused.

By now Shaker is doing what he does before any fight... shaking. He got this affectionate nickname from his brothers-in- arms in Afghanistan. He would shake till the hammer dropped, then hold his own. They trust him to have their back in a fight, a truth that's been borne out many times. They know each man deals with lead in his own manner. If his brothers saw any downside to Shaker, it was keeping him from taking point, just to get at it... and calm the shakes. Sarge knows Shaker has enough discipline to hold back, if that's what's needed.

By the time the three reach the light at the end of the tunnel, their blood's a boil. They're ready for anything.

CHAPTER TEN

The three emerge from the tunnel at the edge of the pit. The gallery busts into applause. This... they weren't ready for!

Sarge holds his hand up against the glare of the sun. He wants to get their bearings before anything else, so he scans the spiked log walls and what gallery he can see from his position.

"What is this?" Rootbeer leans in and asks.

"A bear-baiting pit... and I don't see any bears... I guess we're the prime attraction," says Sarge.

Marcus taps on the microphone. Once he's sure it's on, "You boys had yourself a right long rest. Sorry 'bouts the water but we'ez got plum' tired of waitin'."

Shaker starts to move forward past Sarge, but Sarge grabs his elbow. This is enough to stop him. Now in the pit, Shaker no longer shakes.

Rootbeer yells out, "What the fuck is going on here?"

"Watch ya'll wordin', boys," warns Marcus.

"What kind of game are you playing? ... And why do you think we'll play?" Sarge wants to know, but he also wants to stall while he sizes up the arena. He has no doubt that they are going to have to fight in some way... they need as much edge as they can get.

From what Sarge can see, the pit before them has about two-dozen small mounds spaced all over. The rains of the night before have turned everything to a mixture of mud and sand. Fresh-turned dirt is atop each mound and Sarge assumes the

 STEVE GRAZIANI

heavy rains partially uncovered what they were meant to hide. The big question is... what are they hiding?

"Now if you's hold your piece a bit, I'll git to the particulars. As fer why you'll play... to live."

Gabriel, stepping up beside Marcus on the grandstand, waves down to someone unseen. Two large doors on the opposite side of the arena from the bikers open up. Some ten yards beyond the doors sit the bikers' Harleys. Rootbeer starts to take a step forward, but Sarge holds his hand out to wait. He knows there's more to it than walking across the pit.

Sarge yells up, "OK, say we bite... what's the game?"

Marcus, staying with the ritual, gestures to Pastor Cain.

"How about speeding it up?" Sarge is not much for theatrics.

Marcus smiles and waves the Pastor off. "We'ez obligin' type folks. If ya'lls in such a dang hurry, my guess is that the list of transgressions is too long to be a wastin' time on. You boys now have a chance to be redeemed... So much fer the formals." He points to the other side of the arena. "If ya'll can git through the redemption to that opening yonder... ya'll can go on your way... How's that fer fair?"

The townsfolk break into an ominous laugh.

"Screw your damn redemption, or whatever sick excuse you hillbillies have for this. What's the catch?" Sarge has no interest in the whys of a fight he can't get out of. All he wants is an edge that might give them a chance of winning. It's long odds, but they've faced them before.

Shaker starts to step out into the arena again. Again Sarge grabs his elbow, but this time Shaker throws off his grip.

"We ain't gonna know what we face till someone takes point." With this, he takes another step further into the ring.

Sarge knows he's right. "Take it slow."

Shaker cautiously progresses, avoiding the mounds... then there's a click, followed by a bang! An explosive charge goes off, sending a three-foot square pad pivoting out from one of the dirt mounds... like launching a flyswatter. A vicious flyswatter with numerous one-foot spikes attached to its face.

The pad is rocket fast... but an adrenaline-filled Shaker is as well. Unfortunately he's not fast enough to beat the second pad that he sets off as he escapes the first. Another explosive charge arches it towards him.

The spikes impale Shaker.

Rootbeer starts to rush forward but Sarge uses all his force to slam him back to the log wall.

"He's gone," Sarge yells while trying to restrain his friend.

"Well... your friend done found the catch," comes from the PA system. A mixture of laughter and applause erupts from the gallery.

Rick, Tom and Lisa all wear drop-jawed looks of shock. They stare down into the arena while Hope stares at them with a look of satisfaction.

The kids can't help inching further and further out of the brush... maybe to make sure that what they are seeing is real. They don't trust their eyes. Nothing like this could really happen... and yet, that is exactly what they see.

Hope tries to get their attention, but they are fixated on the gory scene below. She finally throws a loose stone at them.

"You gits seen and we'll all gonna end up bleedin' in that pit," warns Hope.

The boys comply, but Lisa has to be pulled back from the edge.

"Come on... don't jes' stand there!" someone yells from the bleachers. A few other townsfolk echo similar calls for action.

Marcus comes over the PA, "Ya'll heard the good folk... best git to movin'. That there door hain't gonna stay open fer too long."

Sarge glances at Shaker's body. He tries to replay the exact sequence of traps in his mind, all the while analyzing the layout of the many mounds on the field. There's no pattern that he can see. He peers at the log walls around the pit. There are alternating segments of the perimeter that have and don't have stakes.

Another thing that catches his attention is a consistent positioning of mounds in front of the different wall segments. Where there are spikes on the wall, the mounds are slightly farther out than where there are no spiked segments. But there is a mound squarely in front of each. This is all in addition to the many random mounds throughout the field, perhaps to help hide the pattern.

He thinks that whoever set this up took out Shaker by anticipating his next move. He's seen that type of double-tap strike before with IED land mine positioning. Maybe he can play with that knowledge. Catcalls keep coming from above, but Sarge is not about to rush his play.

Rootbeer's antsy to move. Looking at Shaker's bloody body isn't helping, but he can tell Sarge is trying to work things out. He holds his ground.

Up in the grandstand, Marcus appears concerned by the inaction below. He's a politician, albeit a small one, and timing is important.

Standing beside Marcus, Gabriel can see this. "Not to fret... they's jes' thinking out their next move... It builds tension fer the doin's."

With an intense look, Ethan runs up to Marcus. He's holding a slip of paper that he attempts to put in front of the mayor.

Focused on the events, Marcus brushes him off. "Not now."

Ethan remains stubborn on the matter. "It's important," he insists.

For the young Ethan to ignore the mayor's objections means the matter must be of some consequence... especially in the midst of a redemption. Though irritated by the interruption, Marcus finally takes the slip of paper. Once he glances at it, his expression changes. By his face... something serious.

Hope is more captivated by the activities on the grandstand than the gory events in the pit. She grins with anticipation.

Marcus urgently shows the slip of paper to Gabriel, to little effect. Gabriel is more of an in-the-moment person, and right now he's into his creation down in the arena.

Sitting in the grandstand, the town council is clearly itching to know what's in the message. After Gabriel brushes him off, Marcus rushes over and huddles with them.

Down in the pit, Sarge grabs Rootbeer by the shoulders to get him to focus. "We're going to leap-frog the perimeter!"

Rootbeer glances at the log wall around the pit, not clear on Sarge's logic.

"It's a crap shoot... but I think those Punji stake pads will swing right into each of the clear spaces... The spaces with stakes will have a pad fall just ahead of it."

It's still confuses Rootbeer.

"They want us to back into the wall stakes."

"You sure?" is all Rootbeer can say.

"Shit no... but it's a plan. They guessed Shaker's moves."

Rootbeer knows doing something is better than inaction, and he has trusted Sarge for a long time. He nods his understanding and starts to lead out, but Sarge grabs his arm and steps ahead of him. Attempting to go around him, Rootbeer says, "Sarge... let me take the lead."

Sarge stands fast. "Old friend... I'm skinnier than you. I'll take point. If I'm right, back up close to the wall spikes and let the pad fall right in front of you. Get through the clear spots fast!"

Rootbeer nods that he gets it... he's aware of his girth.

"Catch you on the other side." Sarge fist slaps Rootbeer on the chest... and he leads out.

Sarge quickly runs and positions himself directly in front of the static, short wall stakes. As anticipated, his foot trips the mechanism and he hears the click... he waits for a Punji stake pad to pivot towards him, hoping the pad will hit far enough ahead of him to leave room to move. Suddenly the spikes behind him explode forward and burst through his chest!

Gabriel gives a triumphant fist-pump. He knew they would overthink his design and guess wrong. That's why he designed the stakes to appear to be mounted on static-looking vertical logs that blend with the real wall. Of course, just in case, there were Punji stakes that would swing into the non-spiked sections of the wall... if they had chosen differently.

There's little applause from the bleachers. It's hard to keep secrets in a town with a population of 258. A buzz about what was in the note Ethan delivered infects the townsfolk like a fast-moving virus. Fewer and fewer people pay attention to the drama down in the arena.

Before dying, Sarge manages one last yell to Rootbeer. "Just fuckin' run for it!" And Sarge's head slumps into lifelessness.

By now the town council is arguing in the background with no interest in the event, while Gabriel keeps watching the pit.

Rootbeer, after one last look at Sarge, sets off running across the pit. It's amazing how fast a man Rootbeer's size can move when necessary. He zigzags across the pit, explosion after explosion of Punji stake pads, one after another, slamming at him.

Gabriel looks down with fascination... almost rooting for the big man to make it... at least a little farther.

One spiked pad takes a deep bite of Rootbeer's shoulder, sending blood flying. Rootbeer hits the ground but tumble-rolls back to his feet. He manages to keep going. Bloody, but still standing, Rootbeer reaches the open arch at the opposite side of the arena. He spins and holds both hands high, flipping a *bird* to the crowd. He screams out, "GO SCREW YOUR-SELVES!"

A spiked pad, stealthily hung above the arch, swings down and impales itself in Rootbeer's back. He goes limp.

Apart from Gabriel's solitary clapping, there's no applause, no cheers from the gallery. They all seem preoccupied, murmuring growing rumors.

On her perch, Hope has watched the three kids go from shocked observers to willing audience in a short window of time.

Seeing Rootbeer impaled, Rick mutters, "Not fair... he should have made it."

Lisa slaps him, "That was gross!" But her eyes are still glued on the arena.

Hope finds her companions much more interesting than anything happening in the arena until there's a thump on the mic of the speaker system. She shifts her attention back to the pit.

This is what she was waiting for.

Hope triumphantly says, "Here we go!"

Marcus taps the mic. "I 'spec's ya'll got part wind of this."
The gallery goes dead silent.
"Got some right bad news. The roads... both in and out of Redemption, jes' got crushed by mighty rock slides."
The murmuring gives way to a louder buzz. Someone yells out, "Fer how long?"
A woman yells, "What 'bouts fetchin's?"
"Forget fetchin's... What about visitors?" comes from another woman. This last passionate yell brings back dead silence.
In his best mayoral voice, "Don't fret... we'ez gonna set 'bouts figurin' that out d'reckly."
He can tell by the growing buzz of the crowd that this is not going to settle things, but it's all he has at the moment.
A girl's laughter is heard from high above the arena.

Hope laughs at the limits of her angelic lungs. She could care less about the nasty stares from below.
The three kids, caught off guard by Hope's reaction, stare at her in confusion. Luckily, they have already pulled back from the edge and have not been seen.
When Hope stops laughing, she turns and starts back up the path. "I'll be back at the cabin... Things are 'bouts to git right strange."
She disappears up the path, leaving the three kids sitting there... totally bewildered.

CHAPTER ELEVEN

Walking back to Hope's cabin, Tom, Lisa and Rick remain silent for the longest time. It's as if no one knows what to say. Each, in their own way, hasn't settled on what they've actually seen.

"OK... Someone say something," Lisa finally blurts out.

Tom clears his throat. "You're not going to like it."

"Probably not... but it can't be any worse than what we just saw." Lisa is a master of denial, especially when it suits her vision of herself.

Rick shakes his head in disbelief. "Lisa... no one could have pried your eyes off of... *what we just saw.*"

She gives Rick a glare... doesn't he know whom he's supposed to be backing? She snaps, "You taking Tom's side?"

"I don't even know what Tom's side is." Rick thinks it's a stupid question, but he's not about to say that.

They continue walking along in silence.

After a while, Tom says, "I really don't know either."

"Know what?" Seems like anything Lisa says comes off like an accusation.

"Know what my side is. All I do know is that we were all glued to what happened back there." After a second he adds, "I was even aroused by it... a little."

Lisa's face scrunches up in self-righteous disgust. "That's sick! Rick... that's sick, isn't it?"

Rick gives her a guilty shrug.

Her jaw drops before she screeches, "Rick!"

"Look... Tom's hard-on is not the question. The question is what we want to do about it now?"

"How about running like hell? Duh," Lisa spouts.

It's about a fifteen minute walk back to Hope's cabin, and Tom would like to use some of that time to process what they've seen... silently. "Lisa, just honestly think about what you feel... not what you should feel... and, then we can talk about it back at the cabin."

At first this takes her aback, but when she sees no support coming from Rick, she remains silent. After all, it's only a few minutes... she tells herself. She pouts.

As a kid, Tom spent a lot of time over at Rick's house. At home his father wasn't what you'd call kid-friendly and Tom grew up retreating into his imagination to escape his reality. Maybe that's why he has a tickle of a feeling he could take well to the arena's bizarre business. He feels guilty... but not to a great extent.

Lisa pouts along, doing her best not to answer Tom's question. In her head she's well honed to denial. It's taking a lot, because she senses unacceptable thinking. She does her best to ignore it by deciding whom to blame.

His friend, Rick, walks along with the burden of being the most confused. He has a dead equal attraction to both guilt and fascination... the toughest road to understanding.

The trail opens up into the clearing in front of Hope's cabin. They see Hope sitting on the porch, her feet up on the rail. A tray with a pitcher of lemonade and three glasses rests on the rail beside her feet.

As they approach, Hope grins. "Figured ya'll would come back either tearin' at your hair or plum' puzzled 'bouts what you feel... or a mix... 'ceptin' maybe Tom.

What rushes through Tom's head is, *how the hell does she know them so well... or him.* It crosses his mind, *why him?*

Lisa puffs up. "You knew what gross thing we'd see back there, didn't you?" Immediately, she'd like to change what she just said, but that would be bad form.

"Well, darlin', to quote what I might picture you sayin'... Duh. Of course, I knew what ya'll was in fer... I asked you to well think on it afore you tromped along after me." Hope lets out a sigh. "Why don't ya'll take a log."

Rick nods to Lisa and they set a log stump upright and plop down. Tom walks over and sits on the cabin steps.

All remain silent as they sit there. Neither of the boys has figured out the words and Lisa is formulating her denial.

"Ya'll's demons is your'n to be dealin' with... All I'm askin' is if you's can accept what ya'll saw fer what it is... and leave it be at that?" says Hope.

Rick knows his answer: the fascination side won by a hair. He tries to ease the way for Lisa. "Look, we took off on this trip to experience that part of America that's not canned and packaged."

"Yeah, but this is way more than a little different than visiting Disneyland... this is chainsaw massacre different."

The stares of both Tom and Rick break her. "OK... you win... it did catch my attention! You happy?"

"Girl, I weren't tryin' to win anything... My guess is it got both your attention... and imagination." Hope glances at the pitcher of lemonade. "I done forgot my manners. Have some nice cool lemonade."

As she gets up to offer it, Hope accidently knocks the tray off the porch rail.

"Well dang! I can rustle up a new batch right quick."

She quickly gathers the empty pitcher and heads inside.

Tom thinks, from what little he knows of her... *Hope's not the careless type. Come to think of it... she's not the perfect host type either.*

He glances at the spilled lemonade and wonders what was actually in it. If it were him, he'd have a back-up in case his guests rebelled. More importantly, he still hasn't figured out why Hope's putting up with them in the first place.

Hope comes back out with a fresh pitcher, already mixed, and unceremoniously plops it down on the step... lemonade sloshes over the rim. Seeing a skeptical look on Tom, Hope pours herself a glass and takes a drink. Again, Tom is confounded by how she knows what he's thinking. He figures time will tell.

Rick asks, "Back there at the perch, what did you mean by things getting real strange now?"

"*What* do we qualify as... strange now?" Lisa questions.

Hope smiles. "I guess you was all too caught up in the redeemin' to git it?"

"You mean... killing," Lisa injects.

"Whatever... The point is there hain't gonna be more visitors fer a fair piece."

Lisa leans over to Rick, not so quietly, "Except us."

"Don't fret there... If them down below knew I was hidin' ya'll, I'd be plum' treed... kin or no," Hope assures them.

Suddenly Tom jumps up! "I get it!"

"Figured you might be the first," Hope says with one of her smiles, both angelic and lecherous.

"What already?" snaps Lisa.

Tom's now locked eye to eye with Hope. "You really think it'll get that crazy?"

Lisa hates being ignored, which in her head, is happening way too much on this trip. "Hey! ... You two... *What?*"

Both turn their heads towards her for a brief second, and go back to addressing each other.

"Prit' near."

"What a story!" Tom's enthusiasm gets the best of him. He jumps off the steps... setting in motion a clumsy chain reaction.

He lands on a loose log... that rolls from under him... throwing him into a woodpile by the porch... knocking a planter off the porch rail... that lands on Tom's head. Crack!

Tom lies crumpled in the woodpile. He struggles to get to his feet awkwardly. About half way up, "I'm OK... I'm fine... I think." All just before his leg buckles under him. "Or... maybe not... "

Rushing over to break Tom's second fall, Rick is too late. All he can do is help straighten up Tom's crumple.

"Total klutz," grumbles Lisa.

With a nasty side-glance at Lisa, Hope joins in righting Tom. Lisa shakes her head and reluctantly goes to lend a hand.

Once they manage to get him out of the woodpile, Hope gently unlaces and pulls off Tom's hiking boot. His ankle is already swelling. It shows hints of early blues and purples that are going to get worse. Even Hope's gentle touch brings a wince to Tom's face.

"I know it hurts a might." Hope feels around the ankle as gently as possible.

Rick's tone shows his true concern. "Is it broken?"

"Please... don't tell us he broke the damn thing and we're stuck here," Lisa says ungraciously.

Her comment isn't worth Hope's looking away from the ankle. "Right fine friend you got there." She accents it with a wink... that totally throws Tom. It was meant to.

"Best I can tell, hain't anything broke... just a right nasty sprain."

Tom's not a hypochondriac, but it hurts like hell. "You sure it's not broken?"

"Could take you to the town doc... but... "

"No, I'll take your word for it," Tom squeezes out a smile.

"How long?" comes from both Rick and Lisa. It crosses Hope's mind how different two emotional tones can be at the same time. She answers Rick and aims it at Lisa.

"I hain't a-hankerin' fer company fer that long either, some weighin' in heavier than others, but it's gonna take a piece fer him to be up and 'bouts on it." She enjoys how vague that came out. "I got some old crutches up in the cave that he can use fer a bit. But he's not travelin' soon."

"What cave?" asks Lisa.

"That there's my business... I'd stay clear if I were ya'll." As soon as Hope says this she knows she's waved a red flag... and that eventually she's going to have to get in that girl's face.

"Why?" Lisa asks suspiciously.

"Can't you take folks fer what they are? Let's get Tom in the cabin fer now. Then I got doin's in the town." Hope registers a slight hint of panic in Lisa's face. "Nothin' to do with ya'll... so ya'll can breathe."

CHAPTER TWELVE

Hope skateboards to the edge of Redemption and then goes on foot. She would be the first to admit that she has an arrogant manner of walking down Main Street... in her somewhat uppity slow strut. It doesn't bother her. She whistles as she goes along.

Main Street is darn near empty. But something else is different. Curtains that are usually being closed at her passing are now opening. Hope's not sure if it's her imagination but a few of the faces she sees in the windows look hungry. It's too early. She dismisses it to mind-overdrive. Another thing out of sorts... most of the few stores in town are closed. Stranger yet, it even looks like doors are locked. Hope figures it's a form of mourning, whether the people know it or not.

As though oozing out from between the cracks of the buildings, Pastor Cain creeps up behind Hope. He has a lot of practice creeping. He startles Hope by placing a hand on her shoulder. He backs up just in time not to get hit by Hope's skateboard as she spins around. Maybe she helped it forward a bit.

"Cain... that's a right good way to lose a hand... or somethin' else," Hope playfully warns. Her lightness is only in tone... she's never cared for the pious bastard.

He backs away a bit further. "It's Pastor Cain."

"A bit biggity, hain't you."

"You once were part of the brethren, afore you went astray." Pastor Cain is doing his self-righteous best not to allow his true feelings for her interfere with a righteous task.

"It's been a while since I was too young to rightly know what it was... those days are a holler away."

"And now... you know what it's all 'bouts?" There's a part of him that wants an argument... so he could tell her what he really thinks.

"Yep!" is all she says... and she turns back to her walk.

From behind her, fading, "You even use to... "

Hope picks up the pace and starts whistling again, to gain distance from the good Pastor and his words.

A bit down the road she sees Gabriel and her Pa at the Crackerbarrel. She has her next target. As she approaches, Gabriel rolls his eyes and Marcus shakes his head with one of those *what now* mixed with *bad timing* looks.

"I would have expected the Crackerbarrel to have been prit' near packed today," Hope tries to start out cordial like.

"Howdy to you too." It's not one of Marcus' warmest mayoral versions of *howdy*.

Hope looks at Gabriel, "And no hi from you, old man?"

With hardly a glance, "Howdy, girl."

Gabriel always tries to keep his public relationship with Hope separate from their shared understandings. Hope is happy to play along, but part of that includes the occasional dig at him.

Marcus clears his throat. "Hope, hain't usual for you to come to town so often... you gotta point to make?"

"Just a hankerin' to know what's up 'bouts the road?"

"Got word it hain't gonna be fixed anytime soon... Don't suppose you might know anything 'bouts that?" asks her pa, not the mayor.

"I live on a mountain... I don't move 'em. Maybe yer God is just tinkerin' with ya'll fer takin' up his role."

"If so, it might be a dern right time fer you to stay up there on your mountain." This is the most Marcus has said to his daughter in at least a month.

Hope backs up with a curtsey, holding out her sundress. With a mischievous smile, "They's done been fed, so I hain't frettin' too much yet. But, mark my words, things are gonna get right strange afore long."

"Well, thanks for stopping by," says her father.

She turns to leave, and then spins back around, with a nod to Gabriel. "Bye, old man."

"Bye, girl," grumbles Gabriel.

As soon as Hope is out of earshot, Gabriel says, "Teched or no, she's got a fair point. Things are gonna git strange."

"I know... she hain't nearly as teched as most want to think." Marcus thinks on Hope's leave-behind words.

Hope, now almost skipping her way back down Main Street, passes Henry and Marge Poke, a couple in their mid-forties. They're arguing about some senseless nothingness. Hope can't remember if she's ever seen those two argue about anything.

She skips on.

While Hope's out on her errands, her guests lounge around the cabin. They sense it's a bit dangerous to do much else. Tom's half asleep on the well-worn sofa, his swollen ankle propped up on pillows. Rick and Lisa are attempting to play cards at the kitchen table... with mixed results. He is there... and Lisa is somewhere else.

"Gin," Rick says, as he lays down his fanned out cards.

She doesn't seem to notice so he repeats himself. Nothing.

"Where do you think she's off to?" Lisa asks, in a somewhat oblivious daze.

"How should I know? Gin."

"Oh... Is it my turn?"

"Are we playing the same game?"

"I wonder what game she's playing," Lisa meanders.

With an exasperated look, Rick shoves the cards to the center of the table and leans back. He closes his eyes and takes a deep breath, as if trying to refocus.

Rick was always an athletic kid, playing on one team or another most of his youth, all the way up through high school. As far as jocks go, he isn't too bad of an all-around guy. He had an advantage... a kid who felt safe hanging at his house for so many years. They rarely spoke of Tom's father, but Rick knew the score since elementary school. The world unfortunately turned a blind eye.

Rick's friendship first came into play as he took on the role of a big brother to Tom, even though they were the same age. It grew from there. When Tom's father mysteriously disappeared on Tom's thirteenth birthday, there was no more need to hide. Their friendship had already solidified, so it endured.

Over the years, having an overly imaginative, non-jock close friend helped keep Rick's mind open. Of course, there were a few peer-pressure snubbing collisions, especially as they got older, but most were quickly resolved.

As of late, however, their friendship has increasingly become more strained. Rick felt this backpacking trip was a good idea, once Tom proposed it... And Lisa was unable to talk him out of it. It hasn't escaped Rick's mind that perhaps friendships just grow apart. Friends go their own ways as a natural order of things. If that's the case, he figured, it would be a good last trip together.

Lisa's voice drifts back in, "I'm having nightmares of angels with butcher knives."

"Sorry, were you saying something?"

"You haven't been listening!" snaps Lisa.

"Aha... just drifted away for a moment. Look, she's still been nothing but nice to us so far... a bit odd, but friendly."

Lisa's on a roll. "That... that worries me most. Why would she be so open about all of this if she thinks we'll be leaving hear in one piece? Answer me that one."

Roused out of his half slumber, Tom says, "Lisa, you're the one that's starting to sound nuts. Like she said, she'd be in a lot of trouble if they find out she's hanging out with us."

"So... maybe she stops hanging out," Lisa responds.

Just then the back screen door to the cabin squeaks open.

Hope comes in carrying a set of crutches. "Sorta like Hansel and Gretel... I'm jest awaitin' to pop you two in the oven."

Tom laughs, "Don't you mean the three of us?"

"I was a hankerin' to keep you around fer a late night snack."

"That doesn't sound that bad to me," Tom says, with a playful grin.

Lisa stands up with her hands on her hips. "How long have you been spying on us?" When Hope doesn't bother looking at her, she adds, "I have some more questions for you."

"Naw," is all Hope says.

This is not the response Lisa was hoping for. How can you wage a decent fight against... *naw?* She snaps, "What do you mean by... naw?"

"You truly hain't the sharpest tack in the box. Naw means no. It could also mean... why would I want to spy on you and that freaked out head of yours."

Without waiting for some snappy response, Hope takes the crutches to Tom. Then, walking into the kitchen, she picks up the largest butcher knife from the counter.

Lisa stiffens.

Hope walks straight at her, blade in hand. As Lisa's eyes widen, Hope sets the knife on the table directly in front of her.

"Watch out, it's right sharp." Hope glances around at Rick and Tom. "I'll answers what questions I've a mind to... after dinner."

All in a huff, Lisa storms out the front door, making sure the screen door slams behind her.

Lisa's an 'A' lister... that likes another acceptable 'A' lister... that unfortunately is handicapped by a 'D' list friend. She's sure that with the right amount of work, she'll win. Though she's convinced herself it's about her relationship with Rick, at times it's more about who can control Rick. She doesn't understand how much power she gives Tom with this way of thinking. It's been like this as long as Lisa can remember... you only get to keep what you can control. At times she has shinier moments, but those have been scarce on this trip.

With a bit of struggle, Tom lifts himself up on the crutches. "They fit perfectly... Thanks."

Looking partially guilty, Rick says, "You'll have to excuse her, she's a little high-strung."

"Best watch out her strings don't go breakin'... remember, ya'll asked to stay."

Rick gives her a nod and heads out after Lisa.

After plopping back down on the sofa, Tom asks, "Hope, you have any spare paper around that I can use?"

"What fer?" says Hope as she walks to a hutch and starts digging out paper.

"I want to write a story."

CHAPTER THIRTEEN

CRACK!

A stone bounces off the trunk of a dead and twisted ash juniper. It ricochets back and to the right... falling at Rick's feet. He's come out to smooth Lisa's feathers.

"Stand down on the firing line?" Rick quips.

She's having none of it, at least for the moment. She waves him off with the back of her hand and picks up another rock. "They send you out to calm me down? ... The girl that sounds so crazy!"

Another rock gets hurled at the juniper... this one, a wide miss. Lisa takes a deep breath and spins toward Rick. "Am I really being nuts?" There has been so much cattiness lately that it's refreshing to hear Lisa sound sincere.

"Why don't we take a walk... get away for a little while." As Rick says this he doesn't wait for a response. He comes up and puts an arm around Lisa's shoulder.

They start off down one of a dozen paths that surround Hope's cabin, making sure it's not the one to the perch. Rick can feel the tension in Lisa's shoulder start to unwind. She puts her arm around his waist as they stroll. Ah, now this is a hint of the girl he's dating.

They walk some distance silently. Rick knows it takes a little bit of a build up before Lisa will admit anything's wrong... anything of any importance. He lets her go through the process without pushing. The path they are on skirts the base of the hills behind Hope's cabin.

After a sufficient amount of silence to convince herself this is not leading into a lecture, Lisa says, "OK... I'm just confused, frustrated... and a little scared by all this."

They come into a small clearing with a couple chair-size boulders near the base of a red maple. Rick walks behind one of the boulders and, as if it were a chair, pretends to pull it out.

"Care for a seat, my lady?" Rick asks with a slight bow.

Lisa grins. It's nice to have him to herself for a change. She curtsies and takes a seat.

Rick settles down on the rock next to hers. "Go on," is all he says.

After a moment of Lisa looking like she's building up to ex-plode, she blurts out, "It's her being so damn right about us! I don't like that I got something out of watching those three guys killed... I don't like that I don't know what... But, most of all... I don't like that she can see it!"

Rick's lips part to say something, but Lisa's on a roll.

"No matter how bubbly she and her sundress are, there's something seriously scary about her."

"Maybe that's what has us all a little fascinated by all this... there's an uncontrollable scary side to it... And... you'd look just as good in sundress."

Her sudden internal grimace rushes through him, like noticing a trap... after your foot is in it.

"So you do think she looks good in a sundress?"

No use pulling on a foot that's already in a trap. "I'm saying that we're all somewhat confused by this... but we're in it for some reason. Tom's the only one that seems too cool about it all."

"I'm pissed at him too... Weren't for his screwing up his ankle, we could at least have the option of leaving... Maybe."

Rick shoots for familiar territory, "What if I set up our tent... well away from the cabin tonight?"

He's hoping for an amorous comeback from Lisa, but she seems more attracted to something over his shoulder. It's a two and oh count for Rick... not his day. He turns to see what he's competing with.

Nothing... at least nothing he can see... except the brush and trees covering the sides of a mountain. As he stares, Lisa comes over and points about a third of the way up.

"Don't you see it?" she asks.

It's hard to make out any detail, but it appears to be a small ledge with a few trees... a crevice, created by flanking rocks, drifting to darkness. When Rick shades his eyes against the glare, he can even make out what looks like fabric hanging from tree limbs.

"So, what is it?" he asks.

"I think it might be that cave Miss Sunshine mentioned."

There's a new vitality in her voice. Lisa's not much into confessionals, especially about being confused. Conflict suits her better.

When he doesn't respond, she points out what she thinks should be obvious, "If she's hiding anything, it's probably up there."

Rick shakes his head. "I'm not even sure that's a cave... but if it is, she's already asked us to stay clear of her stuff."

"But... " Lisa starts to object.

"It's her mountain... considering we're dealing with some weirdly crazy people... maybe we should listen to her." Judging from his tone, Rick clearly wants nothing to do with the cave.

"Ah... you're probably right," says Lisa, with a small hand pat to Rick's chest.

He hates it when she agrees with him so easily. "I mean it... we need to stay clear of it."

She gives him another light pat on the chest as she passes him on her way back up the path.

"Of course. Guess we should get back before dinner... or whatever she's going to feed us."

Rick shakes his head and follows her. He suspects this is not the end of the matter.

While they head back to the cabin, what he doesn't notice is Lisa stealthily tearing up a scrap of paper from her pocket into tiny pieces and dropping them along the way. Not enough to be conspicuous, but enough to be found if you know what you're looking for.

The clatter of fork to plate dies down. Dinner is over.

There's a lot of silence around the table, for just finishing a good meal... and Hope sets out a good spread. There are still a few remaining golden brown, deep fried meatballs and hush puppies on a tray, and the remains of a colorful salad.

With renewed energy, Lisa is the last one to finish cleaning her plate. One last bite and she collapses back into her chair with an accidental satisfied look.

"Sorry about blowing up earlier," says Lisa.

"Like I done said... it, and me, is a lot to be takin' in. 'Specially in one bite." Hope's willing to try and play nice.

"Speaking about bites, that dinner was good. What was it?" asks Lisa, putting on her best face.

"Mountain oysters and hush puppies."

"Mountain oysters?"

"Yeah, pig nuts," says Hope, deadpan.

"What kind of nuts?" Lisa does her best to remain ignorant.

Tom is happy to offer, "Testicles... pig balls!"

Lisa's chin curls in like a snake recoiling. She stares at her well-emptied plate, wishing she could return its content... in a ladylike way. Neither Rick nor Tom want the aftermath of laughing out loud, so they don't... not out loud.

Rick thinks it best to break things off with, "You said you were going to tell us more about your odd little world."

"What I remember sayin' was... I might answer what questions that I've a mind to... after dinner. Dinner's over... fire away." As a dig, she adds, "Unless ya'll got more questions about that fine dinner."

With an involuntary glance back at her plate, Lisa quickly looks away.

"How long has your town been doing this?" asks Rick.

Hope stops clearing dinner and sits down at the head of the table. "Bin told it started a long spell back... called stonin' back then. Exactly when, can't rightly say. It came and went, but was always not far shy of the surface... always reared its head when bad times showed."

Lisa interrupts Hope, with a hint of self-righteousness, "You mean your people have been killing longer than you can remember?"

"Darlin'... people have been a killin' people fer a fair spell longer than any of us can remember." Hope takes a breath. "Now, if ya'll don't mind I'll finish my piece."

She stares at Lisa to see if there's a response. After none, "Stories were that it was done seen as a sacrifice fer a change of luck. That's back afore it done got churchified. Guess they figured the best way to be shed of occasional bad times was to make it all regular... a treatin' all times as potentially bad... sorta like religious guilt."

Hope pauses. She does have a piece of her father in her. Timing is part of any story. The kids remain attentive, so she goes on, "Nowadays they see it as some kind a purge... Everythin' is right perfect in town... as long as they's have their dose of blood on the side."

Her tone picks up. "These rightly more ambitious doin's started a passel a years back. Then Gabe and his contraptions puffed it up to an art in more recent times. Problem is it's done gotten to be a routine frenzy feedin'."

Rick tries to get his head around this. "There can't be that many visitors."

"You'd be plum' surprised on how folks think us mountain folks entertainin'... Outside the drive-ups, there's skiers in the winters and a passel of backpackers, like ya'll, in the summers."

"Nobody comes looking for them?" asks Lisa in disbelief.

"Now and then... but there's a fair piece of mountain up here... and a well-rehearsed town." Hope's come about as far as she's planning to about the feeding for the town's rituals.

Tom senses this. "Something Rick asked earlier puzzles me."

Hope smiles. Before he can finish asking, "How I come to see things a bit different than those kin in town?"

Tom nods.

"'Cause I'm an artist."

Lisa gasps, "What do you mean by... you're the artist?"

"You heard me wrong. I said... I'm *an* artist, so I can see art. And up here, it's all been made into right strange performance art."

"How did you get such a sick idea?" Lisa says, in a tome that's more than asking.

"From watchin' folks like you... that can't turn away."

"You've had outsiders like us up here before?" asks Rick.

"Don't need 'em to feed people's appetite... But did have a

boyfriend livin' up here afore... hid out, like ya'll. I even lived down in the city with a passel of artists fer a piece... Didn't take to it much, so I came back to my mountains."

Lisa leans in, her attention peaked. "Hold it now... You skipped over the boyfriend living up here thing pretty fast. What was that about?"

"Sex... Thought you'd rightly know 'bouts that by now."

Clearly irritated, Lisa presses on, "I mean, what did he think about... " with a wave towards the front door, "you know... that?"

"He took to watchin', like ya'll. Plum' fascinated by it."

"What happened?" asks Rick.

"Men bein' men... One day he jes' packed up and moved on. I don't have much a-hankerin' to go into that any further." She gives Tom a glance. "I do miss Jared now and then... when I get an itch."

Embarrassed, Tom fumbles with lighting a second candle on the table.

Hope laughs, "Why, Tom... you're turnin' plum' rosy red."

"You two want a room?" taunts Lisa.

With a casual gleam, Hope winks at Tom, "Not yet." Then she turns to Lisa, "But... kind of you to be askin'."

"I have another question... why us?" Rick asks.

"Like I said before... I'd answer what questions I've a mind to... and, for the moment, I'm plum' tired of questions." She stands. "I'm downright worn out fer the night so I'm a fixin' to git some sleep."

Hope's not interested in a *by your leave* so she heads around the table towards her room. She pauses at Lisa. Quietly, she reaches out and sprinkles pieces of torn up paper on the table in front of Lisa.

She leans in and softly says, "Hain't much on litterin' up here in these backwards hills."

CHAPTER FOURTEEN

The glistening white double doors of the church swing open following mid-day services. The townsfolk stream out in their *last* Sunday's best, but a little more disheveled than usual.

There's no customary mingling on the church steps today. On the contrary, most disperse quickly... avoiding each other. There are no real consequences of the town being cut off yet apparent, but the fear of an idea is often more powerful than the reality.

Esther, a hard-looking woman, walks along with her friend, Chloe. "I'm a feared Abigail is gonna get uppity with prices for the necessaries."

Chloe, whose weight hints she relishes supplies, is also distraught. "I know... Went by the bakery afore church and they's already missin' those large pastries I loves so much."

"Might'n be that's a good thing fer you," says Esther.

From the look that flashes across Chloe's face, and her stomping off, it appears that such a coarsely honest statement is alien in Redemption.

Across the way, a rare piece of conversation takes place between two older men, Jake and Aldo. Jake asks almost in a whisper, "Anyone think on askin' that teched young'un of Mayor Marcus?"

"Teched... my ass! That there girl is jes' plain out spoilt. Livin' up thar with her ghosts, she thumbs her nose at the flock prit' near every chance she gits. We'ez gonna fix our problems well afore goin' hat 'n hand to that little missy." Aldo is not the forgiving type.

Pastor Cain creeps up behind Marcus... the man has that consistently nasty habit. Hope had always thought, beside his religion weapon, that habit required the man to wear a cowbell. It was just another of her suggestions that didn't set well with the town... though her pa and Gabriel would lean for it.

Pastor Cain speaks suddenly and insistently as he flanks Marcus, "You seen the services... right peaked. Could hardly drum up a rousin' amen. The town's feelin' so sickly."

"Settle down a piece, Pastor. That's why we'ez fixin' to have a council meeting."

This is all the time Marcus wants to spend with the Pastor... for the moment. He picks up his pace, leaving Pastor Cain well aware the conversation is over. In the politician's style of avoiding unnecessary slights, Marcus yells back over his shoulder, "See you at the Last Chance shortly."

Gabriel crosses the street to join Marcus. As he approaches, "What was our good Pastor whinin' 'bouts?"

"Nothin' much... his sermon, as usual. Thinks folks is missin' the fire in their bellies. Come to it... you wouldn't have noticed, since you found some excuse to skedaddle early," chides Marcus.

"Some of us have work to be gotten to," Gabriel says with a satisfied smile. "So he's seein' ripples in the pond already?"

Marcus replies, half-confidently, "Jes' the newness of it all... bound to settle d'reckly."

"From my experience, when folks start to feelin' antsy, shine is in demand. Looks like me and my still purely might git overworked," says Gabriel.

"Sure you hain't jes' findin' a reason out of the good Pastor's sweet box?" Marcus mentally crosses his fingers and adds, "Let's hope we don't need it... too much of your shine unravels things right quick."

He's right, Marcus muses... *Gabriel's laying groundwork for wanting to spend more time shed of town, and the still promises peace.*

He gives a casual wave at two people down the street but, as Marcus looks on, the two part in an angry huff. *Hmmm... don't go holdin' you's breath,* he thinks.

There are rarely any serious arguments in the town of Redemption. At first they thought it to be the gift of the redeemings. But they've come to know it to be the cost of them. There's an unspoken premise at play here. The redemptions are the price paid for peace and prosperity. It stands to reason that to excuse the barbaric rituals, the people of Redemption have no discord... a monstrous coin. The truth they care not to see is that it's become more about the arena being the reward. They've just become more proficient with putting on *happy faces.*

The Last Chance Saloon wears a number of hats.

At times, it's the stage on which the dark ritual of baiting visitors plays out. At others, a watering hole for locals. But... any outrageous behavior is taboo. Darker, more human nature, if it exists, takes place behind closed doors.

But more often than not, it serves as it does this afternoon, as City Hall and home to the town council meetings.

The large circular council table sitting at the back of the barroom is surrounded by touches of Redemption's history: Drawings or photos of all the mayors of the past 162 years hang on the wall. The photos don't hint at how many of them oversaw bloody redemptions... it doesn't show in their eyes. But what portraits of leaders do?

Other walls in the bar are lined with photos of the real history... Redemption's people. They depict weddings, picnics, celebrations of all sorts, images that lace together a community... missing are photos of the arena.

Marcus and Gabriel are the last of the council to arrive. Aaron is busy bringing out ice tea for the gathering, while Pastor Cain, Naomi, Arlo and Hanna sit at the table mumbling amongst themselves. Hanna, Marcus' wife, gives her husband the evil eye for running late. She uses the evil eye so much it has become toothless... all Marcus does is shrug it off.

Before Marcus settles in his chair, Naomi bubbles out, "Reckon when our mountain road might be gotten to?"

"Was told not to be a holdin' my breath... if that be any sign," responds Marcus, as he takes his seat.

This shouldn't be much of a surprise to the folks of Redemption, considering their isolation. To push them even further down the trough, the road in and out of town is like a fifty-mile hairpin, now only serving as access to one town since the dissolution of the few others it passed through. For most of the state, Redemption and its 258 souls is an unheard-of speck on a map that overwhelms it. Considering their right strange doin's, being a fair distance off the grid is preferred... but not when the mountain moves and roads are cut.

Aaron asks, "Cain't we'ez clear it on our own?"

"Afeard Mother Nature did a purely serious job of takin' it out... we don't have the equipment to right it. We can bring in supplies over the old loggin' road but, as fer visitors, caint be expecting any soon."

Marcus knows this isn't what they want to hear. It's not what he'd tell townsfolk, but it's useless to hold it from the council. The way Redemption is, that's not exactly keeping a secret.

"That's the nut of it... hain't it?" says Gabriel.

They all glance around at each other, knowing he's right. They can farm and hunt and do without many modern things, but no visitors... that's another story.

With unconvincing optimism, Pastor Cain says, "Folks will jes' have to be patient."

Before someone can speak up and say why that's probably not going to happen, there's a knock on the bar door. Aaron goes and opens it to find Charity standing there.

She leans her head in past Aaron and half yells in to Marcus, "Mayor, can I say a piece?"

Charity is the last person Marcus wants to hear from right now, but she can become a royal pain in the ass if she's ignored. After a frustrated shake of his head, he waves for Aaron to let her in, "I reckon it would be OK... but try to keep it short."

She rushes forward.

Charity stands in front of the council like a frog battling the skitters, stepping one foot to the next.

"Girl, you have to go bathroom?" Gabriel asks bluntly.

Charity acts all coyly... irritatingly so.

"Charity, you got somethin' to be said... then out with it," Marcus' patience is being tried.

"Well, ya'll know that second swamp cooler atop Ben's roof?" she says.

"Yeah, what 'bouts it?" asks Arlo.

She does the nervous two-step again, maybe for emphasis, until Marcus snaps, "Out with it!"

"Well... it hain't no swamp cooler at all... He's got one of those satellite disc things hid under it," she says triumphantly. When she gets blank stares from the council, she adds, "Fer a TV he's done hid down in his cellar." This still doesn't get the gasps she was anticipating, so she starts to go on. "He pretends to... "

Marcus cuts her off, "Charity, we appreciate the tellin'... and we'ez gonna take it to thought."

"Jes' thought ya'll oughta knows." She stands there, bursting with passels of things she's not going to get to tell... it tears at her.

After an awkward pause, Hanna gets up and diplomatically ushers Charity towards the front door.

As she goes, Charity protests, "I got lots of... "

"I'm sure you do, dear... but we'ez got more than enough on our plate right now." With this, Hanna gently pushes Charity out the door, whispering to her, "Careful of where you git to pointin'... " and, with a flourish, she locks the door.

While Hanna gets rid of Charity, Gabriel uses the time to pour a little from his jug, *now in plain sight on the table*, into his cup.

Waiting till Hanna sits back down, he says, "Hell... sorry Pastor... It's kinda uppity of Ben, but everyone knows 'bouts that little TV he hides."

Marcus clears his throat, "That hain't the point. I gotta a suspicion that's jes' the tip of the root."

"What are you gettin' at?" asks Naomi.

"We'ez gonna start hearin' 'bouts all sorta things... now that we hain't got visitors to shake a stick at, mark my words. Up to us to cipher how to control it."

Everyone at the table quietly thinks on what Marcus says.

Arlo, not wanting to make big of it, leans over to Gabriel, "You gotta a bit more of the shine in your jug?"

The doors to the Last Chance Saloon swing in and the council, having accomplished not much more than worrying, comes out. Townsfolk are peppered around Main Street, trying to not clump together in an official mob. All watch those who leave the bar.

Marcus leans to Gabriel, "Notice anything different?"

"Outside of they's bein' gathered like vultures?" responds Gabriel.

"Hain't a passel of smiles between all of 'em."

CHAPTER FIFTEEN

Gabriel's 1954 bruised red F100 kicks up a trail of dust on a gravel and dirt country road. He doesn't mind the bruised skin... that goes with it being a truck.

With a rattle Gabriel's truck comes around a bend to find Hope in the middle of the road. With a jerk, he swerves around her. The truck continues another thirty feet, skidding to a stop. It's not that much of a skid. Gabriel's 1954 baby has lost a lot of its pick up. Gabriel is never in that much of a hurry.

He glances in the door mirror. Hope is sashaying up... she waves when she sees his reflected eyes. Gabriel's voice is gruff to friend or foe, but there's a warmer gruffness with Hope.

That voice comes from the cab, "Girl, you's gonna git yourself run over prancin' down the road likes that."

"Gabe... I'd been hearin' this rickety old truck of your'n a fair piece... figured either it or I would git outta the way," quips Hope.

In a defensive, slightly insulted tone, Gabriel replies, "She hain't that old." He sticks his head out of the window. "Hop on in, I'll carry you to your fork... if you behave yourself."

There's a loud creak, one of its bruises, as Hope pulls open the passenger door and hops in. "I take it you's a headin' up to your still."

He sniffs, as Gabriel often does before responding, "Ya figured right. Way things are goin' the town is gonna need some serious num'a-fyin'... and right soon." He grinds his beauty into gear and pulls back on the road.

Other than the rattling of the truck, they ride along quietly for a piece. Gabriel finally says, in his straightforward manner, "You's have anything to do with that landslide the other night?"

"Naw... jes' a stroke ofluck."

"Figured you'd be seein' it that way," says Gabriel.

"Gotta admit... town needs a bit of shakin' up now n' then, don't cha?" Hope more than asks.

"That road goin' out, natural or otherwise, might'n be a speck more shakin' than the town can handle. People is already gittin' on each other's nerves... and it hain't been more than a smidgin of time," confides Gabriel.

"Don't want to say I done told you so... "

"But you will," Gabriel says, cutting her off. "Look, girl, I know you git all caught up in your artsy seein' of things, but if you's could, stay clear of town the next few days... it would be a purely wise idee."

"I'm touched... old man, you is a-worryin' 'bouts me."

Gabriel sniffs, "I'm jest worryin' 'bouts havin' too many things to worry 'bouts at the same time... that's all." With this he slams on the brakes. The truck does a gravelly skip to the side of the road. "Here's your fork."

Hope turns her head and looks through the cab's back window. There are a couple wooden crates containing jugs roped off in the bed of the truck.

"Gabe darlin', you got a spare jug back there?" she asks.

"We've shared a nip 'r two now 'n' then, but it hain't that often you's ask fer a full jug."

"If the town's goin' a crazy as you say, figured it might be a good idee to stock up," Hope says, hoping she hasn't raised a red flag... Gabriel is one of the sharper folk in town.

"Yeah, girl, go ahead and grab one when you gits out."

Before doing so, Hope pulls a baggy of weed from her sundress pocket. She holds out the baggy to Gabriel. "You's got a mighty artistic soul old man... 'bouts time you expand your horizons."

This isn't the first time she's tried to get him to start smoking, but it's the first time the thought dances across his mind to take her up on it. Not this time.

"I'll be stickin' to my shine... fer now."

Hope just smiles, pockets the baggy, and hops out of the truck. She turns back to the window, "Have it yer own way, old man... you usually do." She reaches in the bed and pulls out a gallon jug.

"That I do," Gabriel says as he pulls away.

Charity has lived above the ice cream parlor as long as anyone can remember. Her apartment faces out on Main Street.

Tacky wallpaper of faded angels surround the room. They're polka-dotted with different styles and sizes of crucifixes. On the dining room wall, next to the window, hangs a boardroom size pinup board... on it, photos of many of the good citizens of Redemption. Around each photo are hand written post-it notes.

The dining room table is cluttered with paper clippings, scissors, glue, post–its and notepads. The only dining chair at the table looks out the window onto the late afternoon.

This is Charity's private nook of accountability.

Charity stands at the window with the drapes open just enough for her to use her binoculars. Through the lens she stares at Ben's house. Ben glances all around and opens the storm doors to his cellar. He looks all about one more time to assure his privacy, before he descends through the doors.

Charity utters, "Uh-huh... got ya, again. Wonder what's on?"

Her view moves on to Prudence by her car, just outside the front door of the Last Chance Saloon. Prudence lives in a room above the bar. The young barmaid is fiddling with a grocery bag in the front seat of her car.

Charity takes the binoculars she's using and hangs them on a hook by the window, right next to an even larger pair. With the more powerful ones she goes back to watching her prey.

Prudence peers around, then lifts some of the top groceries out of the bag. She reaches down and pulls a small red package from under the seat and places in the bag, replacing the groceries on top. After one more glance around to be satisfied with her deception, Prudence takes the bag and heads inside.

Charity lowers her glasses, picks up a notepad from the table and scribbles something on the sheet. She rips the sheet from the pad and pins the sheet up near Prudence's photo.

Back to spying, Charity takes up the binoculars once again. She slowly pans down the street looking for more victims. She spies Henry walking along. After he does nothing more than walk, she shrugs and mumbles to herself, "Dang slow day."

Now some movement across the street catches her attention... a brush of drapes. Trying to isolate it, she adjusts the focus of her glasses. Between the split drapes directly across from her apartment, light reflects off another pair of binoculars. They're aimed right at Charity. She recoils from the window.

"Nosy Bitch!" snaps Charity.

CHAPTER SIXTEEN

Hope knows the game she plays. But she's not quite accustomed to this much, or to many guests... especially when one is a catty. Hope finds herself needing to get off on her own more... to avoid overreacting. It would not be appropriate for her; it just wouldn't serve her game. But she's not sure what that game is yet... perhaps she sees them as something to spur creativity... cold or not.

Stars are emerging in the early night sky over her perch. She sits at peace here. There are no irritating questions over right or wrong... no grating female voice. The arena below is silent and dark, as if it weren't there. Off beyond is the soft ambient glow of the town's lights. She can't directly see the town, just its skyprint... more importantly, they can't see her perch.

First, brush rustles... then twigs break... then stones topple ... then Tom comes crashing down through the brush into the last feet toward the perch. He desperately tries to regain his footing with the crutches, but it's like using chopsticks with his feet. Catastrophic failure... Tom slams down next to Hope.

He attempts a smile that won't leave him appearing a total klutz... it doesn't work. But it almost does. Hope smiles, as she shakes her head.

"Reckon a mountain path is a right rough place to be practicin' those things."

As Tom laughs and tosses aside the one crutch left, Hope helps get him twisted around so all his limbs point somewhat in the right direction.

"Thanks. I had to get out of the cabin... got tired of listening to those two waffling back and forth over things. Figured you might be out here."

His thinking brings a grin to Hope. There's a connection here... she knows it. Though it is an unexpected twist.

"Since you already done fallin' in here, might as well rest with me a piece," says Hope, plopping down next to him.

She shoves the jug of shine over to Tom. When he takes slug of it, the burn shows on his face. It brings a soft laugh from Hope and she looks up at the stars.

"Nice n' peaceful like out here," says Hope.

Tom leans forward and peeks down at the arena's darkness. "Odd, considering... but it feels the same to me."

The two remain quiet for a while, allowing the crickets and sounds of the woods to carry on the conversation. Hope lights a joint, takes a drag and then silently passes it over to Tom. He takes it, keeping the silence. With little effort they float on the same wave.

As if trying not to break the evening mood, Hope softly says, "I read some of your writin's... hope that don't fret you too much."

"If you hadn't, I would have asked you to... What did you think?"

"I took a-hankerin' to it. I think you git it... I mean, what I see in it all. It was kind of you to change the place and names in that story of your'n."

"But I didn't change yours," says Tom.

"Kinda like that, too." Hope doesn't fear the world over her way of seeing things, but she does welcome that someone else is aware of her thinking... she would have no other name in the story.

"I hope I get a chance to finish the story."

"Why shouldn't you?" asks Hope.

"With no visitors, Rick and Lisa will get bored soon... And my ankle will heal."

Tom has guessed what Hope sees coming as the result of nature's joke... he has no idea how long it will take.

"That won't be the likes of it... People is downright funny in that way." Hope's confidence is not annoying.

"What way?"

"The fear of not havin' somethin' is a might more fret'n than the reality of it... I suspect the pit will be in use right soon." Hope suspects nothing... it all is within her knowing.

"You sure?" he asks.

Hope takes another drag and stares at him a second. Then, "I 'spec' you know the answer to that... You got yourself a right fertile imagination."

He can't help thinking that she's in his head. If that is so, then he has nothing to fear.

"I like being in my imagination... things can get very bizarre in there... without consequences. You have to hide all that imagination from bein' let loose in the real world."

"Not up here... the rules are prit' near shed."

Tom glances towards the dark hole again. Rules can't get any more shed than that.

"Rick told me a smidgin 'bouts your long kinship... 'bouts ya'll as kids." Hope can see this catch Tom off guard, so she pushes forward with it, "Your pa... how'd he disappear?"

There's silence for a few long seconds. Then Tom looks straight at her, "With my help," he says definitively.

Hope knows this is all he's going to say on the matter. She shows her understanding with a simple nod. Another thing she's pretty sure of... he's never said that before.

The night pauses time.

Hope breaks the pause with, "You remind me of Jared... but different."

"Meaning, I look like I'm ready to run?" Tom says in a light tone... no insult given nor received.

Hope rolls over towards Tom. Her sundress moves smoothly over her skin. He's aware of every inch.

"If you'd a mind to, you could settle here a piece... meanin' after that ankle of your'n heals. Might prit' near be one of a few hollers your imagination can run free like... even the darker parts," she assures him.

Tom's eyes are transfixed on Hope... Her every movement... Her eyes... The drifting of her blond hair. In his imagination he sees Hope as an angel... her soft white sundress bleeds to red.

He smiles.

CHAPTER SEVENTEEN

Sun's well up.

Rick sits on the steps. Lisa is in Hope's chair with her feet up on the rail, like their host often puts hers up. Both look bored... Till the screen door creaks open. Tom comes out, doing a horrible job of not looking pleased.

Lisa leans out and glances behind Tom to see that Hope's not lurking in the doorway. Satisfied, in a voice soft enough to pretend caring... loud enough to be well heard, "I know we're in the woods, but does she have to howl like a wounded animal?"

Rick is not much better. "It wasn't that loud," and he cracks up laughing.

Tom... is just sorry he bothered coming out.

Instead of facing company Hope has headed for the kitchen under the pretense of tea... and the reality of thinking. She stares at the pot boiling, oblivious to the noise on the porch, lost in the game playing in her head. It's her painting and she can control these three... but someone becoming too close means less control, more confusion. Hope doesn't like confusion.

She grabs her daypack from the back of a chair and quietly heads out the back door.

At the opposite end of town from the church is Marcus and Hanna McCoy's home. It's a two-story, white-planked house with a large veranda. In flatland cities, it would be seen as an aged and average house. Up here, it's a mansion, the largest house in town... and well-maintained.

Marcus has an old Chevy in a shed behind the house but, in a town this small, walking is his usual choice. He always likes meeting people, even at those times he acts like he doesn't. Walking lets him encounter more, walking lets him play politician in his small world.

The bulk of Redemption fits in ten-by-four city blocks. Parts of this small footprint are even sparse. Long ago the town supported itself through lead mining, mines that played out two generations back, leaving the town with slightly more buildings than it needed. Adding to that, half the town's population lives outside the town proper.

The mayor strolls along the edge of the street, about half way between home and the center of town. Gabriel's bruised red pickup rattles up beside him and Gabriel leans out the window.

"Town's become right sartifiable. Hop in and I'll save you a passel of senseless jabbering on the way in."

Though a bit confused by Gabriel's remark, Marcus gets in the truck anyway. "What's you talking 'bouts?"

"You's gonna see soon enough." Gabriel pulls out.

As they drive down Main Street, whenever Marcus is seen in the truck, people urgently try to wave him over. Gabriel keeps driving.

"Seems to be folks is gittin' antsy a speck earlier than ya'll counted on," Gabriel warns Marcus. "The council's already gatherin'"

Gabriel pulls the truck to a stop near the Last Chance Saloon, just down the street from the Crackerbarrel.

No sooner than Marcus steps out, Phoebe comes running up. She appears distraught as she belts out, "Marcus... I got somethin' important to... "

Gabriel serves as blocker, "Phoebe, I done told you that has to be taken to the town council."

"That's plum' what I'm doin'," she snaps.

"What Gabe means is you have to tell whatever it is formal-like," Marcus tries with a diplomatic tone.

"But... " Phoebe starts off again.

Marcus decides to hell with diplomacy, "Phoebe... Bring it to the council!" He turns away from her and towards Gabriel, "When we'ez meetin'?"

"In 'bouts a half hour."

"Good... I'm in need of a coffee." Marcus takes off on the short walk to Abigail's Store, which is known to always keep a right fresh pot on the stove.

All Gabriel can do is shake his head, sure that going over to Abigail's and the Crackerbarrel is not a great idea. Then again, how can Marcus feel what's going on without experiencing it. He shrugs and follows.

Marcus approaches two old men, Albert and Quincy, who are in each other's face on the sidewalk. They both are in their mid-eighties. Albert shakes the top of a sandwich board sign as if it were gospel. The sign says 'AL'S SPACE'.

His yell is not as strong as it once was, broken by moments of shortness of breath, "Jes' in case I've a-hankerin to be bringin' my... truck. This here space is smack dab... in front of my store!"

Quincy slaps the back of his hand against the sign, "It's now your son's store, you old fool." His stamina is not much better than Albert's. "Anyhow... you's too dang addled to be drivin'... so I can park... here if I were a mind to!"

"Who is you callin' old... with that rickety... excuse of a body ya'll got." Albert gets up nose to nose with Quincy. If either one of them were to take a swing the contact would probably topple them both.

As Marcus and Gabriel pass by, Quincy starts to look his direction. Both councilmen wave him off and continue on down the sidewalk. Marcus glances at Gabriel, but only gets a shrug in return.

The Crackerbarrel isn't that crowded, but the few that are there... are at odds. Marcus and Gabriel hold back... listening.

Marcus decides to approach Isaac and Abel, despite Gabriel's light pull at his sleeve to leave them be.

"What's you two old friends all het up 'bouts?" he asks.

Gabriel gives an exhausted shake of his head.

Abel puffs up, ready to present his case, "Isaac's two boys was spose to help clear my south field... I hain't seen hide nor hair of 'em so far."

"They gotta a-hankerin' to go fishin'," Isaac defends.

Not leaving it at that, he pulls a handful of seeds from his pocket, "And I got a-hankerin' to do plantin'." With a touch of too much drama, he sprinkles the seeds on the deck. "They's gonna do as much good thar as they's gonna do on my unturned south field."

By this point the two men are back at each other, ignoring Marcus' presence. Isaac goes on the attack, "You still owe 'em fer work they done on your barn."

"You know I'll make that right... even if they's lazed off half the time."

Marcus happily backs away... but backs up right into Esther. Charity hovers close by. Esther is all het up with the store's owner, Abigail.

"I done seen this a comin'... 'cause we'ez a little cut off hain't no reason fer you to git all uppity with ya'll's prices."

"Esther, I've only raised 'em a speck... and that's account of more cost it'll be bringin' neededs over that old fire road. Cain't even guess to what's gonna git broken."

They're not nose-to-nose, but Abigail stands her ground as if they were. So does Esther.

"Those is tomorrow's frets... I's talkin' 'bouts today's prices!"

Of course, Charity has to stick in her two cents... basing it on real knowledge is of little importance. "I know you raised some prices without need last week."

"Charity... would you please get off my deck. All you do is feed on folk's misery," snaps Abigail.

Appearing both angry and hurt, Charity steps away just enough to be technically off the deck, not far enough to miss anything... and close enough to jump back in, if needed.

Trying to be mayoral, and wanting that cup of coffee, Marcus interrupts, "The council's gonna be lookin' to frets like gittin' goods easier... and, Abigail, you got some of that fresh coffee of yours inside?"

Gabriel looks around. Soft edges have become harsher as discontent grows in Redemption.

CHAPTER EIGHTEEN

Marcus, coffee in hand and Gabriel at his side, comes in the front door of the bar/city hall. They're a bit surprised to find most of the council is present. Neither remembers seeing any of them outside.

"When did ya'll git here?" asks Marcus.

Naomi, sounding exasperated, "We had to come in the back door... You should hear all the fussin' out there."

"Naomi... we just came through... out there," Gabriel reminds her.

Walking to the bar, Gabriel pulls a jug from behind it. He very deliberately uncorks it and pours two-fingers in a glass. He knows how this action irks a few on the council... like Naomi, and especially Hanna. He likes that.

Aaron backs in through the kitchen door, carrying a tray with a lemonade pitcher and glasses. He places it on the round council table, and plops down in one of the chairs. The others, who have been standing around, head for the table.

While the others mumble about this and that and pour lemonade, Gabriel saunters over to the wood-louvered shutters. He takes a sip of shine while he opens one panel of small shutters. Only a bit, since the bar shutters rarely get used.

He glances out.

"Hey, Gabe... let's git this goin'," yells Marcus.

Gabriel wanders over to the table with a slight chuckle.

Once everyone is set Marcus raps the table. Hell, he doesn't even know why he does it outside of ritual. Then again, it makes him feel important. But that wouldn't be his public argument. He raps the table again.

"OK... Where 'bouts should we git started? We can take some time fer issues afore we gits to the few that's bound to be outside." Marcus lays out order to address the crisis.

Gabriel gives a loud cough. He's seated on the backside of the table, with one foot up on an extra chair. Gabriel always finds it amusing to watch people plan... and then for life to happen.

With a casual point at the front shutters, he says, "Ya'll might want to rethink your order."

Before Marcus, or anyone else at the table, can question this, the front door rattles as someone unlocks it, making it sound as if it was a struggle doing so.

The door opens. Ethan squeezes in, trying to keep from opening the door too far. He nods constantly at whoever is outside the slot his face is in.

"I know... I promise... ".

He finally gets the door closed and bolted. Leaning back up against the wall, Ethan lets out a deep breath. Then, "There is a passel of folks out there."

"How big a passel, Ethan?" asks Daniel.

"Prit' near... all of 'em."

Marcus shakes his head in disbelief. "Ethan... you sayin' there are 'bouts 250 folk out there?"

Ethan laughs at the absurdity of this. "Naw... jes' those folks we'ez use to seein'."

"So 'bouts a dozen," Gabriel dryly reappraises the facts.

With an innocent shrug, Ethan says, "Well... that's a passel... hain't it?"

There are loud raps on the door. The group looks to Marcus.

"OK... we sees the folks first," Marcus surrenders, as he gives a wave of his hand at the door. "Let 'em in... one at a time."

Of course, the first one to squeeze in is Charity... And she comes chomping at the bit, though she attempts to look sheepish.

Before she can open her mouth, Marcus says, "Charity, why am I not surprised... You already done brought one complaint."

Thinking she might not get another turn, Charity blurts out, "But I know another... much more due a-frettin'."

Marcus glances around the council, reading faces, and looks back to Charity. "So be it... but keep your visits sparse. What da you got fer us?"

Pastor Cain feels he has to lay a little religion on for good measure, "Now, Charity... you know what they's say 'bouts castin' stones."

She puts her hands together as if in prayer, and dances around as if she had to go to the bathroom again. "Yeah... buts I gotta gits this one out."

Marcus starts to lose it. Hanna puts a hand on his shoulder to calm him, and turns to Charity, "Now settle down, girl... and let us know what it is."

Charity nods and takes a breath. "You knows Simon, who parts of the time teaches art?"

"Charity... everyone knows everyone here. So git to it," demands Hanna.

"Well... I hear'd that when he goes out of town fer fetchin' supplies... He dresses up likes a woman."

She finishes this with a look of pride that perhaps her telling will be the best of the day. The recent turn of events has been like a checkered flag waving open a competition for her.

Naomi pointedly asks, "You hear'd... or you know?"

Charity brings her enthusiasm down a speck, "Well... I hear'd... But hain't that 'bouts the same thing?"

Most of the council shake their heads... none bothers to attempt the useless exercise of explaining the difference.

Marcus finally says, "We'll give it due thought, Charity."

"But... " she protests.

"Charity... It's been noted!" snaps Marcus.

If he has to put up with this woman much longer he'll throw her out the door himself. It might even feel good. He figures that will be very un-mayor-like so he nods to Ethan to open the floodgate once again.

Rejected, Charity plods over to the front door... just as Jason comes in. The two avoid eye contact as they pass. Jason, who's a mechanic like his old man, moves towards the council.

As he does, Pastor Cain mumbles an exasperated, "What now?"

His frustration is understandable, considering these good townsfolk showing up to bear witness are the loudest *amens* in church. Regardless of this, he has his little pad out to take detailed notes of the accusations.

Before Jason gets all the way to the table, he anxiously opens his mouth, "I got somethin' ya'll should know."

"Of course you do," grumbles Gabriel, only half interested.

"But... it's important," Jason insists.

Marcus glances at his watch. "Of course it is... so please get to it."

"My pa takes change from the collection plate... and it hain't always in the church's favorin'," says Jason, and pausing as though he's expecting his revelation to astound the members of the council.

All he gets is, "We'll make note of it," from Pastor Cain. And he does exactly that in his little pad.

Jason looks disheartened. He hears the front door being un-bolted by Ethan behind him, meaning his time is up.

A couple hours have passed. Gabriel is on his fourth 'two-fingers' glass of shine. In general, the whole council is bored to death with the steady flow of accusations... real or perceived. Even Pastor Cain's enthusiasm has dropped down to only writing two or three words per telling.

Jane, the town's midwife, has just finished up telling how some fourteen-year old hung a squirrel, "...and so that's why I thought it right important."

Pastor Cain shoves his notepad away, having reduced this down to a one-word description.

Marcus does his best to fake a smile. "Thank ya, dear. We'll think on it."

She gives an honest, appreciative smile and heads for the door.

Ethan's still manning the turnstile into this largest number of telling's in his lifetime. When he was truly younger, he thought redeemings worked... as his long-gone father had reared him. Now that the polish has worn off, he finds that cynicism is in-fectious. Like his mentor, he's taken more to the contraptions than figuring folks out.

Ethan gives Jane a wink as he politely opens the door. His distraction is short-lived when he hears Marcus yell.

"Ethan, be a lad... go out and tell 'em no more fer now... we're a fixin' to hear 'em... but, whatever... jes' tell 'em no more fer now. And... lock the door," Marcus dumps on the lad.

With news that's not going to be taken well, Ethan gives a nervous nod, stiffens his back and squeezes out the door. A key turns in the lock.

Gabriel gives an exhausted sigh and sinks back in his chair. Even for those that don't verbally sigh, they emotionally do so after the overload of the last few hours. Everyone breathes for a speck of time.

Aaron breaks the silence, "I vote fer the sex-toy tellin'."

"Naw... I was partial to the hung squirrel one... then, maybe 'cause it were the end," says Gabriel.

There are a few laughs around the table... but not all.

Hanna is not one to laugh. She's more of a believer than her husband. She knows Marcus is pragmatic and she tolerates it, but she has drunk all the Kool-Aid. Hanna truly believes in the redemptions. She has a cold, hard face that may have been softer in younger days. She appears to always be in control of her emotions, or hiding them. Hanna only has one bright red button... Hope McCoy, her stepdaughter.

"There were a few noteworthy tellin's in there," Hanna coldly says. There's a chilly hint of a call to arms coming.

"Hanna there is right... I got a few marked down right here." Pastor Cain waves his notepad. "If they wasn't our good God-fearin' neighbors, some of these tellin's would have 'em teetering close to... you know."

Gruffly from the shadows, Gabriel speaks up, "Now, ya'll skeered of the word... redemption? Hell, that's what this here meetin' is all 'bouts."

"Well, if Hope hadn't... " Naomi catches herself.

This is a hammer slam on Hanna's red button. She glares at Naomi for a long second... she bites her lip... she takes in a deep breath... and, like a boiling teapot taken from the fire, the invisible steam over her head dies down. She decides Naomi has cut it off quick enough.

Hanna rarely would discuss Hope and, even more rarely, call her *daughter*. Hope is the daughter of Hanna's sister, Rachael. And Rachael was not Hanna's favorite sister... even though she was her only sister. When Rachael passed on some ten years ago, Hanna took control of things and moved right into her sister's shoes, including marrying Marcus.

Hope knew her father didn't know what hit him, but at nine she couldn't get through to him. Hope got her imagination from Rachael... that's always been a sore spot. Now add to that her rejection of the town... and Hanna sees red.

Most hold their breath to see if someone was going to blow up. No one is more pleased than Marcus that it has passed. He can hold his own with the council and the everyday mayoral duties, but he doesn't have the same control at home. And, as crazy as Hope gets, she still reminds him of Rachael's creative side. She's his daughter.

"Bringin' us back to the nub... anybody got any idee how we'ez gonna deal with our itch?" Gabriel asks, with his usual tendency to get to the point.

The more timid Arlo speaks up, "I know it hain't never been done before, least not this way, but how 'bouts we put a team together. They drive on down to the flats... "

"Over the fire road?" injects Aaron.

"Yeah... over the fire road. And then they snatch people in a moonlight hunt... you know, folks that wouldn't be missed, like homeless." Seeing skepticism, he quickly adds, "And... of course, only ones that is rightly redeemable."

Arlo is on the shyer side, but the grin he has says he thinks he hit gold.

"We haven't lived up in these hills so long without bein' much bothered by tinkerin' with things down on the flats. That might be a right good rule to stay by." Marcus is being neighborly.

He's half a mind to tell him how stupid that would be... but what good would it do? He glances over to Gabriel to suggest he mind his manners. Marcus is sure *stupid* would have been one of Gabriel's kinder words.

The consensus of looks stands behind Marcus, so Arlo lets go of the idea... reluctantly.

"Anybody else got a dog to bring to the game? That gatherin' of righteous citizens out there is gonna grow like rabbits," says Marcus, dancing around the issue that's almost a foregone conclusion.

Hanna impatiently stands. "Let's git to the core of things... The only ways that arena is gonna git filled is if we'ez put an eye on one of our own."

This is the elephant in the room. Dancing around it will serve no purpose. Yet all sit quiet. Finally Pastor Cain speaks up.

"I... we... do look to one of our own... it's gonna mean redeemin' someone's kin."

"Hell... in these parts we'ez jes' 'bouts all kin in some way," says Aaron. He may be exaggerating, but not far off the mark.

"Pastor's right, hain't any way around that stump. Might be we could pick someone with the least close kin," offers Marcus.

Hanna's quick to add, "But they has to have fair reason fer bein' redeemed."

Gabriel quietly grumbles, "Since when?"

He gets a mixture of both knowing and offended glances.

"We'd be gittin' reasons enough to find someone... how good the reason is in the speechifyin' of it." If Marcus knows nothing else, he knows how to spin wording. "If we'ez gonna do this, I'd suggest we git to it afore folk's blood gits more het up."

Naomi reaches for an upside, "Might'n be takin' of one of our own will right temperaments amongst folks a smidgin... least fer a spell."

"And maybe we'll find sunshine in a gully-washer, too," quietly grumbles Gabriel.

"Gabe... got two things fer you. Can you gits the arena up and ready fer tomorrow?" asks Marcus.

"If I use an old toy, it's doable." From Gabriel's tone, it's clear he's disappointed in having to use an oldie, but these are unusual times. "What's the other thing?" he asks.

"Put a damn locked box out front fer the tellin's."

"Hell... sorry, Pastor... Some folks up here cain't write too well," responds Gabriel.

Aaron perks up. "They can draw stick figures, with names on 'em showin' what they think was done wrong."

Gabriel grins, "That might be more fun fer us... sorta like that game of figurin' out puzzles... What's they call it... charades?"

"Naw... charades you act out. My mother used to play that. But, Gabe, you's part right... it's sorta akin to it. Be right more fun than today's tellin's," says Naomi.

Then... they get to deciding who to kill next.

CHAPTER NINETEEN

Tom's the kind of writer that if he was on a computer in a coffee shop, others would be turned off at the exuberance with which he hits the keys. He's the same with pencil and paper. He sits on Hope's steps scratching away with fervor. Crutches lean against the rail and his healing ankle stretches out before him.

It's drifting into late afternoon and no one has seen hide nor hair of Hope all day.

A hickory nut hits the back of Tom's head.

It barely fazes his focus. One hand, out of pure reflex, slaps at whatever hit him and returns to its chores. Another nut hits Tom.

"What happened to your ridiculous banter when you think you're coming up with something original? Your incessant searching for the next stupid idea?" Lisa has a way of making *good morning* sound snippy. She throws another hickory nut.

She and Rick lounge on Hope's swinging loveseat. The chain holding it creaks with every move. A light snore comes from Rick. The two of them look like melted ragdolls, one awake, one asleep. It's been a lazy, and lifeless, day.

Lisa lets out a bored sigh. She doesn't like hearing Tom... but, even more, she dislikes the silence of his not trying to impress her. That's what she usually thinks is his motive... any guy's motive. She throws another hickory nut.

In a slow turn, Tom looks at Lisa, "I'm not searching... I'm finding." He pivots away, leaving her with little ammunition.

Lisa doesn't know what miffs her more... that he's talking over her or that he's not paying attention to her. With a nasty wave of her hand at Tom's outstretched leg, "Ain't that ankle of yours getting any better?"

Rick stirs. He opens his eyes and twists his neck until it makes a slight pop... first one way and then the other. "Ain't?" he asks lazily.

Lisa throws the rest of the hickory nuts, planned for Tom, onto the deck. She huffs, "We stay up here any longer, our minds will deteriorate into thinking like these hillbillies."

"Careful what you be sayin' 'bouts us hillbillies," comes from the woods. Hope meanders out of the bushes flanking the trail to town. "'Specially since we'ez 'bouts to put a show on fer ya'll tomorrow."

Tom sets aside his writing. He's more pleased to see Hope show up than to hear of renewed redemptions. Rick and Lisa glance at each other, more affected by the potential of more bloodletting. Neither will admit it yet.

A glint of concern washes over Rick's face. "There haven't been any new visitors... have there?"

The concern moves contagiously to Lisa. The glare of her eyes grows to more of an accusation than concern. Tom just smiles, pretty sure of what's going down.

Hope squats down in the dirt. She takes a stick and starts scratching at the ground... without a smile or even eye contact.

It has its intended effect on Rick and Lisa. They glance nervously at each other. Tom watches with amusement. Hope at last raises her head and laughs.

"Gotcha!" She stands. "Hain't worth frettin'... done told you that I'd have to answer fer ya'll bein' here. Though it might be a passel of fun seein' one of ya'll in the arena." She pauses, allowing Lisa to throw her a nasty look. "Jes' teasin'... No, the crazy doin's I told you of is 'bouts to commence."

Whatever emotions on their faces a few seconds ago now make a complex shift as they look back and forth between each other. They all know, that to different degrees and for different reasons, that's why they are still here... whether they admit or not.

Hope watches all three with a careful eye. She sees Tom as the most detached from making judgments about what is coming. Rick is still a bit of a puzzler... torn between fascination and revulsion. Hope's not sure how that will play out. The easiest for her to read is Lisa... there's a darkness there. Despite all her huffing and puffing, she's the one with the most bloodlust.

Sounding a bit bewildered, Rick says, "Bad as it sounds, that's what we stayed for... right?"

Lisa's only willing to offer her silence as an agreement.

With a little effort Tom gets up on his crutches. "Hey... fair lady, how about a walk?"

"I'm plum' tickled with the idee."

When Tom gets over to Hope, there's an invisible spark. Then they head for a path that's a little less exacting for his crutches.

Disregarding Rick's nudge, Lisa can't help adding a dig, "Your ankle seems much better... with her."

Hope and Tom grin as they continue on the path.

Lisa peers at Tom's notebook, which remains on the step.

After a bit of walking, it's clear Tom's ankle is healing.

They get to a clearing and Hope stops. She knows the walk will lead to a question... but tires of waiting for it.

"So what's pressin' on your mind?"

"Why us?"

It's the question Hope expected. They had all danced around it, even Tom... probably, for fear of an honest answer. If it had come from either of the other two, she wouldn't be concerned about the *honest* part of it. Tom's earned a bit more.

"I hain't quite sure... I means, the painting is in the works. Maybe I sees this as all comin' to an end... and I want to share it. You know... tree fallin' in the woods an' all. Like I done said... I hain't quite sure. That'll have to do."

She gives Tom a little nudge and adds, "And you is right good with my itch."

CHAPTER TWENTY

Normally the bleachers around the arena have about an eighty-five percent attendance. Most days a few folk are bound to be absent, busy keeping the small world of Redemption turning. This is not one of those days.

Everyone is here... and happy to be in the bleachers, not below them. Like a wildfire, the word has gotten out that they will be redeeming one of their own... only a few know whom. The crowd is abuzz with speculations.

Up on Hope's perch, the three kids inch closer to the edge for a better view. Lisa shoves Rick over to claim her fair share of real estate... there's nothing timid about her hunger now.

The humming noise of the crowd below mutes anything shy of a yell up on the perch. Rick leans back out of the bushes, asking Hope with a loud whisper, "Any idea of who it is?"

Hope finds this an odd question, considering they know none of the people from town. She wonders if giving names to the victims enhances the experience.

For her, anyone put in the arena will be someone whom she not only knows, but also most likely has history with. Will it enhance her experience? She thinks not. Hope's focus has always been more on the predator than the prey... Though she does get a kick out of the imagination Gabriel puts into his contraptions.

As an answer to Rick's question, Hope takes a last drag on a new joint and tosses it to him. "Hain't any of ya'll... is all I know."

Listening to this, Tom, knows that's probably not true. He doesn't know how yet, but he senses Hope is the puppet master in this whole game. How far her tentacles reach is still a puzzle, but that's part of her fascination.

The townsfolk's buzz grows to a chatter... then the chatter drops to silence. The council takes the grandstand. The keyed-up crowd holds the silence tightly. It's quick to find a new level as both Marcus and Pastor Cain come to the podium.

Marcus taps... thump... thump.

Marcus' tapping on the live mic earns a few laughs from the audience. The man has never tapped on a dead mic... yet he has to check every time. He and technology are not close friends.

Thump... thump... as he taps on it one more time to be sure, "Looks to be a mighty crowd this mornin'."

He doesn't get the usual friendly town banter back... just a silent hunger.

"So ya'll wants me to git to it... very well. Ya'll know we hain't had visitors. But it's come... and come... and come to the council's knowin' that there's a few rotten apples in our holler... "

Pastor Cain leans into the mic, cutting Marcus off, "And we'ez rightly aware that everyone here is akin to a kin. But please keep it a mind that the redemptions are about a greater good. 'Cause of this we'ez felt... well... "

Marcus retakes the mic, "What the good pastor here is sayin' is we hain't airin' dirty laundry... ya'll just gonna have to take our word fer their deservedness. We also hain't to take kindly to any feudin' over those who rightly end up in the pit."

A man from the crowd yells, "'Nuff rules... gits to it!"

Others follow it with like yells. The fear shows in the crowd. Before, this was a celebration... Now there's a solid touch of frenzy.

Marcus knows when to speechify... and when to shut up. He turns back and gestures for Gabriel to join them at the front of the grandstand.

Gabriel hesitates and then gets up. With a lackluster walk, he joins Marcus at the rail. He's not happy putting in an *oldie* on such short notice... wasn't even given enough time to give it much of a facelift. The only thing he was able to do... and it was a deal breaker... was to demand a cover for the reveal.

Ethan and Daniel work the pit below. They watch Gabriel.

Without much of a drumroll, Gabriel flips the back of hand up... that's enough.

On cue, the boys in the pit pull levers on counterweights placed at both sides of the arena. A mighty stone block drops from an armature. Ropes snap taut against the stone's weight. The cordage is so evenly spaced it whips the parachute-weight cover off of Gabriel's Run in one fluid wave... one from each side. The crowd applauds, a little more harshly than usual... Gabriel only admires the smoothness of the drapes' separation.

What stretches across the pit is Gabriel's Run... A gauntlet created by barrier walls on each side with sharp blades embedded in the barricades to keep the prey on the path. The four-foot high walls are built atop frames with tractor tires for ease of use. Down the length of the gauntlet are spring-loaded, arching headsmen's axes made of sharp harvester blades.

Gabriel hated having to use another arching device so soon after the bikers. It was the only ready-to-go rig he had that didn't need tinkering... just blade sharpening. Even dull, the blades would be deadly, but Gabriel had to have them glisten.

The toys have been shown... now the crowd quiets for the entrée. All eyes shift towards the dark hollow that empties into the pit.

Gabriel had abstained from choosing the sacrificial lamb so he could tend to his contraption. Since life holds so few surprises, though this doesn't qualify as a big one, he hasn't bothered to ask. He waits at the grandstand's rail... watching, like everyone in the gallery.

Lisa scoots out so far that Rick and Tom together have to pull her in... again. Even Hope leans forward in her short patio chair, binoculars in hand, to see who comes out of the mouth.

At previous redemptions there was applause, but now there is only an eerie silence coming from the light at the end of the tunnel.

By his nature, David is a rather invisible man... even in a town with so few folks. He's the town's apprentice baker. Until the town's main baker dies off, that's all David will be... even though David has quietly, invisibly carried the baker's load for years. Now... it's academic.

As terrifying as it should feel, David battles confusion at this stage. After all, weren't the redemptions for the good of the town? They've existed all of his life, though he can't remember local folks ever being targets of the redemptions... after all, isn't the ritual for the sake of locals?

Maybe it was true generations back, but in his life they've always looked outward. The redemptions have gone through other changes over David's twenty-six years. When he was a boy he recalls them only being once a year. Then they started becoming twice... then quarterly. Nowadays, hardly three weeks go by without someone seeing the pit... And sometimes, like the past few weeks, the pit has been right busy.

Like most of the townsfolk, David enjoyed the ever-increasing redemptions, especially since it's always been strangers. He was more than happy to believe they were just... and needed. That belief confuses him... now that he's been singled out. For all he knows, most everyone likes his bake wares. He can't think what else he did to ruffle the town... for that matter, he's almost invisible to most townsfolk.

There's no grind of rolling doors behind David as he slowly walks towards the mouth of the tunnel. There is just a big man, Jake... and Jake's shotgun. With a glance over his shoulder, and a look of resignation, he continues forward towards his fate.

David at last emerges into the sun and hard shadows of the pit... as so many before him, the glare is disorienting. His appearance was a bit slower than Marcus would have orchestrated it... but even a mayor can't control everything.

Seeing David in the pit, Gabriel leans toward Marcus, "Well, there goes those great little cinnamon things he makes."

Attempting to sound like a mayor, Marcus snaps, "Gabe, this here is serious doin's."

"They was serious cinnamon things," replies Gabriel.

The crowd's reactions are caught up in the same confusion. They were in fear of not having redemptions, but now seeing one of their own down there has a sobering effect... many of them are going to miss those little cinnamon things. The reality that each of them is in the bleachers instead of in the pit sinks in... the applause grows.

Lisa squirms backwards out of the bushes and looks over at Hope. In a loud whisper, "Who's this guy?"

Hope concludes the name must enhance the experience... the why of it doesn't make any sense to her. Hope has already guessed that if any one of them were after the full effect of the bloodletting it would be Lisa... not that she would have any sense of the art of it.

Might as well give her the full show... Hope dryly says, "Doubt you know him... but his name's David."

From the moment David steps into the pit and sees Gabriel's Run and the glistening harvester blades, his belief in redemptions slips further. His movement slows, but the barrel of the twelve-gauge touching his back resumes his long walk to the mouth of the gauntlet.

Marcus hates dead time. He figures he might as well make use of David's slow walk to get to the formals... even though he's not sure the crowd actually cares.

"David... " Marcus sees David stop, look up and casually wave his hand. "Naw, boy... You can keep on movin' along."

Marcus clears his throat to get back to the formal, "As I was 'bouts to say... David, fer reasons we hain't goin' into all public like, you have been called to redemption... fer the sake of our redemption."

He takes a speechifying breath... "Now, hain't jes' you, David, but for everyone here... Ya'll gonna have to trust our judgment on this... since we'ez agreed it best to keep the particulars private... to spare kin."

Pastor Cain steps up next to Marcus as a show of church support. Marcus tastefully blocks the good pastor from the mic.

"As I was sayin'... we'ez favors this way to ward off any feudin' and hurt feelin's... Now, David, you 'bouts ready to be redeemed?"

Now at the gauntlet's mouth, David looks up. Confusion is on its way to terror... but not there yet. He searches for words. Generations of redeeming rush through his head. Is he playing his part? Damn, those blades look sharp... who's gonna cook his cinnamon rolls? All of this rushes through his mind.

He nervously clears his throat. All are listening. David stutters out, "You mean you hain't gonna tell me what I did?" David is good at being invisible, even in his words.

Marcus shakes his head, without meaning to, at David's poorly sculpted last words. In an attempt to bring the poor boy's spirits up, "It might'n not be all bad news... we had one fella make it all the way through the run... though it were long ago."

Gabriel leans into him and quietly says, "Missin' 'bouts twenty pounds... and he died fifteen minutes later."

Ignoring Gabriel, Marcus holds up a small air horn, like those from a sporting event. Somehow it ended up in Redemption, who knows how long ago, and Marcus has had it on a shelf forever. He thought, with reverence for the new, hopefully temporary doin's, it would be a fitting touch... plus he thinks it will add pizzazz.

"OK, David... when you hear the horn, git to goin'."

The crowd starts chanting. At first it's a low, guilt- muffled chant, but it quickly gives way to a much louder coliseum hunger.

David staggers back from the starting line... till he hears the hammer cock on the shotgun. For someone so invisible, with so few kin and even fewer friends, David shows spunk by simply not being a quivering mess... but willing bravery is too much.

A shrill blast sounds!

When the gun barrel nudges David across the starting line, he thinks to himself... *maybe I'll be blessed.*

Instead of going full bore through the gauntlet, David starts off by trying to outthink it... he's probably not the most gifted person to outwit one of Gabriel's inventions.

David sees the first mobile blade will swing in from the left. He hugs the right side of the gauntlet, at least as much as possible, considering both walls are lined with blades. As he comes parallel to the spring-loaded headsman's ax, he hears a *click*. With amazing speed the blade arches towards him. David squeezes backwards, feeling the sharp pain of one of the static blades as it slightly penetrates his side. The arching razor strikes down between David's legs... missing by less than an inch a part of him he greatly values.

Up above, Gabriel grins. Even though it's an old game, he remembers every detail of its operation, every click of its voice. The first blade was spaced to allow someone to do as David did. The boy will be unwise trying that maneuver at the second.

Near the next loaded blade are deeply cut grooves on both gauntlet walls... there will be no squeezing by it.

Everything is overwhelming David. The chants rising louder and louder from above, the growing fear inside him and the total confusion over why he's there... All convince David there is no choice but to trust in fate... and go for it full bore. Going all out may not be the best strategy, but it will turn off the racket in his head. Fear is greatest in the mind... maybe it will ease with action... or at least soften.

He skins his way by the second blade... the third nicks his trailing hand but doesn't slow him. He hesitates at the next and pulls back just in time to save his nose. He has to climb over this one. Here the thought of jumping out of the gauntlet crosses his mind... but the man with the shotgun will ensure that won't work. He hesitates and catches his breath.

The pounding of feet on the bleacher above grows, urging him to keep up their bloody entertainment.

Exhausted, David shoves off again.

He beats the next blade by a hair. David's not so lucky when the fifth one is tripped. It slices down just behind his right shoulder, deeply skinning a five-inch slash in his upper back. David staggers towards the deadly sidewall. He collapses to the ground inches shy of it.

There are cheers from above, celebrating his making it halfway... and urging him to keep going. David knows nothing about halfway marks, all he is aware of is he is not done... and the pain. He accepts that he is dead. This is the first calm fraction of time he's had all day.

Good thing everyone's eyes below are glued to the arena. Tom, Rick and Lisa's heads are out way too far. Tom is the first to realize how exposed their fascinations have left them.

Getting Rick back is easy, but it takes the two of them to coax Lisa's withdrawal.

Unaware with what's going on with the kids, Hope is consumed by the show below... that she has set in motion.

Resigned, David plunges forward. A diagonal blade glints as it brushes him. But luck can only go so far. The next blade swings in and slices into David's right Achilles tendon, almost severing his heel. Hobbled, he struggles on hands and knees to keep moving. He trips the last blade he need worry about... it takes off his head with his shoulders still attached.

At the final strike of the gauntlet, there's a moment of silence in the gallery. Perhaps it's for the loss of one of their own... perhaps it's for the loss of those little cinnamon things. The silence doesn't last long... blood has the ability to prime applause.

The three kids, each battling their own emotions, back out of the bushes.

"Gross!" proclaims Lisa, with a cheering voice.

All look over to see Hope standing at the edge of her perch. She has her eyes closed and fluidly waves her arms as if conducting a symphony.

CHAPTER TWENTY-ONE

It's funny how such an event causes people to retreat into their own thinking... even Hope, who has been through it countless times. For her, David's killing is just a starting brush stroke in a painting that had become stale.

Lisa is scary. She paces around, almost giddy. Words couldn't express how excited the redemption has made her... and if they could, she surely wouldn't speak them.

In the corner, sits Rick, the most tormented by the war in his head.

As far as Tom goes, he seems the least lost in his conscience... but he seems lost in the room, wandering around looking over and under. He checks on a table near Rick. "You see my notebook anywhere?" he asks.

As though snapping out of a daze, Rick looks up... After a second, "What?"

"My notebook... have you seen it?" asks Tom once more.

Rick, not focused, "Thought I saw it on the porch."

Tom glances at the front door. "I thought so too."

As if to put out a tiny brushfire, Lisa walks to a table by the fireplace and shoves a book to the side to expose Tom's book. "Here's your damn book... Keep track of your own shit."

She avoids eye contact.

Hope retreats into the practical... pulling dinner together instead of listening to the kids' idle talk. This much non-stop company is an unusual experience for her. It doesn't distress her... still; it's a lot of prattle in her sanctuary. She goes from cupboard to cupboard looking for something that doesn't want to be found. Finally, she turns and takes note of the room.

Tom is by the fire writing in his book. Rick is still in the shadows with his demons. Lisa has settled into doing her nails at the dining table. She tries, badly, to look remorseful. Satisfied that all are preoccupied, Hope steals out the back door.

Lisa quickly gets up and goes to the kitchen window, as if she were waiting to make the move. She watches Hope disappear up a path and makes a mental note of it.

Sun is giving way to twilight and Main Street is overly busy for Redemption. Some of the edge has been taken off. Folks are more at ease coming out of the shadows. There's still a hint of sharpness in the air, but not as many accusing eyes.

Prudence is clearly the most attractive woman in Redemption, outside Hope. She loves the attention thrown her way on a twilight stroll, or hanging at the Crackerbarrel. The problem this evening... she was one of the few people that actually paid any attention to David... for other than his baking.

They had been casual friends as kids. His pa passed some time back, and being from another holler originally, David had little local kin. Somehow Prudence had become sort of a distant sister, or close cousin. David was also one of the few guys, regardless of age, that hadn't repeatedly hit on her after her first rebuff.

This evening finds Prudence at the Crackerbarrel, among a few others. She appears pensive.

Isaac leans in and asks, "What's got you so quiet, girl?"

Sounding less than her bubbly self, "Hain't right that they's don't tell us what a person did."

This sparks Isaac. "I hain't quite right with killin' one of our own... but it is a redemption. Still... seems we should know the worth of it."

Isaac is in his mid-forties, and one of the few in Redemption who's spent time out of the holler. Long time back when he tried living down on the flats, he ended up doing a tour of duty in the service... court encouraged.

There's the grumble of agreements in the background.

Abel speaks above the others, but shy of being on a soapbox, "It hain't right. Oughta know what yer bein' redeemed fer... it's breakin' tradition."

Marcus was right the other day... most of the time Isaac and Abel are good friends. Especially when it comes to the hunt.

"Enough of this don't ask, don't tell rule," spouts Albert. He and his cane sit in the background, near the oak that breaks the edge of the Crackerbarrel. Albert has so many lines that he blends with the tree. Isaac gives an odd glance at the old codger, wondering where he picked up his wording.

What started as a grumble is becoming a movement... among the six at the Crackerbarrel. Prudence started with a simple and heartfelt concern. As things grow she sets David aside... and inches towards the mob.

A woman off to the side yells, "I want to know what dirty thing he did." Nothing indicated this to be true other than David was a loner.

What started as, *right to know,* now comes across as, *blood is not as sweet without self-righteousness.*

"What he done is to have less kin in these parts... " Prudence's words are not as loud, but heartfelt.

Charity, not to be left out of gossip, joins the group on the deck. "You're right... What are you gittin' at?"

"They're feedin' us someone that'll make the least waves in the pond," spouts Isaac.

"No matter what he done?" finishes Prudence.

Marcus pauses in the distance... taking it in from afar.

Isaac is on a roll, "That there tattle n' tell box in front of the bar is plum' full of tellin's 'bouts folk."

"Probably darker than David... " Prudence is getting fired up now. Her passion is over David, while the rest are just getting fired up for the sake of it.

"Yeah... They's got lots in that box," injects Charity.

Abel lets out a laugh. "Woman... half them slips in there was writ by you." From muffled grins to snickers and guffaws, the others join in the laughter.

Charity retreats mumbling, "It hain't no such way."

"Back to serious doin's," Isaac continues. "We could most likely pull *one* outta that box with real needs... then the redemption would have real meanin'." Isaac is half believer, half hunter. None around challenges his use of the word *one*... for now.

Marcus comes walking up on the crowd, pretending he's unaware of what's being discussed.

"Right fine redemption, don't ya'll think?" He holds a smile even though he knows it'll be of no use... mayor habits.

Isaac steps up, "We'ez jes' jawin' that over... Some here think David was chosen over his shyness of kin... not over wrongs."

Abel joins in, "What we'ez sayin' is we'ez a-hankerin fer a truly right redeemin' instead of doin's jes' to keep us quiet."

"So you're sayin' that the redeemin' of David, which reasons were kept quiet fer ya'll's safety, hain't settled anything?" Ever a politician, pretending he's hearing, while covering his ass.

Isaac ramps up a notch. "What he's sayin' is yer bound to ritual by havin' true reasons fer bein' redeemed." He steps towards Marcus, almost in a challenging manner.

From somewhere in the rear a woman says, "And... not some plain out rumorin'."

Charity slaps at this comment with the back of her hand, as though she's shooing away a fly.

Marcus can't remember if even his race for mayor was this cantankerous. Actually, he barely remembers the last time he ran for mayor... against an opponent. The job doesn't pay that much and dancing is too fast for most to have a hankering for.

Even if it's a wasted effort, Marcus tries to dredge up some logic. "I want you to think on this fer a piece... If we'ez start redeemin' everyone that has some taint, we'ez gonna run outta folks... we'ez only got 258 souls."

"257 now... or is that 257 and a half?" comes from Abel.

"That hain't half funny," snaps Marcus.

Albert spouts again, "Enough of this don't ask, don't tell rule." He is still sitting, and blending, with the tree.

All glance at the odd old man.

Marcus takes a deep breath preparing to get back in the thick of it. "OK... OK... I done got an idee of what's frettin' ya'll. Let me take it afore the council and we'ez gonna work things out... You can take my word fer that."

CHAPTER TWENTY-TWO

Pastor Cain should have known the hunger of his flock needed to go hand in hand with being pious, that any token show of redeeming would not hold for long. He prides himself in being able to herd the flock... and he failed. Not again. The best way to control them is to get ahead of the herd, appear to be in the lead, and nudge them where he wants.

He stands at his pulpit, shaking his head with a well-rehearsed degree of drama. He raises both hands outstretched, slips of paper in the grasp of each. Little does the congregation know, the slips in Cain's hands are simply blank pieces of paper. Real is unimportant, especially in religion.

The council hadn't bothered going through all the tellin's yet, perhaps for fear of what they might find about themselves. The first day of tellin's at the meeting produced some head-scratchers, but not much truly worthy of redemption.

Then again, there wasn't much against the Goodridges or the bikers. Pastor Cain figures *worthy* falls within the telling... his telling of it.

Marcus grins at the building dramatics below. He knows exactly how righteous the good pastor can get... when needed.

Strategically, Marcus had stowed away in the church loft before services. It was best not to have the whole council together right now. This way they can keep shifting the ball till they figure things out. Three are missing from today's service, Gabriel, Aaron and Marcus... though not so much.

Floating higher up than Marcus, Hope straddles the roof's crest. She listens down through the steeple as she occasionally does when she's expecting change... or wants a good laugh. She sits there waiting for the fireworks below.

At the pulpit, after a sufficient time, Pastor Cain squeezes his eyes closed and vigorously starts shaking both his raised hands... as if being touched by the spirits.

"The Lord works in mysterious ways!"

He gets a round of warm up *amens!*

"Now... we hain't planned on the roads goin' out." He shakes his hands, full of folded papers. "But without such a mishap we might'n not come to realize we'ez have a bushel of folk with some right serious sins... sins, worthy a-dealin' with."

The fire is catching. He gets another round of *amens* and mumbled agreements.

Hiding in his blind, a look of disbelief crosses Marcus' face. He wonders what good this line is doing. Start them down this path and the townsfolk will clamor for too many heads.

Pastor Cain is a believer... but has always been pragmatic. Marcus starts to wonder if, like much of his flock, the good pastor is becoming too true of a believer. He can hardly yell down a voice of reason from the shadows.

Cain times his beats, "Ya see how the Lord's being downright good to us."

He shakes one of his full hands. The fire's aglow. Fervor grows as the congregation peers at the slips of tellin' papers.

One man yells, "Let us sees the gifts!"

It's followed by louder *amens.*

Hope listens to the echoes of *amens* waffle up through the steeple. She closes her eyes and drifts away. A hand comes to rest on her shoulder.

When she opens her eyes, she turns to Jared. Angered, but keeping her voice down, "You bein' up here is downright teched! I told you not to follow me."

"Don't worry... I'm invisible." Jared gives her an affectionate pinch, hoping that will curb her irritation.

Hope's not that much of the angry type, she tends to roll with the flow... and adjust to it when needed. She shakes her head with a smile, "You'd be prit' near startled by how fine a hawk's vision 'comes when it's hungry."

Jared has a rugged mountain-man look enclosed in a twenty-year old friendly face. It isn't his good looks that hooked Hope... it's his quirky dark side.

"If things are about to change, like you expect, then I want to be here with you." Jared is not to be dissuaded from sharing in Hope's visions.

Hope knows the words she delivered to the township last week would begin the next stroke in her painting. She hopes Jared doesn't become a casualty of it.

More *amens* drift up from the congregation below.

Hope closes her eyes.

So far Cain has had complete control over his audience. He's well versed in playing to people's lowest common denominator, their fears. It's a strategy that works, whether a tiny town in the Ozarks or a nation. Pastor Cain knows how to build on fears... and when needed, ease them down.

"Might'n be the Lord's way of sayin' it's time to be cleanin house," preaches Cain.

There's a round of evangelistic declarations like, 'Amen', 'That's right, Lord,' and 'It's time fer redemptions'.

The pastor takes a breath at the pulpit to tell all to settle and refocus on him. Once he has them back in his grasp, Cain throws the slips of paper from both hands in the air.

There's silence as the congregation guesses about their contents.

"We'ez hain't exactly eatin' cobs here... we'ez got prit' near enough house corn to feed the arena fer a long spell." He pauses to allow the shift to commence to take hold.

A woman does a quick stealthy squirm out of her pew seat to snatch up one of the slips of paper has fallen on the floor. When she opens it, she's bewildered by its blankness.

Pastor Cain catches this. "And we'ez should not be found guilty of spreadin' false witness. I hain't bringin' the tellin's out here in public, but we'ez got lots."

The woman quickly stashes the slip under her leg, as though none of a dozen folk saw her take it.

Marcus, in the loft, tries to gauge where Cain is going.

"What we gotta remember is that we'ez got plenty... so we don't need to git all het up over the roads bein' out... or rush to over-redeemin'." He pauses a second to see how well his turn is holding.

"What's you tryin' to say, preacher?" comes from someone in a back pew. From the relative silence, this is a question on others' minds as well.

"I'm a sayin'... we shouldn't be rushin' to use the arena when we'ez been so blessed with such abundance."

Marcus has a light laugh, shy of anyone hearing, at Cain's backdoor attempt... even if he doesn't think it will work.

There's a growing spread of disgruntled mumbling from the pews. Pastor Cain can tell he's lost his audience. He surrenders with, "We'ez gonna take a good long look at all the tellin's."

Hanna McCoy is quick to add, "And we'ez gonna make 'em accountable... all of 'em!"

Those who don't think they could possibly be on that list, which includes most in the church, are just as quick to add their verbal support.

Hope leans away from the steeple and has a belly laugh, without a grain of concern over being heard.

She's been up and down all morning. Nervousness and boredom mix as Lisa paces around Hope's cabin.

Even though he doubts it will do much good, Rick suggests, "Settle down... you're doing yourself no good."

"Where does she keep disappearing to?" snaps Lisa.

With less patience, Rick says, "What does it matter?... Outside a few words, she's still been nothing but kind to us."

Tom's rather casual about it. "You know anyone else that could show us something like this?" His tone hints that he no longer even finds the activity in the arena abhorrent behavior.

"You ever think she might be out there arranging for us to be the next in that pit?" accuses Lisa.

"She's not!" Tom loses his casualness.

Lisa stops pacing and stares at Tom. "Then... after all these years, why is she keeping us around? ... Tell me that."

Tom's not sure how much of what Hope has shared with him should be passed on to them. And something else he's not sure of... does Hope have plans for Rick and Lisa, which he's going to be immune to? He's not going to breach that.

But this seems innocent enough, "She thinks this is all coming to an end... and she wants to share it with someone. What's wrong with that?"

None of them bother bringing up the ethics of getting off on watching a total stranger get gruesomely killed.

Lisa is losing steam. "Well, I think she's hiding something up at that cave of hers."

Rick joins in, "I told you to leave that alone. We're her guests, and till Tom's ankle heals, we're going to act like guests."

He hopes that will put an end to it... he knows it won't. But his snapping at her does set Lisa aback.

To avoid a later headache, Rick adds, "Anyway, how do you know she isn't watching us?"

He knows this show of allegiance will allow her to quiet down... while saving face. He's right. She glances around, gives him a little shrug, and goes back to pacing.

Tom quietly mumbles to himself, "You mess with her, and I'll help put you in that pit."

This gets a snapped glare from Lisa, as though she heard him. He gives her an impatient, but innocent sounding, "What?"

Abigail's is a fine place for Marcus to catch a bite to eat... and to catch chatter after the midday services he supposedly wasn't at.

Most folks in town know there's two times to leave Marcus alone... when he's speechifying and when he's eating. Just as he cuts into a slice of ham, he sees Charity approaching.

Marcus holds up his hand towards her, "Charity... I'm having my lunch. And I hain't listenin' to tellin's." She still inches forward, so he adds, "And no questions."

There's a 'but' on Charity's lips, but Marcus' unwavering held up hand causes her to swallow it. She sulks back to the counter.

The door swings open and Gabriel enters. When he sees Charity near the counter he almost leaves... but.

"Hey, Gabe," Marcus loudly says.

After a second of hesitation, Gabriel comes over and takes a seat with Marcus. The two can feel eyes on them. Marcus snaps a hard glare at the room and folks go back to their business. Even so, Marcus and Gabriel keep their volume down.

"I hear'd the good pastor didn't have much luck headin' folks off." Gabriel had lobbied to be one of those not to show up for midday services.

Marcus gives him a disappointed sigh. "Let's jes' hope the good pastor don't go followin' his flock."

"Sounded like the redemption yesterday didn't buy even a speck a time," Gabriel warns.

"Hopefully it was jes' church fever," Marcus says, with limited conviction.

"From what I hear'd, they was prit' near callin' fer a mud pit of blood." Gabriel would rather talk real versus hopes.

Marcus thinks on it for a couple seconds. "If we was to step things up in the arena... and they's see more kin in there... they'll settle."

With a doubtful shake of his head, Gabriel says, "Think you's lookin' fer sun in a gully washer."

"You might be right... but can you handle a couple days of redeemin's?" Marcus truly believes he can weather this.

This is unfortunately like a knife in the gut for Gabriel. What's the good of redemptions if he can't come up with new creations? It becomes nothing more than killing people... at least in Gabriel's way of thinking.

Marcus can see the wound. "Gabe... it would only be temporary-like."

Trying to help, Gabriel finally says, "Only if we'ez start pittin' folks against each other like."

A slight burst of energy picks Marcus up. "That's a dern sheen of an idee... The winners gits relieved of their sins... the losers gits redeemed fer ours."

'What 'bouts my creations?" Gabriel still has to ask.

"Mark my words, old friend, it'll settle right quick... And we'ez got the Forth of July comin' fer you's to come up with a sartfied eye popper."

Gabriel likes the idea of focusing his energy on a real eye popper... and he has one in mind. And the boys can handle the mundane doin's in the pit. But he doesn't have much trust in Marcus' view of things settling.

With little enthusiasm, he says, "Like I said... sun in a gully washer."

CHAPTER TWENTY-THREE

A twig lightly snaps under Gabriel's foot. He pauses and smells at the air... there's a slight hint of smoke. He unslings his old double-barreled twelve gauge.

Gabriel has an old ATV gathering dust up at his still. He uses it when hauling's needed, but normally prefers the walk through the woods. It's not that far from where he parks his truck, by country standards... and it's a peaceful trek.

Not that Gabriel is that concerned by someone messing with his still... he has quite a heritage of shine brewing and privacy. Gabriel doesn't bring his shotgun to the ready, but he readies his shotgun to do so if need be. He steps lighter as he comes over the ridge leading down to his clearing.

Off to his left is a rustic, half moss-covered shack for crashing in when he gets fed up with being around town or samples too much of his own shine. A large, open-posted roof extends from its side, covering a couple generations of old stills, miscellaneous still makings and part of a cord of dried wood. There's an empty rack for dressing deer near a heavy, almost-worn round butcher-block table.

Gabriel takes it all in as he comes to the edge of his clearing. In the distance to the right is another open-walled shed with panels of tin as its umbrella. This covers his main still. A young fire is burning under it. Gabriel glances around... no movement.

Silently, an acorn flies in and hits him on the head.

"Old man, how you fixin' to have good squeezin's if you lets your fires burn out?"

Gabriel turns to find Hope sitting up in an oak. With little effort, she shinnies down. While she's doing so, Gabriel turns away and heads for a rickety wooden bench.

"Now you think you can be schoolin' me 'bouts shine... jes' 'cause I'm your only friend here 'bouts."

There's a coil of copper tubing, aged dark, mottled with patches of oxidized green, draped over the bench. He kicks it off and watches as it springs around like wire jello.

As Hope heads towards Gabriel, she teases, "You sure weren't that friendly like the other day in town."

"We were right friendly in the truck," he defends, in a tone saying it's how it's supposed to be, and it's best she accept that.

Gabriel takes a seat and Hope plops down next to him. The bench groans, but holds.

"Jes' means, in the past week you're only one outta three." Hope says this in jest. She well knows the dynamics needed between her and Gabriel... in order to have something between them at all.

It's true, he doesn't get much opportunity to be friendly with her. But Gabriel figures Hope is best taken in small doses. As much as he grumbles, they're doses he values.

"You hain't countin' all I done said behind your back."

"Admit it... life would get right boring without me around... come to think on it, how things cookin' in town?" she asks.

"Hell, girl... why do you think I'm here?"

Gabriel gets up and saunters over to a wood firebox about the size of a large ice chest. He lifts the hinged lid and grabs a jug of shine.

"Came up here to restock... and hang a piece."

"Folks shakin' sticks done gotten that bad?"

As he makes his way back to Hope, "Somethin' awful... you're 'bouts the first smile I'd seen today." He sits. "Everybody's eyeballin' everybody... and your pa's got a dang strange idee fer fixin' things."

Mocking a girly tone, she says, "Tell me... tell me."

"Not likely... you know my thinkin' on that." Gabriel is known for being secretive, especially regarding things arena- related. It's mostly guarding his creations, but that naturally rolls over to hill mystique. Only lately he's losing the zeal for it, and shortchanging the events weighs heavily on him.

Hope senses this and, even though he has never partaken before, it seems a worthwhile time to try once more. She pulls a baggie from her sundress and begins rolling a joint.

As each preps their offering, they silently enjoy each other's presence.

While Hope is busy rolling, Gabriel struggles with a cork that doesn't want to leave its jug. An echoed pop and it's out. He takes a good swig, sets the jug on the bench between them, and slides it over to Hope without words.

Before taking his offering Hope holds out the joint, "Figure if there be a good time to be startin'... now's 'bouts the right one."

"All these years you've been tryin' to win me over to your ways." Gabriel eyes the joint a couple seconds. "You know somethin'... as downright strange as folks are gittin'... I think it's 'bouts time to take you up on it."

"Artistic as you be... took you too dang long," she says with a satisfied and long overdue grin.

As Hope lights the joint Gabriel pours her a small jar of shine. They trade. Once Gabriel takes the joint he inspects it like an alien object, peering at it from all sides.

"It hain't gonna do you much good lest you git to inhalin' it," teases Hope.

"I'm a gittin' to it." Cautiously, he takes a small puff. He coughs and blows out a tiny wisp of smoke.

Hope laughs... but in a friendly way. She offers, "Next time try holdin' it in a piece."

He surrenders to trying it her way. One steady long drag is followed by a contorted face... his version of holding it in. After holding it a bit too long, an exhale bursts from Gabriel. After he gathers his breath, Gabriel tries to get serious.

"Hope... with everyone so het up in town, why don't you let me tell folks you is at least thinkin' 'bouts helpin' out?" He knows this is probably going to fall on deaf ears, but it's worth a try.

"'Cause I hain't a mind to... and I'm right surprised of you askin'." Hope's not angry. But she did hope he was more understanding of her state of mind. Then again, he's never pretended to be interested in much more than his version of art... his creations.

The effects of the weed come on quickly... Gabriel's smile broadens. "A few in town could use this to soften up the edges." After a second uncontrollable grin, "Hope, serious-like... if you hain't gonna help out with the doin's... which is your call... At least stay clear of town fer a piece. The good side of folks hain't showin' much."

"Don't rightly think even this can soften most in town." Hope has waited long enough for the buzz to kick in and loosen Gabriel's tongue. She gives him a pleading face, "I hain't gonna ask you what you're fixin'... but can't you jes' tell me what's a cookin' in my pa's head?"

Gabriel thinks on it a second... and then another second. At last he says, "That's mighty powerful stuff you got there... Oh, you were askin' 'bouts your pa." He pauses another second. "Hell, you's gonna hear right quick anyhow. Your pa done thinks a rush of redeemin's will cure folks... I thinks he's looking for... sun... "

"I know... in a gully washer," Hope says. She's well aware of how often he throws that phrase around.

This pulls a laugh from Gabriel, not something that happens all that often. Maybe the weed is having some effect.

Even in the short time they have been talking, the skies darken by a few shades. Very distant flashes sculpt clouds on the horizon. Hope glances in that direction and gets up.

"Guess I gotta be gittin' afore that storm rolls in."

"Hope... mind my words 'bouts stayin' clear of town," says Gabriel. He takes a moment trying to remember what he wanted to tell her. "Oh... Yeah... Watch out on the path... I done set a few new traps."

Hope steps up to him and peers in his eyes, "Oh, yeah... yer good." She hands him a couple spare joints she had been rolling. "Jes' in case it gits real crazy like."

As Hope starts up one of the paths, Gabriel appears to have something else to say... But he's a bit lost.

Hope glances over a shoulder, and with a grin, "I done already seed your traps."

"Girl... you do have an eye." He wonders how she knew that was what he was searching to say... or did he actually say it. He sits back down on the bench to figure out what he's going to do next. After glancing at the joint they were smoking lying on the bench, he decides what the hell. Gabriel lights it up again.

After a few more drags, he's getting the hang of it. *Shit*, he suddenly thinks... he promised to meet Marcus about tomorrow's doin's. All he has to do is figure out his way back to town.

CHAPTER TWENTY-FOUR

Lisa is stir-crazy. Perhaps it's the storm brewing afar. She has been patiently waiting much of the day for the kind of privacy she needs... and waiting is not her strong suit. Normally the last thing Lisa wants is to be ignored, but today she'd like to be unnoticed... even if she were to disappear for a while.

From her position on the porch, she can easily steal a peek inside from time to time. Tom's where he's been most of the day, sitting at the table, scribbling in that notebook of his. Rick is the problem. Every so often he comes out to see how she's doing... she's trained him too well. She's in luck... Rick has dozed off on the sofa.

After one more peek inside, Lisa grabs a flashlight and the binoculars from the porch and sets out on her own.

Driving down Main Street slower than usual, Gabriel watches how antsy the town is getting. He can't hear the words but body language speaks volumes... a woman spinning away from another a little too fast... a man walking with his fists clenched... another woman in the distance throwing up her hands and turning away from another man. His nice bright red truck isn't even catching a wave. Folks aren't winding down.

Gabriel's prize Ford finally gets a wave... from Marcus. He waves back, grateful for the first contact since he has forgotten where he was supposed to meet him.

No wonder Hope is so strange crosses Gabriel's mind. He imme-diately rethinks... *Hope is Hope, shine or smoke aside... she's jes' a truly strange girl.*

Marcus waves again, as if he thinks he's being passed by.

He is. Coming back to the moment Gabriel pulls over near Abigail's... maybe a couple spaces further.

As Marcus walks up, Gabriel sticks his head out of the window, "Sorry I'm late... I think."

"Oh, I knew you'd get here... you always do."

Already feeling a little undervalued, this is not the thing he wants to hear. He thinks... *maybe one day I won't be there.*

One drop of rain is quick to turn to many. Marcus covers and rushes into Abigail's. Gabriel gets out and saunters inside, relishing the downpour as he goes.

Once inside Gabriel gives everyone a friendly eyeballing, which in itself gets a few bewildered looks in return. Gabriel is not always one of the warmest characters in town... except to a few close friends. To many he's happy to show his curmud-geon side. He settles at Marcus' table.

Marcus appears a bit puzzled as well. "You OK?"

With a grin wider than usual, "Better than most."

With a deep breath and a shake of his head, Marcus dis-misses Gabriel's odd manner. It's time to get to business.

"Gabe, you done set up the arena fer tomorrow's doin's?"

Irritation scrunches Gabriel's face. "I said I would... and I did. Don't rightly likes it much. Ethan and Daniel will handle the fixin's... and I'll be up where I'm supposed to be... anything else?"

"OK... don't go a gittin' so het up 'bouts it." With a hint of concern Marcus asks, "My friend... you gittin' uppity 'bouts re-demptions all sudden like?"

Marcus knows that at times Gabriel's artistic notions leave him on a different plane than townsfolk. Even so, he's always been able to guide him in the right direction, but lately Gabriel seems more distant.

Gabriel thinks on this a moment. "Naw... I'm a smidgin het up 'bouts it bein' less creative, but that hain't it... Maybe we'ez jes' been at the trough too long."

"What's gotten in to you today?" asks Marcus.

"Jes' talkin with your daughter... " Seeing Marcus cringe, "Yes, with Hope... Don't go lookin' at me that way, she's your'n. Anyhow... done run into her out 'n 'bouts."

Marcus uncoils a bit, "Hope you done told her to stay clear of town fer a piece."

"'Course I did." He pauses, not quite sure this will go over, "I even brought up the idee of her helpin' a piece."

"And what did she say?" Marcus asks rhetorically.

"Hope... She said prit' near what we'd expect from Hope... when somethin' gits in the girl's head."

Marcus is like a bobble-headed dolly in his agreement.

"But... some things she said got me to thinkin'... this is a bear that's gonna turn on us. We needs to puzzle out a way to back it down... not feed it."

"This Hope's high notions?"

Gabriel laughs. "Hell, no... she were, how'd she word it?... Plum' fascinated. She done sees her idee of a painting in 'bouts most things."

Actually, Hope often seems pleased when life shifts wind... as if she were orchestrating it. He ponders this... *no, that's beyond even Hope. Or... is it?*

Marcus' neck is getting sore from agreeing, it's time to move on. "She's a downright strange one when she's a mind to be... Now, back to the arena."

Gabriel knew Marcus listening was like searching for *sun in a gully washer*. Exhausted, he asks, "What's you want to know?"

Lisa had explored a few paths in the limited windows of time she found for herself, but hadn't been able to retrace her steps to the vision she had seen before on the hillside. There are many paths and branches of paths to explore. She had come close to giving up, but when Hope went for supplies the other evening her curiosity was refueled.

The storm wasn't in Lisa's plans, even though it clearly loomed in the air before she left. Now, a mile out from Hope's cabin, it's getting both dark and wet... and she's on her own. The drizzle was irritating, but not enough to deter her... this heavier rain is another story. Hillside runoff is starting to obscure the path with a river of mud. The heavier the rain becomes, the more disoriented Lisa gets. After slipping on the path, she cusses out Hope... for all the good it will do.

Struggling to get up, wet and muddy, Lisa catches a slight glint from somewhere up the hillside. She wipes water from her eyes and the binocular's lenses... still cursing Hope under her breath. It's not clear where the glint came from, but she can see the shadowy crevice in the rocks even through the grey sheets of rain. Getting up there in this weather is another matter.

Amazing how the same conditions that obscure ninety-five percent of something can reveal the hidden five percent. A flash of lightning briefly reveals a thin suspended line from the crevice above... a rope.

Lisa figures it must join the path around the bend. This storm would normally have Lisa running for cover, but finding this cave she's not supposed to find has become an obsession with her. She trudges on.

Once she makes it around the bend, without falling off the mountain, Lisa finds what she was hoping for... a rope, a way of ascending the hillside. Not only a rope suspended from rebar stanchions, but crudely carved steps in the hardpan leading upward. With her goal in sight, the rain doesn't seem to bother Lisa. She knows there's something darker about that smiling blond in a sundress to be discovered, as if Hope is not strange enough as is. She sets out on finding what.

Water and mud cascade down the crude steps carved in the hillside. It splashes over Lisa's well-soaked hiking boots.

Outside of the obligatory family camping trips that most kids either relish or hate, Lisa hadn't spent a lot of time in the great outdoors. She's healthy and can hold her own, but cross-country backpacking would not have been her first choice for killing a month. She's only on the trip to protect her territory. She even tries to convince herself that she only walked through the dark door Hope opened as merely a strategic relationship move... she knows what she denies.

Her dislike of Hope has grown from seed to root.

For a city girl, climbing a mountain, she's not doing badly... it's amazing what being driven can do. With a good grip on the rope suspended like a rail, Lisa climbs the last few steps onto a large rock ledge. She's drenched, bruised and scrapped.

Now she sees what the glimpse of fabric was. A drape of burlap hung from a stick stretching between two rock faces.

Darkness is behind it... she knows it.

Darkness is catching up outside as well... if she's going to do this she best get to it. Lisa switches on the flashlight and reaches out for the burlap. Her hands shake and not solely from the rain. She jerks the fabric to the side, with a heart that's expecting the bogeyman to burst out at her from the darkness... but darkness is all she gets... the mouth of a cave.

After a second to let her heart settle, Lisa aims the beam in and steps forward. It takes a second for her eyes to grow accustomed to a world defined by a small beam of light... and all its dancing shadows. Once they do, ambient light filters in and she gets a sense of the chamber. From the boulders outside, she expected to be in a natural cave. Instead, it's the relics of an extra-wide mining tunnel. Accidentally or intentionally, the boulders outside toppled down from higher up the mountain, obscuring the cave's true nature.

Lisa takes stock of the stone cold room. A cot, a table and a single chair rest near one of the walls. Judging from the dense cobwebs, they haven't been used in some time. A couple arteries of smaller tunnels branch off from the room. One tunnel has already collapsed and the other, with a maze of webbing blocking it, appears not to have been used in ages.

On another wall there are rows of crudely built wooden shelves. A patchwork of jarred fruit, bagged staples and canned food rest on them.

Lisa's nerves have settled. She glances back at the cot. A dusty kerosene lantern sits on a stool by its head with a box of wooden matches leaning against it. The natural coolness of the mine and Lisa being soaked brings on a chill even if it's a balmy summer night outside. Lisa shakes off the loose water and wipes her hands on her pants... to almost dry.

Her fingers tremble from the cold as she fumbles with the matches. After a few tries she gets the lantern lit. It illuminates things a bit more, but the cave retains many of its shadows.

Holding the lantern high, Lisa moves over to the shelves. From the disturbed dust near the jars, she can tell this is Hope's hidden pantry. Part of her was hoping to find human skulls lined up... she realizes that would be too simple.

She listens... other than the echo of her own movements, there's a heavy silence to the room, like sound was shrouded in the same cobwebs covering most everything else. Lisa moves away from the shelves, working the perimeter of the chamber to see what else, a slice more incriminating, she can find.

She comes to the smaller branch-off tunnel that has not collapsed. After peering at the collapsed branch, she looks up at the rotting wood support beams. They seem shy of being able to keep the mountain at bay. A flashlight beam through the layers of cobwebs discloses little more than a jog in the tunnel.

She lightly brushes her hand through the sticky webbing and decides no one has entered in a long time... from the supports' precarious nature, she sees that's for good reason. She passes on the tunnel and moves on.

In a particularly jagged section of the wall are a number of long animal pelts hanging from metal spikes. The stiffness of the pelts gives the appearance of dark treasures hidden behind them. Leaning in just far enough to reach the first pelt, she yanks it off the metal spike... and jumps back. It hides nothing but coiled ropes.

With similar caution, Lisa does the same with the next three pelts. The most incriminating thing she finds is a bear trap. She reminds herself that Hope is the girl who decorates trees with dynamite, so a spring trap isn't true evidence.

She pauses at the next one in line. Two boot tips extend out from under the floor-length skin. Despite logic, watching the boots slows Lisa's hand as she reaches out. With a snap, she rips the hide away. Something dark falls towards her... she recoils. Nothing more than an empty backpack topples to the ground.

Lisa bends over and takes a deep breath. She glares back down the line of spikes, and around the room... not much incriminating to show for all her effort. Frustrated, Lisa stands and kicks the pack. Before it tumbles away, something catches her attention. Kneeling down and holding the lantern close, she turns the pack over to the frame side.

Stitched on a top strap is the name 'Jared'.

Lisa jerks back, sending her off balanced... and falling on her rump. As she gets up, her eyes never leave Jared's name.

"Hain't safe to go a pokin' around where you don't rightly belong," comes from somewhere in the dark behind her.

Startled, Lisa drops the lantern as she spins around.

A burst of lightning silhouettes Hope looming in the doorway to the cave. Without a word, a terrified Lisa barges past her and out the cave's entrance.

Hope walks over and picks up the still glowing lantern. She stares at Jared's pack for a second and scans around the mine for other telltale signs. Satisfied, she takes Jared's pack and a stick from against the wall. She walks to the mouth of the tunnel that delves into the mountain. Using the stick to brush away a path through the cobwebs, she heads deeper into the mountain.

Hope goes around the bend in the tunnel and into a cavernous back room. Cluttered all about the room are numerous dusty skis and a pile of backpacks. Hope tosses Jared's pack on the pile. Then she says to herself, "Lucky girl."

Returning to the larger front section of the mine, Hope picks up an ax near the shelves.

"Time to put away some old brushes."

With a few well-aimed blows of her ax, the supports leading into the smaller tunnel cracks. Rock and dirt come tumbling down, leaving Hope in a temporary cloud of dust. When it clears, the back of the mine is sealed off.

Hope grins, gathers a few jars of fruit from the shelves, stuffs them in her pack, and takes one last glance around the cave. She knows that even its time is coming to an end. With a pleased nod, she's off.

CHAPTER TWENTY-FIVE

When Hope arrives back at the cabin she finds a muddy and wet Lisa more than a little worked up. She has already woken up the guys and is gathering their things. Neither Rick nor Tom appears that bothered.

Undisturbed, Hope goes into the kitchen and casually places the fruit jars from the cave in the cabinet.

Still packing, Lisa keeps one eye on Hope's every move. For Lisa, she's seen the elephant... now it's time to get out while they still can. How this is playing out chafes her since Hope is being infuriatingly casual about it all.

Though she's trying to focus on her packing, Hope's silence is just too much for Lisa. She blurts out, "So... What have you to say for yourself?"

Hope turns from the counter and strides directly toward Lisa. The action sends Lisa cowering back, almost falling. Hope pulls up just short of her frightened guest. She looks Lisa up and down, with a side-glance at something Lisa hides behind her.

Caught off guard, Lisa awkwardly feels for the kitchen knife in her back pocket. Like most who don't regularly use weapons, she forgot it was there in the heat of the moment.

"Before you ran off all half-cocked, I was 'bouts to tell you there's bobcats and other varmints that like cool caves... You were plum' lucky you didn't run afoul of one up there."

Hope knows that's not where it's going to stop, but it's a reasonable place to start. Lisa is like a deer caught in the headlights.

Hope backs away a few steps. "I'm right cautious when I'm goin' up there... but it's prit' near the best place to store my preserves."

"That's not what I saw stored up there!" snaps Lisa.

Stepping back towards the table, Hope says, "I 'spec you're meanin' Jared's pack?"

Lisa pounces, "Exactly! The same Jared that just up and went away... without his pack."

Lisa glances to the guys for moral support, but Rick only seems half behind her. Tom appears fairly unconcerned either way.

Trying to remain polite, which is not her normal tack, Hope keeps her voice calm, "In a sense, he did... I jes' didn't figure it were any of your business where he went to." Giving Tom a wink, "Still don't... but I'm bein' on my best behavior with guests."

"I'm sure you didn't," Lisa snaps. Since Hope has noticed it, Lisa has had her right hand on the knife in her back pocket... looking like she's ready for a quick draw.

Having avoided it long enough, Hope waves at Lisa's hand, "Would you please put that thing on the table afore you cut your cute little ass with it."

Rick shakes his head, steps over to Lisa and gently takes the knife from her pocket. He looks at Hope, "Maybe she's got reason to be concerned."

"She's done clum' the wrong tree."

Hope takes a seat at the table and gestures for them to join her.

Rick gently nudges Lisa towards the table, but she's not having it. She plops down on the cot where she was packing their things. Ricks sits beside her with a shrug.

Hope rests her elbows on the table and gets to explaining, "A piece back, Jared come back up here fer a visit... and I welcomed the company." She gives Tom a flirtatious glance. "One night he got a head full of shine and took a-hankerin' to see what Gabriel was a fixin' in that barn of his."

Tom's been around Lisa enough to know she inevitably turns situations to dramas... So much so, that if it were important, it would likely be missed. For that matter, he often stops listening, but anything about the arena catches his interest.

He asks, "You mean the things for the pit get built in that barn behind the arena?" He had only seen a piece of it from the perch.

In rare unison, Rick and Lisa say, "Tom... shut up."

Having hooked her audience, Hope might as well finish the tale. "Anyhow... he got himself good and snared. Jared ended up in the arena."

After an appropriate dramatic pause, Hope puts on her best sincere voice, "One of the few times I didn't watch the doin's."

Lisa hisses, "And you just let him get killed in that pit?"

A flash of lightning from the storm brightens the room for a millisecond. A crack of thunder follows.

Being polite is a strain for Hope. "Awful het up over jes' a name... hain't you? Anyway, darlin'... that's a piece of art down there... it has its own life. Why would I go messin' with it?"

Hope pauses, reaching for what she figures will be understandable terms. "If I'd said somethin', I'd be well up the creek."

"So they never connected him to you?" asks Rick.

"A few had their suspicions, but he hain't been in these parts fer quite a piece... I was fixin' to let out, but nothin' come of it." For the illusion of normalcy... theirs, not hers... she adds, "That's why I jes' preferred sayin' he up and let out."

She's melted Rick and Tom was a non-issue. Lisa remains stone-faced. Hope figures it's less the issue at hand... and more about her losing. To cap off the defeat, Hope says, "Guess I kept the pack fer rememberin'."

His mind caught up in contraptions, Tom has remained quiet. Then he says, "Sounds pretty reasonable to me... sorry about your friend."

In a grumble louder than a whisper, Lisa says, "That's if you believe her."

Hope glares at her. The girl truly does require a taste for... one she doesn't have. "Like I done said... if I wanted to see ya'll in their hands, I'd jes' would a let you go on your pretty way to town the other day. You can take off... or stay. But Tom hain't in much shape fer travelin'."

Tom waggles his still-wrapped ankle in the air... even if he is faking just a little.

Rick stands and slaps his hands as if finishing a huddle. "Sorry about... Jared. I guess we'll stay a piece... because of Tom." His tone says he was just looking for an excuse to see more of Hope's weird world.

Lisa appears much less than enthusiastic... but keeps her peace.

More lightning flashes as the storm rumbles on.

Hope pops up. "Now that ya'll are satisfied, I'm gittin' a touch of fresh air... I'm plum' talked out fer now."

Without waiting for a response, one way or another, Hope heads out the front door.

Lightning flashes... and Lisa sees that same frightening silhouette she saw at the mouth of the cave. The weak spring swings the door closed softly.

Hope smiles... as though that was a planned effect. The rain cascades off the porch roof in an almost continuous sheet. The effect is mesmerizing, like viewing life through a rapidly changing funhouse mirror.

Hope stands there, less captivated by the water sheet than her dilemma... Why is she really protecting these guests? It's a matter she figures she'd have worked out by now... if anything, it's a bit more of a puzzler.

She's borderline bored with Rick... and well over the border with Lisa. It would be easy to feed them to the town's appetite... except for Tom. Hope likes Tom's company, even if it's a complication.

More important... Having a witness somehow seems a needed stroke on the canvas. Hope reminds herself that she's made bad strokes before. With a grin, she also knows how flexible she is with her art. A flash of lightning washes Hope's face with an eerie polarized black and white glare.

It's one of those summer evening storms that are exhilarating, but not cold. They are great for sitting on a well-covered porch and drinking a drop of shine. Ingredients of a right fine evening at the McCoys'. This isn't one. The porch, the storm and the shine are all present... but the tension of the town killed the *right fine* part.

Pastor Cain leans in, as if to emphasize his words. "So, everythin's set... the who's and the how's of it all. And we'ez all complete fer the gatherin'." It comes off as an overdone recap.

No one else, Marcus, Hanna nor Gabriel, bothers leaning in.

Gabriel sips from a jug, looking as disinterested as possible.

Seeing Pastor Cain glance at him, he says, "Don' be lookin' at me... I hain't got any interest in the who's... and I prit' near don't have much to say on the how's lately."

"Pastor, we have done settled all this... But let me remind ya'll that what we'ez 'bouts to do is herd in the town's thinkin'... We cain't be doin' this regular," Marcus says, hoping the pastor will see the finality of it... as well as this meeting.

His tone must have worked at least halfway. Getting up to leave, Cain says, "Understood... At least those in the pit will now truly belong there."

Hanna, being a good hostess, stands to see the good pastor away. Before she leads him to the stairs, Hanna turns back to her husband, "I differ, dear... we got lots of sinners who we needs to be dealin' with."

She turns away with little interest in a response.

Once Marcus is sure she and the pastor have turned the veranda's corner, he shakes his head in exhaustion... from the day, from the situation and from his wife's zealousness.

"Sun... in... " Gabriel starts. Marcus's glare ends his words.

This time it's Marcus who leans in, "Gabe... you got yer head on right fer this?"

Gabriel realizes his meeting with Marcus earlier might have come off a little strange... what he now knows is it's best not to smoke before meetings.

To answer simply, he says, "I'm fine... jes' put off over things bein' so average like."

As the two of them stand, Marcus puts a hand on Gabriel's shoulder, "Put yer mighty creative mind on the somethin' fer the Fourth. Trust me... this will settle."

The two walk around the veranda towards the front steps and Gabriel jests, "If we'ez doin' it anyway... sure wish we had done it afore we lost those fine little cinnamon things."

They reach the front steps to find Charity standing under an umbrella near the front gate, rain pounding down.

Gabriel quietly says, "She's all your'n."

He lifts his light jacket over his head and rushes past Charity for his truck. The jacket was more against Charity than the rain. Once Gabriel passes, Charity turns to Marcus and raises an arm, ready to speak...

"Charity... Go home!" Marcus pivots and goes in, closing the door behind him.

CHAPTER TWENTY-SIX

The storm blew through, leaving the earth breathing in a humid summer day. It left a rather muddy pit in the arena, as well. This doesn't bother the raucous crowd filling the bleachers. There's not even a small percentage missing the spectacle today. The clamor is a mixture of friendly and hungry, all happy to be in the stands and not below them.

Marcus and the town council are in place on the grandstand. In silent protest, Gabriel appears bored. Ethan and Daniel slosh around below, readying the same elements that are the source of Gabriel's boredom.

There's a large oval rack in the middle of the pit. Ethan places a long pole, with a sickle blade at its end, in the rack.

It's the last of the weapons to join a slew of menacing-looking toys that Gabriel had collected over the years. It's an odd collection with only one thing in common... death. A headsman's ax, spears of various lengths and cutting edges, swords of all shapes... even a mace, are among the stockpile of weapons. There is one other thing they have in common... Gabriel had all their edges sharpened.

Extending up from the middle of the rack is a wide, twelve-foot long pipe. It's capped by what appears to be an oversized patio heater head.

Marcus comes up to the mic and thumps it, as usual. Pastor Cain looms close behind him, just in case there's an opportunity to share the mic... and speechifying.

More increasingly, it takes longer for the audience to settle down... perhaps they're starting to understand the stakes. Marcus thumps extra hard on the mic, as usual well aware it works. The effect is reached, and the crowd's uproar dies to a murmur.

Tap, tap... "I sees you's all fired up a bit more than regular. Want ya'll to know right off that we've shed some of the old rules of the redemption fer somethin' different."

He pauses in anticipation. There's a momentary silence that comes with the shock of suggested change.

It's broken when a woman yells out, "What fer?"

"Woman... give the man a chance to talk afore you git all het up," yells a man on the other side of the arena.

Marcus figures one for two isn't doing bad thus far. "I was 'bouts to say... 'cause we'ez putting our own townsfolk down there, we reckoned to put folks in the pit with 'bouts equal sins... "

"And what?" interrupts the same obnoxious woman.

"Woman!" chastises the same man across the way.

"The what is a chance... They gits to choose betwixt themselves who gits redeemed... and who gits forgivin'."

Marcus rests for a few moments, allowing the crowd to breathe... the way he knows them to do. He didn't bother to mention that by structuring the doin's this way... with having a chance, sinners would be unhappy, but more cooperative. And more cooperative means a better show... that's good politics. Experience has also told him to feed the audience with only a few pieces of change at a time.

The grumbling of the masses rises and falls... and repeats its modulations a couple times. A more consistent hum or yammer is a sign of most being on the same page... they aren't yet.

A man yells out, "Jes' git to it... and we'ez gonna tell you afterwards what we'ez thinks."

"Fair enough... Now, keep in mind that those findin' themselves in the pit is prit' near apples to apples, sin-wise... and they hain't been chosen outta convenience," Marcus tries to assure them.

Another faceless woman yells, "We'ez gonna be the judge of that, too."

"Are we havin' a redeemin'... or not!" comes immediately from another irritated woman.

Marcus wonders if that guy Caesar got more respect at the Coliseum... probably not.

Josh stares down at his swinging feet. As the toe of his sneaker sweeps past the gridded rows on the floor, it creates a rippling visual moiré effect. The cold stone holding chamber has not been made friendlier for the sake of locals... except for a recording of whiny fiddle playing coming over the crackly speakers. This mountain version of Muzak is more to mask what's said, or done, in the arena than to soothe.

Josh is in his early thirties and clean-shaven, which is somewhat unusual in these parts. He sits on the metal bunk surprisingly calm, but not looking up. He doesn't want to exchange looks with his cellmate.

On the other hand, Benjamin, who sits on a nearby bunk, studies Josh carefully. He's also in his early thirties, with a reasonably trimmed beard.

Josh is relatively new back to Redemption, only returning a year ago. He had unfortunately gone to explore the flats some four years back. Down there he got in some trouble that landed him for a couple years in the county jail. After that he didn't last long on the flats before coming home. His family's farm being well outside of town, combined with Josh being on the shy side, left him not knowing that many townsfolk... at least, not more than face knowledge.

The town's unofficial, but understood, rule is to use only those who have been away, and choose to return, as minor links to the outside world. It creates less unneeded temptation. Being a cut-off artery, for long before the landslide, Redemption occasionally has to send someone to the flats for the various supplies that only the outside world can offer. Josh qualified as one of the drivers.

Josh angles a glance up toward Benjamin, who's still staring at him. "What?" he asks self-consciously.

"Hell... outside of church, I thinks this might be the longest spell we'ez been in a room together," says Benjamin. Considering his predicament, he also seems to be taking things calmly.

"You got any... " Josh starts to say quietly.

"You gotta speak up... too late to offend anyone."

Josh clears his throat and raises his voice some. "I was askin'... got any idea why you is in here?"

"Whatever it were... I'll bet it got somethin' to do with my wife."

"Oh... you're married." Josh had thought he was getting a hint of interest.

"Not rightly so... and she'd be all het up to use it on me, now that everyone is a hangin' out their laundry."

Josh thinks on this a second, then, "Oh... up here?" The last part of that just slipped out.

"What they got you in here fer?" Benjamin asks.

Josh peers down at the grating. "It's a big mistake... that's all it is."

Benjamin nods towards Jake, the council's muscle standing just outside the door, shotgun in hand. "Time fer manure seems prit' near over. Things don't rightly matter now."

Though Josh tries to keep it at bay, a grin slips out. Still not looking up, "Someone done told I've gone by a club named the Back Door when I was down on the flats."

"Ah... now I gits a glimmer," says Benjamin, but not in an accusatory way.

Not feeling as intimidated by the truth now, Josh looks up, "How'd you know 'bouts that club way up here?"

"My dear wife done turned over some magazines I gits now and then."

Josh appears puzzled.

"The kind of magazines that's come with plain wrappin'... A friend of mine from these parts took off a long time ago. He sends them to me," says Benjamin, with no hint of embarrassment.

The shyness is finally wearing off Josh. A warm smile dawns, "Well... guess it's right nice to finally meet ya."

Benjamin glances around the hard cold room and says, "Cain't rightly agree with you on timin'."

"And... afore we'ez gits to today's doin's, I wanted to remind ya'll that the weapons and that plum' pretty mushroom thing in the pit is thanks to our town genius, Gabriel," Marcus announces.

The crowd's antsy... they grumble and murmur.

Gabriel doesn't even bother getting up for the impatient, lukewarm applause. He simply tips his hat from his chair.

A man yells out, "Jes' get on with the redeemin'!"

Marcus covers the mic and glances back at the council, "Right testy, hain't they."

Hanna snaps at him, "Then give 'em what they wants... and stop your speechifyin'."

There's a jolting clank from below.

Benjamin and Josh stand inside the mouth of the tunnel, still lit by the neon above them. Without a word, Benjamin slaps a passionate kiss on Josh. It's not rejected. They separate just as abruptly.

Another clank and the doors open with a hollow grinding squeak. Everyone in the stands strains their necks to see who will come out. Josh and Benjamin emerge, holding their hands up against the sun.

Momentarily there is silence from the bleachers. Marcus thinks, only so briefly, that maybe his plan of seeing kin in there is starting to work. Then a woman lets out a scream like she has just won the lottery. This is Benjamin's wife. She jumps up and down clapping her hands till kin help settle her down. The rest of the townsfolk crack up laughing.

Marcus' heart sinks... just a speck.

In addition to the new items in the pit there have been some changes to the grandstand, as well. An oversize clock from the old gas station is mounted at the front of the podium. A big red button that belongs in a carnival rests atop it. Josh and Benjamin take all this in... as Jake, and his shotgun, coax them towards the center.

The crowd cackles high and low. The cackling becomes more pronounced, in various degrees, by the nearness of kin of those in the pit. That's a little misleading since there are not that many original clans in Redemption's early history, so most people in the stands are a bit akin to each other.

The general area around Benjamin's wife is the most active and weighted towards rejoicing. Apparently Benjamin has stepped on a few toes outside of those making accusations in the tellin's.

Josh's much smaller area has kin that are less vociferous. Maybe they're more understanding... at least, Josh hopes so as he walks towards the rack. His knees shake. It should help to remind himself that he, as all here, has cheered the bloody redemptions from these bleachers many times... it doesn't. His knees shake even more. But to his credit, Josh is still on his feet, walking to his fate... for a ridiculous reason.

There's more arrogance to Benjamin's movement. It's shy of a stride, but up from a walk. The occasional hand gesture in the air makes it clear he's lost reverence for the tradition of redeeming. He has a few particularly obscene silent gestures reserved just for his wife and kin.

Pastor Cain makes note how his profane gestures draw more cheers then his preaching does.

Marcus steps back up to the mic. "Benjamin and Joshua, how is ya'll doin'? Never mind... it's a no account question. So, let's jes' git to the formals. We'ez hain't goin' to be airin' dirty laundry... "

This meets with a growing clamor of discontent, and more than a few catcalls, from the gallery. Marcus has hoped to keep this minus the dirt, partially because each person may view deserving sins in different ways... he doesn't need the post-redemption debates. He should have been able to tell from the Crackerbarrel the other day, that wouldn't fly.

"OK... OK... we'ez gonna give a hint at things... Jes' don't go pushin' fer details," Marcus says and he steps away from the mic to gather his thoughts.

Pastor Cain and Hanna rush up to him... no doubt to be sure he adequately paints the two in the pit with sufficient darkness. They huddle for a few seconds, with Hanna being very animated about her opinions.

Gabriel can be seen seated in the background laughing, softly, at the hypocrisy.

A frustrated Marcus breaks off and comes back to the mic. He thumps on the mic, even though it hasn't been turned off. Clearly uncomfortable, he searches for the right wording, "Alright... Benjamin and Joshua, you's both been found to be... perverts." Much of the crowd breaks up laughing. "And that's all I is gonna say on the matter."

A smattering of boos come from those who want to hear more titillating details. They're disregarded by those who want to get on with the redeeming and quickly die out.

"Now lets me git to the important stuff... the rules. Actually... there hain't any. One of you's gits to live and the other gits redeemed."

Gabriel leans forward in his chair and loudly whispers, "You's forgettin' the clock part."

"Oh, yeah... there is one. You got three minutes from when I hit this here buzzer to git it done... If you's both still standin', then that mushroom-like thing will explode, sendin' ball bearings all 'bouts the arena." Marcus pauses at what he just said and he glances back at Gabriel.

The audience drops it's yammering a notch. A man yells, "What's you mean... all 'bouts?"

Gabriel can't pout all day. He quickly steps up to the mic, "Don't ya'll fret... it's designed to cover jes' the pit."

Gabriel is enough of assurance that anyone can ask for... at least in regards to his toys. No one has been *accidently* killed yet.

Ethan, Daniel and Jake decide it's a good time to get clear, and head for the tunnel.

Tom took some private time the other night to do some rearranging at the perch. When not around Rick and Lisa, his crutches become amazingly less restrictive. He had managed to uproot a bush and replant it near Hope's picnic blanket.

He pulls back from his bush and glances at Hope, "Gladiators... This keeps getting better and better!"

"I thinks it takes some of the flair out of the doin's... You should-a seen some of the right colorful inventions old Gabe done come up with," she responds. As Tom starts to go back in his bush, Hope adds, "And don't go thinkin' I'm snookered by you rearranging my deck."

"Didn't think they'd pay attention down there," he says with a grin.

Hope and Tom aren't alone at the perch. A few yards away, Rick and Lisa are too glued to the arena to care about talk.

Hope cocks her head, "Watch out... That's a speck of what Jared done thought."

Left alone in the pit, Josh and Benjamin peer at each other... and then at the weapons rack... and then up to the grandstand.

Marcus places his hand over the ridiculously big red button. "An' we'ez commencin'... Now!"

He hits the button... an air horn blasts. Then, there's a sudden, loud tick-tick-tick blasting from the speakers. Everyone freezes for a brief moment, trying to put a finger on it.

Gabriel displays one of his first smiles of the day. He has rigged the speakers to the ancient clock on the podium... for a three-minute window. He figured it added a touch of flair.

Tick-tick-tick...

Benjamin gives Josh a quick, "Nice meetin' ya," and grabs at the rack. He pushes a few nasty-looking choices out of the way, settling on a medium-length spear with blades at both ends. To get a feel, he tosses it back and forth between his hands. He looks at Josh.

Tick-tick-tick...

Josh sets down one sword and grabs a short sickle-like blade. It feels too short and he takes a longer staff, with a sickle blade at the end. After a couple swings, he tosses it down.

Gabriel, not at all pleased with this form of game, sneaks a peek at the fiasco playing out in the pit. He sighs and shakes his head.

Tick-tick-tick...

"Make up your dang mind... we'ez only got three-minutes."

"That hain't fair!" snaps Josh.

"Just grab somethin'!" yells Benjamin

Tick-tick-tick...

Enough being polite... Benjamin charges at Josh, spear at the ready. Josh grasps the first thing his hand touches... a short rod with a nail-spiked wooden ball hanging from its end... a hill folk's mace.

Josh barely manages to parry Benjamin's attack with the mace, but in his follow through the spiked ball swings all the way around to take a bite of his own leg.

Kin or no, the townsfolk break out laughing. Marcus wonders if they're more enthusiastic over kin than visitors. What kind of box has he opened?

Neither of the men are weapons graceful. At least, Benjamin appears like he's not going to hurt himself. He attacks again.

Josh swings in cautious defense, but seems more on guard against his own weapon than that of his enemy. Benjamin's blade slashes his shoulder. His shirt soaks up the red. Now Josh

CHAPTER TWENTY-SEVEN

A breath of ease has settled over the town this late afternoon. It's as though all the townsfolk were playing Russian roulette and the chamber has clicked for the day.

Marcus and Gabriel stroll down Main Street, testing the waters. They get the occasional congratulations as they go... but the calm feels fleeting. Behind all the smiles there's an edge of fear.

As the two approach a smallish gathering at the Crackerbarrel, Gabriel stops and tips his brim, "Glad to say I got work to git done fer the Fourth." The smallish gathering is not small enough.

Marcus knows his friend's true motivations and can hardly blame him. Gabriel's art is in his hands... and in his still. Marcus's art is in people.

Before Gabriel leaves, Marcus asks a redundant question, with a grin, "Sure you hain't gonna tell me what's you're workin' on?" It's a friendly dig... he knows how much Gabriel hates that overdone question.

They part company with no answer given.

Even before getting to the porch of the store, Marcus notices something has caught everyone's attention. In a little park across from the Crackerbarrel, Pastor Cain and Hanna supervise some project. A couple townsmen are digging a long hole. It now has Marcus' attention. As he starts across the street, the two men hoist up a beefy pair of antique stocks.

Marcus stops in his tracks when he sees the pastor and Hanna are being exceptionally obnoxious to the two men. They're insisting that the base is well packed and can handle the weight of serious resistance. A couple of kids run over, jump up and try to hang on the contraption. Hanna shoos them away.

Marcus thinks back on history and he reckons they haven't used stocks since the late eighteen hundreds... up here, maybe the early nineteen hundreds. It must have come from Jake's.

If Redemption has anything that resembles a museum, it is Jake's, the muscle man's old, closed body shop. While the Last Chance Saloon functions as city hall, Jake's shop functions as the city hall's basement. It's the catchall of the town's history.

Hanna catches sight of Marcus, so there's no escape for him. He smiles and says, "What, my dear, are you doin' with that dern antique?" He knows the answer almost as fast as he knows he shouldn't have asked in the first place.

Pastor Cain attempts to intervene but Hanna moves past him... snatching the pastor's notebook on the way. She shakes it in the air, like a schoolmarm with a wooden ruler, "'Cause we'ez got all levels of transgressions in here... and we'ez cain't kill all the sinners."

He knows her well enough not to be baited into this. Marcus's never been quite the believer his wife is... and she can get right heated about it. With a smile and nod that says *we'll take this up later*, Marcus strategically retreats.

Not having been able to see what's happening in the park with her binoculars, Charity comes outside. She heads for the Crackerbarrel where there are more ears to listen to her.

Unaware of what a small circle of folks there is talking about, Charity pries herself into it like a crowbar. "Now that's a purely fine idee," pointing to the stocks. "I know some folks that would be prit' near perfect fer... "

The circle peels away from her.

Taking in the insanity growing in the town, Marcus makes a slow turn. Ever an optimist, he's sure it will wear thin soon... if not after tomorrows doin's... then by the Fourth.

Charity raises a hand, "Oh, mayor... oh, mayor... "

Lisa paces around, indoors and out, like a caged cat. She's torn between wanting to see more and wanting to run. This can be a problem. In Hope's view... it makes her unforeseeable.

Unpredictability is part of art, but like many artists, Hope wants to edge the control in her favor. When Lisa passes her one more time, Hope speaks out, "You know... we oughta go fer a walk together."

The first thing that rushes through Lisa's mind is *absolutely not*. She doesn't say this... instead, she just stares at Hope in puzzlement.

Hope repeats herself, "A walk... you and me... how's that sound?"

"Dangerous," Lisa says.

"I promise not to the perch or the cave or anywhere with a mighty drop off." Hope gives her a grin, "Ah, come on... If I'd wanted to do ya'll harm, I'd have gotten to it by now. I got somethin' I thinks you might wanna hear." Teasing it a little more, "'Bouts you folks getting oughta here." She can tell this will get Lisa to bite.

After a long pause, Lisa says, "Sure... why not?" But she's not ready to go yet. On her way back into the cabin, "Just give me a minute to tell Rick I'm going."

She figures this will take some of the risk out of a private walk with a nutcase... maybe not much. Hope doesn't object since it has no bearing on her plans.

Once inside, Lisa heads straight for Rick. She grabs his sleeve and aggressively coaxes him into the kitchen. In a whisper, "She wants me to go for a walk." The way she says it comes off very ominously.

"So?" responds Rick.

She glares at him... with a look saying that was not the right response.

"OK... if you don't trust her, then don't go."

Rick is searching for safe ground, where there probably is none. He surrenders, "OK... What do you want me to do?"

She pulls him to the kitchen window and waves towards the trails leaving the cabin clearing. "I want you to watch what path we take, and if I'm not back in a half hour, come find me."

He gives her paranoia a supportive nod, "Fine... a half hour. I got it." He hopes he doesn't fall asleep on the sofa.

That being settled, Lisa starts rummaging through the things on the counter. After tossing some miscellaneous items aside, she holds up a butcher knife. She attempts to hide it in her back pocket, but it's too long. Tossing it down, Lisa grabs another one. The serrated edge catches on her designer jeans. "Dammit!" and that one goes flying onto the counter.

Rick is having a hard time holding back a laugh... the desire to have a place to keep his feet warm tonight makes him try.

Lisa finally finds a blade that doesn't damage her two hundred dollar jeans... or stick out like a sore thumb. That it's so small it would be useless against a large, angry cat doesn't seem to dawn on her.

Rick still holds his laugh as she puts it neatly in her back pocket. The temptation is too much.

"Lucky there's no clock." It comes off too flippant for Lisa. She gives him a cold stare that puts his warm feet into question.

Hope sits on the steps waiting for Lisa to set up whatever safeguards her crazy little mind comes up with. She reminds herself to be nice... at this point in the painting. The screen door slams behind her and Lisa storms past.

Over her shoulder Lisa says, "What are we waiting for... let's go."

Be nice, Hope thinks... like a mantra.

As Lisa turns, Hope points, "That there parin' knife is right dangerous... if you take a spill... or run into a squirrel."

Reflexively, Lisa feels at the blade so close to her ass... she decides on taking her chances. She waves for her host to take the lead. As Hope passes her, Lisa gives a quick glance back at the kitchen window to see if Rick's watching. He appears bored or sleepy, but he gives her a slight wave.

At least Hope's not heading off on the path to the perch. Then Lisa remembers that most of the trails she explored while looking for the cave passed some precarious terrain. She pats the tiny knife in her pocket.

The trail is too narrow for the two to walk side by side, which is fine with Lisa... she prefers following at a safe distance. Hope's been silent for the last five minutes walking... she knows it plays on Lisa's nerves.

As though she can read Lisa's mind, Hope says over her shoulder, "Silence is mighty loud at times... hain't it? Don't you want to know what I got you out here fer?"

The way that sounded, Lisa isn't sure she wants to answer... now that they're well away from the cabin. But she came for a reason... might as well get it over with.

"I can't wait."

Hope talks over her shoulder as she goes. "I knows you and Rick is gittin' right fidgety to get back on the road."

"I know... you're going to remind me of Tom's foot... I don't think it's as bad as he makes out."

Hope shrugs, "On that one... think you're plum' on the mark... he does have a hankerin' to hang 'round a piece."

"That's not the only piece he has a hankering for," Lisa says, like a bad punch line.

How the hell does he put up with her? crosses Hope's mind.

"What I was gittin' at is... I've a mind o' keepin' him 'round a piece, too." Hope stops and turns around to face Lisa. "I got my suspicions that it wouldn't ruffle you much... but that brings us to Rick."

Lisa's now on her home field... scheming. And she feels comfortable. "You leave Rick to me."

CHAPTER TWENTY-EIGHT

Today's getting off to a slow start... Hope and Tom haven't gotten up yet. Rick and Lisa show little more energy, lazing around on the front porch. If they're leaving, there's little sign of it.

Hope finally comes out looking bright and shiny in her sundress. She stretches her arms wide, with a satisfied yawn.

Lisa cringes, then putting on a fake smile, "Look who's sleeping in late."

"And... look who's still here 'bouts," Hope throws back to her.

Her first inclination was to comment on who still has a dark appetite, but that would have been playing too much on Lisa's field. She knows pointing out Lisa's hunger to her is more part of the art... and she likes the dig.

"Rick wanted to stay a little while longer... *a very little while*," Lisa says, though she has been more convincing.

"Figured if it was happening again today... I have to see it," Rick offers, knowing his girlfriend sandbagged him.

People stream into the bleachers. A buzz of excitement and rumors prevails. Maybe it's just their relief at having missed today's callings... again.

Near the back of the grandstand, the council is in the middle of some kind of commotion.

"Why am I hearin' 'bouts this now?" demands Marcus.

He's used to thinking on the fly... not that things are normally that hectic in Redemption, but it's still irritating.

Gabriel steps up. "Those two old oaks got right insistent... in front of a passel of kin of those you's throwin' in the pit today."

"But they don't have much sins to be washed," Hanna interjects, wanting to see dirty blood stain the sand.

Marcus knows the church is politics, but straight politics trumps that. Kin are hard enough to manage without adding in that he turned away those that would take their kin's place. That would lead to giving him a horrifically bad day.

"Hanna, we done gotta honor their wishes or they's gonna take their ruckus out into the streets... plus there's the kin."

Being overruled, she stomps away... with Pastor Cain close behind her.

With a hand on Gabriel's shoulder, Marcus asks, "But with shotguns?"

"They's insistin' upon their own ways," he responds.

Aaron adds, "Either one of them most likely could outshoot most of us." There's a nod of agreement on that point.

Gabriel points out, "In their day... Anyways, I made sure they's only using lead slugs instead of shot... and I had the boys prep the pit with hay bales."

Without shot, there wouldn't be a broad spread pattern. And there will be barriers enough to make it an interesting bout... without ricochets.

"What if one of them has a heart attack and shoots into the townsfolk?" asks Marcus.

"God works in mighty mysterious ways," Gabriel says glibly. He has always been pragmatic about the religious aspect of the arena.

Having had enough of a huddle, Marcus approaches the podium just as the townsfolk settle... good timing is a right good sign, he thinks.

Thump, thump... "I see ya'll done made it in time."

The loud hum of the crowd tells Marcus that the rumor of the line-up is spreading. In a town this small, there's never time to get ahead of things. Somebody stubs their toe at one end of town... and by the time you get to the other end of Main Street, word is they've lost their foot.

"Afore ya'll gits too lathered up over what's doin', let me set ya'll straight. We do have a change in the menu today... Two of our older folk done volunteered to use the doin's to settle an old dispute."

Marcus pauses for the expected grumbling of the crowd... it doesn't disappoint. The folks of Redemption take to change like tooth pulling. He silently keeps count in his head... timing. Now is about right... before the first heckle.

"The way I sees it, they's takin' to the arena by choice is a might more powerful than a regular like redeemin'." Truth in politics is consistent... from big government to the smallest theater in the hills. "They's even said they's a doin' this fer those found right guilty." He builds, "What we'ez got here is our own sin-eaters."

He found his hook, though he doubts many will apply for the job.

Hope leans forward in her beach chair, getting a rush from the turn of events... the same rush she gets when a particular crimson red takes on a hard glow next to the deepest of blacks. She also knows her father's mind... and how this sin-eater angle must have pleased him to come up with. He's probably thinking of how to play with it further.

Tom pulls back out of his bush. Seeing Hope so focused, he doesn't want to break it, so he goes back to the show.

There's the familiar clank of the tunnel doors being un-bolted... Everyone leans forward in their seats. Their eyes are focused on the mouth, when another bolt unlatches at the entry arch to the arena. Both portals open simultaneously.

It crosses Gabriel's mind that the boys have done a right fine job of timing.

Albert enters from the south... Quincy from the north.

Even Marcus is impressed by the showmanship of it. The two oldest fixtures in town are determined to have it their own way... but if it plays well, that's fine with him.

They are both armed. Albert carries a twelve gauge pump and a double barrel one is slung over Quincy's shoulder... so he can use his cane.

When Gabriel said he had the boys put out a few hay bales, it was an understatement. There are a dozen or so stacks of bales... a perfect combat game grid for a couple agile combat-ants. These aged gladiators may very well pass out going from one to the next.

The columns of hay, though none over six feet, are well laid out to catch errant slugs fired from almost any direction within the pit.

Marcus sees it's his cue, "Now folks, I give to ya'll... "

"Shut up... up there!" yells Albert. Then he coughs.

Quincy nods his agreement.

A man in the bleachers with a handlebar moustache yells out, "This 'bouts that stupid parking space?" He gets a round of laughter, so he adds, "Hell... bet ya'll cain't even lift them there shotguns."

"Heard nuff outta you too, curly beard... yeah, I can see that far," snaps Quincy.

So far, everything the two do draws laughter.

Marcus taps on the mic, "Anything you wants from us to get it started?"

"Jes' that ya'll watch n' learn... and that you stop tapping that damn mic," Albert yells up.

Gabriel walks near Marcus and, with a quick reach, he switches off the mic. "They's done got this far on their own wits... best let 'em be."

Quincy tosses away his cane... the adrenaline of the moment has given him a little extra boost. He unslings his double barrel and starts to walk forward. Albert matches his advance. It's not exactly a gladiator's explosive charge... slower... and somewhat steady.

When each gets to the first stack of hay bales, both stop. Their orchestration has quieted the masses... so far. Both lean their shotguns against a bale. Then each reaches down and withdraws something from between the bales.

Total puzzlement washes over Marcus' face as the two old guys put on what appear to be Mickey Mouse-type caps with exaggerated red ears.

"Still a wonderin' what they's want those fer."

Apparently Gabriel has known about the caps a piece longer than Marcus.

"You look like a dang fool in that there hat," says Quincy.

"Ya gonna have to speak up," responds Albert.

"Hell... Your ears should be right big enough."

This gets another laugh from the gallery. Marcus watches his audience. They're captivated by what these two old coots might do next. It's not out of kinship, since these two have done their fair share of irritating most townsfolk. Missing so far is the loud hunger... he knows it won't last.

"So what's you wanna do now?" Quincy asks loudly.

"Let's put on a show," counters Albert. The adrenaline has gotten into his system as well... enough to get him up to half-speed.

The crowd's fascination is broken when the man with the mustache yells, "Is we supposed to wait till ya'll keel over of old age?"

"They's gittin' hungry... like you said, let's give 'em a show." Quincy gives Albert a nod.

They walk-run to the next pile of bales, which stand closer to each other... with their shotguns at the ready. The irregular tops of the bale stacks allow them to be seen... or not. Unfortunately, their absurd hats pop up before their eyes.

BOOM! Albert's hat goes flying off. While Quincy repositions himself, Albert reaches down and raises his hat high. A large hole is in the middle of the right ear.

He yells out, "Guess you done got first blood."

There's a laugh from behind the stack... and Quincy hobbles to another stack.

Albert gets a bead on him but doesn't fire, waiting for the right moment. Quincy's head starts up and BOOM... the shot kicks up a chunk of hay, but misses its mark.

"Gittin' old... hain't ya," comes from Quincy's concealment.

He moves a few bales over and slowly rises, his shotgun ready to be leveled. BOOM... a shot sends his hat in the wind.

The novelty of good showmanship and any respect for age are quick to wear off. There are yells for more action, not only from the man with the handlebar mustache.

Not timed in answer to any other calls but their own, Quincy and Albert walk out into the open. Standing squarely facing each other, they hold their shotgun barrels down, but poised to be raised.

Quincy says, "Keep your finger clear till you's full up."

Irritated, Albert snaps back, "I know... I done learned that seventy years past."

"Yeah... from my pa... were that long ago, weren't it?" says Quincy with a touch of melancholy. He counts, "One... two... three."

On the count of three, the two snap their barrels up and fire simultaneously. It would be hard to tell which man's round struck first... but both their hats fly away from their heads.

Marcus has expected righteous outrage over the lack of blood by this point. But at first, there's murmuring, speckled by pockets of applause. The applause grows for their respected skill, especially by those who shoot... and a dern good show by those who don't.

Both Albert and Quincy take a full circle bow. As they do, Quincy ejects his shells and loads two more. Then they take a stance and give a knowing look to each other, words reserved in silence. Their shotguns come up and discharge... BOOM!

Both slugs hit their targets... center mass. Two old men who have been friends, enemies, opponents and all the things that have passed between them over the years, topple to the ground.

As Quincy falls, his double barrel goes flying. When it hits the ground, the second barrel goes off. The slug hits a weapon in the rack that looks like a garden weasel... The wheel of spikes spins... a single spike flies off the wheel... it rockets through the air and embeds deep into the throat of the man with the handlebar mustache.

Marcus stands there glancing between the two old men dead in the sand and the man slumped over in the stands.

He glances at Gabriel who shrugs with a grin. Then Marcus peers back into the pit. "Damn... that was movin'. I think we'ez jes' seen our first dual hillbilly euthanasia."

"You're 'bouts right... they was right pigheaded 'bouts hidin' some serious ailin's," says Gabriel. He had done what he could to aid them... he'll sleep well tonight.

Marcus thinks it's been a mighty interesting day so far... and that's just the first match.

CHAPTER TWENTY-NINE

Lisa pulls out of the bushes, appearing unsatisfied. "What next... they going to have beheadings of the homeless?" It's not only the townsfolk who prefer self-righteousness served with their blood.

Hope shakes her head, knowing that Lisa missed the beauty of the last match. The show is wasted on her... trying to explain it to her would be useless.

Tom had pulled back, as well... for the intermission. He sits quietly... thinking. Hope figures he understands... and doesn't want to bother his appreciating it.

She can only see Rick's feet... he's either not wanting to miss the start of the next match or he's asleep. Hope lights a joint and takes a deep drag. Grabbing her binoculars, she decides to take a closer peek at the micro strokes below.

The arena is in intermission. Folks have brought their lunches and there are picnics spread throughout the stands. Except for where the man with the mustache was... there, a crew is cleaning up.

Prudence, the bar waitress, is missing the usual number of buttons from the top of her blouse. She's surrounded by suitors of all ages... some old enough that flirting is just a way of feeling like they're still young. *Good luck, fellas*, Hope thinks, with a smile.

Having a microscopic view of the pit proves interesting. She takes another drag. Young men, busy as ants, flash across the lens of the binoculars. They make it a true halftime as they rush to clear the bodies... rake in the blood... and move the bulk of the hay bales to the outer edges of the pit.

The last item must have been at Gabriel's orders... no use having visibility even partially blocked during the doin's. The first match was custom ordered. Now the arena is back under Gabriel's cap, even though he tries to show little interest.

Hope's view of the arena moves on. The woman who calls herself Emily the Soothsayer has apparently dipped into the shine too much... again. She staggers about on the bleachers... if it weren't for the other townsfolk, she would tumble over the rail and into the pit. Seems like a soothsayer should figure out what comes next when she picks up a jug.

Her glasses drift over to the grandstand. No shortage of pic-nickers there either. She can only imagine their conversations. Her step-mother Hanna is chastising anyone that doesn't agree with her... using religion as her blackjack. No wonder her pa is having an affair with Prudence. Of course, he has no idea that Hope knows... or that many townsfolk suspect.

Hope knows her pa is just as busy trying to convince ev-eryone, except Hanna, that black is white, and that these events will have to taper off... All the while keeping his good old boy mask secure.

That's odd... Gabriel is staring directly at her, not a casual glance, but a true stare. Once he knows he's been seen, Gabriel still takes a few seconds before breaking it off. Odd.

Then Hope notices binoculars lie on the deck next to Gabriel's chair. Hope thinks back... she had been too caught up in Albert and Quincy's unique offering to remember seeing Gabriel using the glasses. She's truly unsure if he had used them to watch her perch area.

Tap, tap... nothing comes over the speakers. Marcus appears suddenly vindicated. Gabriel quickly moves over and switches the PA system back on. He knows there will be no end to Marcus' thumping now.

Thump, thump... "That were a rightly interestin' match. They had it their way... we'ez gonna miss those two old oaks."

A yell comes from the stands, "You's speakin' fer yourself... they's weren't much more than hot air." It's clear that any hint of reverence has passed. "Git on with it!"

Just then the tunnel doors open and Charity stumbles out... at the urging of Jake and his shotgun. There are cheers of approval, not surprise. More than a few expected to see Charity in the pit... if not now, then very soon. Her appearance pleases many, but what puzzles most is whom she will go against. All eyes watch the mouth of the tunnel.

There's a collective gasp as Ethan escorts Abigail into the arena.

As Charity heads towards the rack, she keeps turning around and around. Occasionally she squeaks out, "I don't belong in here... I know a passel of those that do... I hain't one of 'em." Her pleas fall on mostly deaf ears.

Abigail walks much more calmly. She's not the most agile of women... some would even call her right hefty.

She tells Charity, "Well... you's here now, so stop the whinin'."

Once near the rack, Abigail stops and glares up at Marcus, aware that they both know she's been stabbed in the back. The Crackerbarrel deck in front of Abigail's store and café has seen too many seasons of Charity's rumor-mongering. Abigail knew Charity's name had to be on their sinners' pole... her crime was bribing the council to move it up to the top.

Seems Redemption's charter makes it illegal, by local rules, to make a bribe... but not against the law to accept one. It's a rule that rarely gets brought up, for practical reasons. It's also a rule that sleeps in the shadows till needed.

Abigail's always been tight with a dime, never forgiving debts and rather ruthless over financial matters. She's as ruthless as one can be in a tiny town, and... always with a smile. Under the pretty face of Redemption, pre-landslide, boil quite a few resentments... and few are allowed to surface.

A woman in the stands yells, "How fittin'... big mouth versus big... "

Marcus drowns her out with, "Now folks, let's keep it civil-like." The best way to control a herd is to lead them. "Let's git right into the officials of the second half of the doin's."

"Then do it," someone yells.

"Charity... " he sees her working up to saying something. "We'ez already been through all this... so keep your peace."

Pastor Cain hands Marcus his little notepad with a list of transgressions. He sighs as he takes it. Marcus is pretty sure he could handle the words without a list... but it's the official way of doing it.

He reads, "Charity you's accused of bearin' false witness against old man Rogers... and bearin' false witness against Prudence... and bearin' false witness against Beatrice." He glances over at Pastor Cain for an answer.

The pastor shrugs, "Twenty-six."

With a shake of his head, Marcus turns back to the mic, "Let's jes' say three's enough."

Charity sputters, "But... but... but... "

Glares can burn and Marcus feels Abigail's. She wants to get on with it.

"And Abigail... you's accused of the evil of bribin'... and of prit' near hoardin' the trough."

"That mean you're gonna return the money I done give you?" Abigail yells.

There's a mixture of laughter, cheers and some grumbling from the gallery. Charity is exactly what is said of her... and more. She's often a pain in the ass. But, she's a mighty fine tool for rumors... receiving or sending.

On the other hand, Abigail is a pleasant enough skinflint... but she holds a paper on most everyone and everything in town.

Handing the notepad back to the pastor, Marcus ignores her question. "I've done explained the rules yesterday while ya'll were sittin' up here... they's the same. You got three minutes from the horn."

Ethan and Jake leave the field to the women.

The horn blows, the mob cheers and the clock ticks.

It comes to Charity that her dramatics don't serve her now, so she gets to the weapons rack as quickly as Abigail.

At the rack, Abigail pulls out a few bladed weapons before quickly settling on a sword... more akin to a scimitar with its curved and heavy-ended steel. She has the bulk for it.

Charity is being choosier... but that's not her main problem. Holding one spear, she points to another, "Abigail, how 'bouts that one?"

Tick... tick... tick...

"Charity darlin', I really think that mace thing over there is more fittin' you," says Abigail calmly, gesturing as it as if picking out Tupperware.

With a glance at it, Charity smiles, "Thinks you's plum' right... thanks."

Charity reaches far over to grab the mace handle... out in front of Abigail. The scimitar swings down on her neck. Mouth still open, Charity's head topples to the sand... with a thump.

Abigail thinks, *How appropriate... Charity's open mouth was her biggest problem.*

The crowd applauds and laughs. A few mourn the loss of her rumorin'... as they say, nature abhors a vacuum, so no doubt someone will take up the banner, or megaphone... if anyone lives.

Abigail strides triumphantly towards the tunnel, owing nothing to anyone.

The council gathers before separating into their individual directions. Marcus seems a bit distant... as though he's talking to the air, "Cain't ya'll see... we'ez gonna run outta people."

"We won't run outta sinners!" Hanna's harsh voice brings him back down.

Seeing his chance, Gabriel peels off. He steps over to the rail and peers down at the pit... then up at Hope's perch.

Hope stands at the edge with her spyglasses on Gabriel's face. There's a sadness she rarely recalls being there. She brings the glasses down and gives him a parting wave.

Turning to head down the trail, Hope stops and glances over at Lisa. She looks like seeing the elephant this time got to her. Rick consoles her.

Hope moves on, not even waiting for Tom. She figures each person should have solo time after what the town calls a redeeming... and she calls art. She feels a hint of sadness, perhaps an overflow from Gabriel.

CHAPTER THIRTY

Contrary to the norm, the Last Chance Saloon is fully packed... and it's not pretend partying. It's not happy partying either. There's the chilliness of a New York City bar on Friday night... everyone with their own singular agenda. And many are getting a bit more sauced than they're used to.

Marcus and Gabriel try to isolate themselves by sitting at the bar instead of the council's table, which is occupied by Hanna and her following. People constantly bump into and jostle them... with little success, they try to ignore it.

Marcus grumbles, "This jes' cain't go on like this... we'ez all gonna be at each other's throats."

"Careful with your wordin'... gonna be like takin' a bone from a dog... you is liable to gits bit," Gabriel warns.

A drunk slaps Gabriel on the back. "Dern fine redeemin'... keep it up."

Ignoring him, Gabriel leans to Marcus, "'Specially by drunk dogs."

Aaron, behind the bar, comes over and leans into the two. With a soft voice, guarding against extra ears, "This here hain't normal... I'm prit' near outta store-bought liquor. Hell... most of the time, it's fer visitor nights. Nobody drinks that much... at least, not here."

"Speak fer yourself," Gabriel admonishes. "On that subject... reach me my jug."

While Aaron reaches under the bar, he asks, "That's what I was 'bouts to check with you on... you got any squeezins' near by?" Sliding the jug over to Gabriel, "Other than your private stocks... I mean."

"Certain I got a few jugs over at my shop... Way these folks are a goin', it won't last," Gabriel replies while uncorking his jug.

"Any little bit will help... they's bound to wind down," says Aaron, happy to get anything.

Marcus and Gabriel glance at each other... Gabriel is the first to strike, "Sound familiar?" Not wanting to rub salt in the wound, Gabriel turns back to Aaron, "I'll send one the of the boys when I sees 'em... thought I spied Ethan a speck back."

Aaron nods his appreciation, knowing this is the best he's going to get from Gabriel, and Gabriel is not someone to push.

Cyrus, a bulky butcher, stumbles up and puts an arm over Marcus' shoulder. "You shore comin' up with good fixin's... fer the road bein' out." He slurs his words.

With a spin on his stool, Marcus pushes Cyrus lightly back, but remains in his face. "Ya'll's jes' missin' the point!"

Cyrus holds out his arms ahead of himself to keep his proper distance. The stationary position makes him stagger slightly. "And what's that?"

Gabriel, not turning from the bar, gives Marcus a warning nudge, which is ignored. As if arguing with a drunk does any good, Marcus says, "We'ez jes' cain't keep puttin' our own in the arena... don't ya'll git it?"

Marcus is losing his mayor's cool... he's actually meaning what he says, not just politicking.

The only response he gets is, "Why not?"

Gabriel has had enough of this... he spins around with a snap. "'Cause it hain't right... plus, we'ez gonna run out of folks... you dimwit!"

He's not sure if he's reacting to the stupidity, or if he figures Cyrus will leave rather than get double-teamed... probably both.

Straightening up and attempting to sound a little sober, Cyrus says, "Sin is sin... hain't it? Mayor... you's startin' to sound like you's against the redemptions." He takes a breath, realizing he's getting into deep waters. "Ah... I's jes' a bit drunk... keep up the good work, Mr. Mayor." And he retreats.

Before Marcus can say anything, Prudence backs into him. He snaps a glance towards the council's table. They're looking glum but not looking at him, so he sneaks in a playful pat to Prudence's curvaceous bottom. Staying within propriety, she gives him a flirtatious nudge before stepping back... a bit.

"Don't rightly gits this crowd... they's always polite- like flirty... but I's done had my bottom pinched five times this evenin'."

"Five?" grumbles Gabriel.

"Well... might'n be a speck more than five," she grins.

"Sorry, Prudence... it's prit' near gittin' outta hand," says Marcus.

She grins, "Didn't say I was all that het up 'bouts it."

She moves on, lest she wants to make it six... and in front of his wife.

"You frettin' over what stupid Cyrus said?" asks Gabriel.

"Naw... But a drunk's mind sometimes pours out right dark truth." Marcus' looks of concern are becoming more frequent.

Gabriel suggests, "Thinks we done grabbed onto a boulder that's already movin'... all we'ez can do is stay out from under it." Enough preaching, with a chuckle, "I think your back-to-back redeemin's done backfired on you." Then with a glance towards the council's table, and a touch more caution, he adds, "You might want to keep your objections on the quieter side... or they's gonna lump you in with Hope."

Seeing Ethan at the far end of the bar, Gabriel yells, "Hey, Ethan... over here!" He tilts his head as the boy approaches. Is Ethan staggering?

When Ethan at last makes gets to Gabriel, he snaps to a poor version of attention and adds a sloppy salute, "What's your wish, old man?"

Both Gabriel and Marcus are baffled by Ethan's air of independence. Gabriel remarks, "Thought you didn't drink."

"Thought so too," Ethan slurs, with a similar, puzzled grin. "Anyway... what can I do fer you?" Then, clicking his heels together, he delivers another salute... almost poking himself in the eye.

Ethan is enjoying the experience, and the crowd is wearing on Gabriel. "Never you mind... I'll see to it myself. Go chase a girl," he says.

Ethan's smile widens... he gives a third salute and totters away to look for the kind of trouble a young man wants.

"I leave you to the masses... keep out from under the boulder," says Gabriel as he gets up to leave.

"If I can, old friend... Don't get lost in that thing you're a buildin' fer the Fourth and forget your ways back." Marcus knows the temperament Gabriel has for getting isolated away with his toys.

Gabriel exits past the council's round table where Hanna is holding a darker court. The antics of the partying mob are just feeding her fury.

Marcus watches his friend pass Hanna... and her grimace. As mayor, he should go over there and try to shape things... as her husband, he's fine where he is. They're already upset about not frying some sinner tomorrow, because Gabriel needs to set up for the Fourth... best leave it be.

It's quieter than usual at Hope's cabin this evening, partially due to Lisa's brooding... Seems that last match between the women has gotten to her. Not that she knows anything about the two women, it's just the idea that two women would kill each other throws her. Being an equal opportunity artist, Hope is amused by Lisa's discrimination.

While Lisa broods, Tom helps Hope finish clearing the dishes away. Once they're done, Hope tosses her painting/kitchen apron on the counter.

"I got a chore to git done," she tells him.

"Anything I can help with?"

"Nope... this is a solo thing... hope it don't fret ya."

Lisa comes out of her rut and back to the moment... suspicion is a powerful stimulant. "Where you sneaking away to?"

Hope's *I hope it don't fret ya'* tone changes while she gathers her jacket and a light pack. "If I were a sneakin' away... you wouldn't know it."

She stops before leaving and turns back, "If it were any of your business... maybe it is... I'm a goin' to check on ya'll's safety."

Lisa glares at her.

Hope's not interested going into the details, especially with someone so clueless of the creativity. But there's something about seeing Gabriel earlier that has tweaked her interest... or concern. Lisa wouldn't understand.

She gives them a flippant, "See ya'll later."

CHAPTER THIRTY-ONE

NO TRESPASSING, KEEP OUT, BEWARE OF TRAPS, are among the many signs plastering the exterior of Gabriel's very private barn. Only a few in town get inside, and even fewer have keys. Since Gabriel's art is death, not many wish to test his traps, and most suspect he has many. This barn that houses his horrific creations is peacefully nestled behind the arena.

One more time might jes' be the charm, thinks Hope. She has come to the barn many times in the past, but yet to get a peek inside. Hope has always thought this odd, considering the kindred spirit she thinks they share.

She could have always gained a peek on her own, but it's never bothered her that much, and she wouldn't betray his trust. His privacy is a brush stroke in his art... she's willing to accept that. But today's different... the boulder is already moving... maybe he'll be more receptive.

Hope leans her back against the barn's smaller door and steadily bangs on the wood with the heel of her boot. She yells out, "Come on, Gabe... I knows you're in there."

Bang... bang...

She knows he's in there since the three exterior padlocks are unlatched and the door is bolted from inside. If it were Ethan or Daniel, the only two others who have keys, one of them would have come to the intercom immediately, if nothing more than to shoo her away.

She's been here seven minutes. Not hearing Gabriel's voice yet is a good sign to Hope... means he's thinking on it. Or... he's passed out.

The intercom cracks, "Go away... whoever you be!"

"Gabe, you damn well know who this is!" She continues her annoying and loud tapping with her heel. "You got your best all- time admirer out here... And I have a joint." In a less grandiose tone, she adds, "And time is runnin' out."

After a few more moments of silence from within, a bolt un- latches... and then another.

Hope backs away.

The door opens wide enough to let out a slash of bright light... and then Gabriel's head. He glances back and forth and then, "Git on in here, girl."

Hope cannot hide her surprise, even if she is pretty sure it would work this time. At last, she's going to see behind the cur- tain. Gabriel opens the door just wide enough for her to slip past. After he takes another glance around, the door closes. Bolts squeak as they're latched.

Hope stands wide-eyed, staring at his massive workshop. She's stepping into Gabriel's mind... a well-cluttered zone. Her shoulder is brushed as Gabriel passes by grumbling, "Anyone sees you come here?"

"Howdy to you too... I don't rightly remember you bein' this paranoid." She starts moving after him.

He talks over his shoulder as he walks. "Others go seein' me let in someone new, after all these years... I'll have all kinds tryin' to git in."

She senses there's more to it but, being a guest, figures it's best to let it work its way out. They weave through isles of racks, heading towards the heart of the barn. Racks of all sorts of junk... junk just waiting to become creations. The two arrive in a wide-open area.

"Wow!" Hope's amazed by the cavernous size of the inside. It's larger than her imagining of it was... and she's got a serious imagination. She calculates it's the size of three large, high barns. From the outside, it appears so much smaller. Then she realizes, from the roofline, that half of it was built under the arena bleachers. The hanger-like space curves into the arena... it's deceptive.

They arrive at the heart of it all... Gabriel's long worktable.

Hope grins like the Cheshire cat as she sees dozens of drawings tacked to the walls. The details of some of them are astounding... schematics of horror. Mixed in with the detailed renderings are even more thumbnail sketches on various size scraps of paper. There must be at least twenty feet of a high wall papered by ideas.

Hanging on a distant wall, like a well-organized shop, is a collection of cutting weapons, everything from antique swords to unrecognizable, gruesomely sculptural tools of death.

Various crossbows hang like screwdrivers in a row. Axes have their place, as do spears. The high, factory-style lighting shows how sharp the cutting edges are kept by the boys. It also shows spatters of dark brown on the handles and joints... dried blood. It's a menagerie of the grotesque... in neat order.

The counter in front of her is half-covered with mechanical parts in various stages of becoming something... and tools. At the far end, there's a boxy-shaped item covered by a tarp. Here and there are some odd items for a shop of horrors. Hope picks up a heavily dinged brass bugle. She gives Gabriel a puzzled face.

"Don't ask," he says, unwilling to share his mind.

She has a feeling that might be his answer no matter what she were to pick up... or it's something she really doesn't want to know. Hope prefers believing the former. He reaches out and takes the bugle from her and places it back on the counter where it belongs.

"OK... You got your way in... what's on your mind?"

Without a word, Hope zips past him on a beeline for a flying saucer, draped with red, white and blue cargo parachutes... at least, that's what Hope's imagination sees.

Its profile does resemble a high-peaked flying saucer. At several points around its wide perimeter are workbenches. One bench rests near an exposed part of the hidden treasure. A metal panel is open, exposing a maze of gears.

As she approaches it, Hope asks, "You gonna give me a peek?" She plans on stopping if he says no... but she's hopeful.

Gabriel passes her with more agility than she expected. He definitively pulls the parachute over the exposed area. "Then what kind a show would you have up there in that perch of your'n?"

Hope cain't think of an argument to this... right is right.

When Gabriel reaches down to retrieve an unattended wrench, Hope glances around, looking for her next piece of mischief. From a new angle, she sees a keyboard sticking out from under a covered box on the counter. Off she goes.

"If I'd known you had what I think that is, I'd come knockin' earlier."

She stops and turns. Hope poses with the tip of the tarp in her fingers, awaiting a verdict. No answer is enough for her. With a playful, dramatic flourish she disrobes the box... it is a computer, as she imagined.

Knowing Gabriel, against all odds, he probably has found a way to have Internet in the boonies.

Gabriel knows keeping up with her energy would be like catching a fly in a pastry shop... he's too tired for that. He ambles over and sits on a stool at his counter.

Hope can see in his tread that he's carrying some weight, and perhaps it's trying to work its way out. In a more down-to-earth tone, she asks, "Why'd you let me see it?"

"Guess it don't matter... Sorry, girl, I'm a smidgin' surly 'cause of how things are gittin'... It's right further down the road since last I saw you."

"You workin'... or hidin' out?" she asks.

"Supposed to be gittin' some shine, but had enough of that crowd inside... They're celebratin' their own end... and don't rightly even know it."

Relaxing a bit, Gabriel takes a jug and a couple jars from under the counter. He pours each of the two jars a quarter full and hands Hope one.

"Was gittin' in some fine-tuning on the piece fer the Fourth," he says, while nodding over at the flying saucer.

"What's you mean by things comin' to an end?" Hope asks, though she is well aware of the answer to her own question.

With another nod to the flying saucer, he says, "Figured this is 'bouts the last contraption I'm gonna make... things is jes' spinnin' outta control."

"You don't believe in redeemin's no more?" asks Hope. Religion had never been much of a topic between them. While thinking on it, Gabriel pulls up another stool for Hope.

As she takes a seat, he says, "Never did... I weren't a serious church go'er. Jes' liked makin' the contraptions. Weren't in my mind to argue the reasons. It's been a way up here fer longer than I can remember."

Gabriel takes a swallow from his jar... its bite doesn't register on his face. "A few in town are believers and a few are too-

good believers. But there's more that are jes' a-hankerin fer the blood. There are a handful in town that's hain't the feverous type, but they's few."

"To tell the truth... I always seed the arena as a piece of absurd human art... figured the same fer you," she confides as she takes a sip of shine.

"Guess I don't dwell on it quite like you... and you have mentioned your art-thinkin' afore... more than once," he reminds her.

This is probably one of the longer stretches the two have talked face to face with each other... getting at anything.

She shrugs off her concern, "What I done figured was it's come along enough to need a fresh twist fer an endin'."

"You take out the road?" asks Gabriel. There's no threat in his question.

Hope takes another sip and grins through the burn.

Gabriel shrugs, "It don't matter much now... but you gotta admit... when it was workin', things was right sane and peaceful. Almost... too dang peaceful."

It crosses her mind to thank Gabriel for being such an important color in her pallet, but she decides he might not take it in the way she would intend it.

Gabriel sees her gears turning. Either from the shine, or from having a breath of someone truly different to talk with, his spirits rise, "'Bouts time to be movin' on anyway... keepin' our secrets."

"We'ez racked up a fair number on each other... hain't we?"

He takes his jug and tops off her jar. "Like that fella, a few snows back, that you had livin' up with you."

Not ruffled, "So you know'd 'bouts Jared?"

"Yep... Don't get me wrong... he kept his mouth shut 'bouts you... gotta give the kid that. Guess only thing I didn't know was the why's of you setting him up... Figured if you wanted me to know you'd a said so."

Hope takes a sip of shine... no matter how long she's known shine, she can't shake the burn. When her breath settles, "I was a touch more sore-like back then... His vision of art and mine parted ways... and it seemed a right simple solution."

In this too predictable world, Hope's cockeyed view of things often catches Gabriel's interest... more so now that it's darkening. His interest shows in his posture, as he leans forward. It tells Hope to finish it out.

"He done started recordin' redemptions... then he put the memory chips on weather balloons. In his head, it was somethin' 'bouts bringin' the chance of chaos into the picture. I didn't agree... he lost."

This brings a chuckle from Gabriel, "Like I done said, figured you had yer reasons." After another slug of shine, he adds, "Like you must have yer reasons fer the three kids up at your place now."

BANG ... BANG ... BANG... comes from the distant door. Startled, both look up.

Gabriel presses the intercom on his bench and snaps, "What!"

Ethan's voice comes through, "Aaron done sent me fer those jugs of shine."

Gabriel is aware that leaving Hope hanging might be a touch mean, but he does just that. He digs out three one-gallon jugs from under the bench. With one under his arm and one in each hand, he heads for the door. It's well out of sightlines, so he doesn't bother telling Hope to hide ... she has enough to think on for the moment.

It takes a lot to catch Hope off guard because of her perspective on life... everything's a twist in the fabric she sees. She

usually sees the twist as interesting, if not outright exciting... but this caught her off guard.

She had a gut feeling on the perch that something was amiss... now all she has to do is adjust to it. The revelation is not that much... if he had wanted the kids he would have already have told the council. Question is... why did he tell her?

Hope can hear Gabriel making short work of Ethan's needs.

Seconds later footsteps approach. Gabriel saunters back and remounts his stool, happy not to have any more to do with townsfolk for tonight.

While he was gone, Hope has lit up a joint. She offers it to Gabriel.

He waves it off, "Not right now... don't mind if you leave one fer later. That stuff's right interestin'... if I don't have much to do." He takes a swallow of shine, "So... What's on your mind 'bouts those kids?"

"It's been a playin' in my head while you was fetchin' shine... and I'm betwixt n' between 'bouts it. They's play some part in things... jes' hain't visualized it yet." She pauses to take a drag. "More's the question... what's you gonna do 'bouts 'em?"

"Don't rightly know it would do any good if I was to do anything. Your pa has a dang fool notion if we was to play things out like he's got in his head, everythin' would right itself."

"You don't see it that way... do you?" she asks.

He lets out a sigh, "Not rightly."

Hope chuckles, "Sun... in a gully washer."

The humor doesn't register with Gabriel this time. "Lot's a buildin' up to the doin's on the Fourth... they's gonna want to make it a big deal."

"You know who's gonna be redeemed?"

"I'm like an old time executioner... I stay shed of the choosin'. Those that's you got up at the cabin would fill the needs fer the Fourth... as far as bein' right important. And they'd take the place of some townsfolk." After a breath he adds, "Hope, you's done it afore... a passel of times."

Gabriel knows as much as he chooses to know... after all, he is a senior member of the council. He stays on the outside over some matters because they're not about his creations... conscience can be a pest. But he does have a sense of their thinking... Maybe the hint of being fed from the outside might nudge things one way or the other.

Hope realizes he's grasping, she's just not sure why... outside of killing all the folks they know. After all, the end is the end.

"Would it rightly change the seasons? I hain't goin' back to the old days."

After another swallow, Gabriel answers, "Yeah... You's probably right." He puts the jar down and corks the jug... a mountain way of saying *time to move on.*

Hope gets up, pulls a joint from her pocket and places it on the workbench. "What's you doin' 'bouts my guests?"

"Most likely nothin'... You's prit' near right... things is probably rollin' downhill too fast to git in the way."

She didn't get the solid answer she wanted, but Hope doesn't see getting much more out of him. If the corking of the jug wasn't enough, Gabriel starts back towards the exit end of the shop.

Hope takes one last peer around at Gabriel's grand shop... then she follows. While walking, Hope says, "Gabe... I'll let you know if things up above change."

"Fair enough," he replies.

CHAPTER THIRTY-TWO

The screen door creaks when Hope comes in.

"Look what the cat dragged in... Wonder what Jane Bond's been up to?" asks Lisa indirectly via Rick. The attentive boyfriend, Rick sits at the far end of the sofa, massaging Lisa's feet. Tom is nowhere to be seen.

It's right dangerous to be pokin' the bear, crosses Hope's mind... especially this evening.

To irritate her, Hope smiles at Rick, "You givin' rubs out?"

She passes by Lisa on the way to the kitchen. She gets a glass of water, leans against the counter and just watches the room. "Where's my Tom?"

"He went out... exercising his ankle, I guess," says Rick.

Kicking Rick's hands away, Lisa springs up, "You know, every time you go skulking around out there, you leave us in danger... don't you?"

"You're right... I could hear the two of you a country mile down the trail. Then again, I could always solve that." Hope's meaning is lost on neither.

Pretending not to get it, but speaking more timidly, Lisa asks, "I thought you said your people never come up here?"

"Never's a long piece... You done seen what's goin' on down there. Best to figure some might be out lookin' fer folks on their sinner's list... or some sinner's out looking not to be found," says Hope.

"So now... we're in hiding?" snaps Lisa.

"Not rightly, but it would be best to keep your senses 'bouts you... and not piss off your host." Hope puts her empty glass on the counter. Not interested in further conversation, she strides through the room and out the door.

Rick puts his hands on Lisa's shoulder to ease the resentment that's boiling in her... she slaps them away.

When Rick said Tom was outside, Hope knew exactly where he would be. Walking down the trail to the perch, she tosses around what Gabriel had said. With the right nudging, it might be an ideal time for her and Tom to let out. It's just a matter of convincing Tom... and coming up with a plausible reason his friends didn't make it. But does she want that weight hanging over their union?

A pebble hits the back of Tom's head. He smiles. Picking up a small pebble of his own, he tosses it over his shoulder, blind.

"Get your chores all done?" he asks.

"Prit' near most of 'em," she responds as she comes the last few feet down the path.

With a slight chuckle, "Don't tell me you've killed Lisa already." He has no idea how close to home he's hitting.

Hope settles down next to Tom. For a while they share the night sky that hoods the arena. A sketchpad rests near Tom. Hope reaches over him in a sultry manner, ever so slowly.

"You mind?"

Pressing forward into her slow reach, "Be my guest... it's your book."

There's plenty of glow from the moonlit night for Hope to see the pages she thumbs through. Some are a mixture of writing and thumbnail sketches. She passes these by and settles on a page with a larger sketch. It's his interpretation of Charity's beheading... in black and white.

The image not so clean like in a graphic novel, or comic books, yet it's much more than simplistic. The foreground and background pattern flow where neither is more important... half black, half white. The downed head simply blends with the bigger picture. After staring at it intently, Hope says, "Think you got the feel of the piece... and all from memory."

"Some memories are difficult to wash from your head," he says.

"You... you know what I done said... 'bouts maybe you stickin' around a speck?" Hope fiddles with asking.

With most, Hope is fine with her wording... Tom's a little different. Her dating opportunities are limited.

"Thought you said it was all coming to a finale? Didn't know if that was the circus... or us?" asks Tom.

"This place is purely comin' to an end... rightly so. Jes' 'cause one piece of the absurd is a comin' down don't mean there hain't other craziness out there to experience... and I hain't against company," Hope says, doing her best to get to the point.

"So you're going to intentionally look for other people's insanity... though it might be hard to top this?" He's finding it hard to believe that this makes sense to him... but it does.

"Sorta gotten it into my blood... and I'm prit' near sure there's plenty of dark art out there."

Tom thinks on the enormity of what she's suggesting... to travel in search of the bizarre. Not just the bizarre, but also the blackest of the freaky. As absurd as it sounds, it has a creative, exciting, sociopathic appeal. Then he wonders if he can keep up with Hope... or be a casualty of one of her paintings.

"OK... I'm in... if you really want the company."

Hope flows with almost any outcome, seeing them as strokes to a bigger picture, but she finds herself hoping on this question. She's pleased... and her pleasure shows itself with a serious kiss on Tom's lips.

When they break, "I take it... you want?" jokes Tom.

Hope leans back with a satisfied, "Yep."

The moon bounces off gathering clouds on the horizon.

"Once we get Rick and Lisa away from here, where we off to?" Tom's bubbling of innocence, especially for someone that finds death fascinating.

"That's tomorrow... this is now." She thinks of how to word this next part. "You know Lisa has her mind plum' set on gittin' away... that last redeemin' got to her." Tom patiently listens for the point. "Well... your ankle is comin' along right good... but it hain't in the shape fer hill travelin'."

"What are you getting at?" Tom asks.

"You done already said things was a comin' to a crossroads between you and Rick... maybe this is the time. Might be that we'ez outta let them go their own way," she suggests.

Tom doesn't quite want to consider the cautious twinge that tingles down his spine. From hints he's gathered in the past days, it crosses his mind that Hope has been supplying the town with victims for some time now. The same Hope that had a boyfriend end up in the pit. Maybe power in numbers is not such a bad idea, at least till his ankle is better. Then the worse thought flashes through... maybe she needs food for the masses below, and his friends are on the menu.

Of course, he doesn't want to think of all this. After all, he's just connected with a magically strange girl.

He finally says, "I wouldn't really be able to go till my friends were safe, even Lisa. We'll just have to find a reason to get them to stay long enough for us all to travel... once we're clear, then we split from them."

"Of course," Hope says, knowing she'll just have to shift her thinking a smidgin... it's just brush strokes.

The two arrive back at the cabin. When Hope and Tom start up the steps, she puts out an arm for him to stop. The screen door is closed but not the door... sound carries. They're softer when they step up on the porch.

Lisa has her pack out. Everything she plans to put in it is neatly spread out on the bunk. She rattles on while taking inventory.

"I've had it this time, we need to go. This has gone way beyond crazy."

The first thought Rick has is, *when wasn't it crazy?* But trying to be reasonably supportive and keep his feet warm at night, Rick says, "Tom's ankle does seem like it's getting much better... "

She cuts him off, "Now... with or without Tom... I mean, your friendship is on the downslope... and I know Hope wouldn't mind having her itch scratched, as she calls it."

As with many in a relationship, Rick often chooses the *go along... get along* path. But challenging his friendship is a bruise to his ego. It's OK for him to dump Tom in his own time, but presuming it of him is something else.

"We're not going without Tom... as soon as his ankle's ready, we're out."

Creak goes the screen door.

"Ya'll up and leavin'... again?" Hope says in a perky voice.

Rick preempts Lisa, "From what you've been telling us, the sooner we get going, the better. It's just a matter of Tom's ankle."

With a backhanded wave at Tom, Lisa says, "His ankle looks much better. Hell, you're going out on moonlight walks." Her argument is not going to be influenced by the crutch under Tom's arm.

The crutches were a last moment touch that Tom grabbed on the way in. Holding one up, he says, "Every time I stay on it too long, I'm back on this." He hobbles to a chair, for punctuation.

"His ankle is mendin' right well, but it hain't ready fer cross-country... while totin' a pack," says Hope.

Lisa snaps, "What are you suggesting... we just hang around till someone finds us and we end up in that pit?" She's on a roll, "Or... till you decide it's all *art like* to give us to them?"

Hope visualizes it... and it doesn't seem like a bad idea. But she says, "I done told Tom I'd take care of ya'll... and that's what I plan to do."

Lisa storms to the other side of the room.

"She's still upset over the earlier killings. So... what are you suggesting?" Rick asks in a more open manner.

Ironically, the one that's most conflicted about the activities in the pit is always trying to be the most neutral. Hope simply views him as being indecisive.

"The Fourth of July doin's are in two days. There's gonna be a mighty to-do 'bouts them and a lot of hoopla after. Tom's foot should be prit' near ready by then. Ya'll would find plum' empty hills that afternoon." Hope figures this is enough to hook them.

Rick and Tom listen... Lisa pouts, but still keeps an ear to the conversation. Rick has been won over, but he still asks, "What about the people you said were scouring the hills right now?"

Hope smiles, "Scourin'... is a speck strong. My cabin is off limits. So hangin' around here would be a right fine idea."

"We're prisoners," grumbles Lisa. She takes her empty pack and tosses it back to its resting place.

Hope steps over to a cupboard and pulls out a dusty Monopoly game. She waves it in the air, "Ya'll like board games."

CHAPTER THIRTY-THREE

Fourth of July

Two backpacks are full and leaning against the wall waiting to get used. A third rests near them, still empty. Lisa sits at the table, nervously tapping her foot against its leg.

Her continuous tapping irritates Rick, but he knows saying anything will only bring on an argument, so he tries to appear busy by thumbing through an old library copy of *American Psycho*, no doubt acquired by Hope while living down in the flats.

The door to Hope's room swings open and out comes Tom. His ankle seems greatly improved. Hope has made sure he stays off of it... in the most pleasant of ways.

Making a visual point of glaring at her watch, Lisa barks, "And where is her highness?"

"She's coming... or at least she was," Tom says grinning.

"I'm sure she was," grumbles Lisa, as she goes to Tom's backpack. She takes it up and tosses it to Tom. "Fill it up... time for us to get the hell outta here."

"Ya'll got a fair speck of time... the doin's hain't till this afternoon," comes from the bedroom. Hope walks out with a lazy, satisfied yawn. "Hain't gonna be safe till after the doin's. You done seen our secrets... you might as well see the big finish."

"Wouldn't it be better if we go during the event... that way we know where they'll all be?" asks Rick.

Hope plops down on a stuffed chair and props her feet up on a log footstool. "It's gonna be a fright harder to git outta these hills without me... and I'm gonna see the finale." She gives them a checkmate smile. "Ya'll can join me... or hang here... or try to go on your own. It's up to you."

As they come down the path to the perch, it's clear that Lisa is angry... situation normal. She didn't want to stay alone at the cabin, but is not about to be a happy participant. She kicks a rock. It rolls down across the perch... right to the edge. All three watch it teeter precariously on the lip. It settles without falling off.

Hope glares at her. "Careful... ya'll hain't outta my woods yet."

Rick and Lisa go low and scoot over to their box seat hiding place, while Tom slides into his bush. Not bothering with precautions, Hope walks to the edge and peers down into the arena.

The bleachers are beginning to fill.

Gabriel's toy has also filled out... or more like up. It's the same diameter as Hope remembers, but it's much higher. The face is a mystery since it still wears a parachute drape. Gabriel walks around it, checking this and that. Ethan and Daniel follow close behind, awaiting any last minute orders.

By Hope's calculation, Gabriel has been fiddling with this contraption for about a year. She remembers it was just under a year ago that he brought a loaded flatbed into town. It was all cloaked in mystery... and heavy tarps, and caused quite a buzz around town for some time.

Gabriel remained close-lipped and the buzz faded away with time. His creation is now going to see its day. Hope wonders if he had a sense of the ending even back then.

The council filters up onto the grandstand. At one point, Hanna, Hope's estranged stepmother, glares up at the perch. This strikes Hope as a bit strange... but she hasn't paid much attention to the woman in ages. Not since Hanna wanted to redeem her for refusing to continue supplying the town during the winter months when visitors were scarce.

Hope had never been that close with her domineering stepmother, and became even further distant once she discovered how to see the world in her own way. Marcus is not up on the stands yet... probably still pulling together all the fixin's.

The gallery is settling in with its usual loud chatter of anticipation and relief. A few yell down at Gabriel to tell his secrets before the unveiling. No one expects an answer... it's a ritual these days, almost as much as the actual redeemings.

Gabriel had taken the redemptions from the Stone Ages of hangings into the world of reality entertainment... A world in which appealing to the lowest common denominator is gold. He holds a position of true honor in town, even for those who don't care for him that much.

At present, down in the pit, Gabriel doesn't feel any sense of honor. He's more attuned to the idea of achieving long-term survival. If it's all going down, he doesn't want to get caught in the wake. As a way to distance himself, he's already told the council that if they keep at it, they will have to be satisfied with the gladiator matches... and Marcus signed off on it.

Gabriel can see Hope watching from her ledge. He had hoped she would have gotten the hint at the barn and cleared these parts. Realizing that their ways were sliding downhill, he has come to terms with letting her guests off the hook, as well. If they choose to hang around, it may be another matter... they may become more acquainted with the town's ways.

Even though it isn't dusk yet, Ethan and Daniel, on Gabriel's orders, set off a half dozen homemade tube rockets. Standing out against the dance of grey clouds and blue sky, the burst of fireworks brings cheers from all. It's meant as an opening salvo... everybody knows more fireworks will follow the show when the evening drifts in.

Aaron gets up from the council and walks to the mic. He taps on it only once. "Forget that... the dang thing's always rightly on."

It's met with call outs from the gallery the likes of, "Where's Marcus?" and "What's ya'll doin' up there?"

He waves his hands in an appeal for silence... or at least something close to it. "Settle down, ya'll... Marcus will be out in a speck. He jes' wanted me to git things goin'... till he can show up."

There are a few more yells about Marcus and Aaron's being there, but most settle for waiting to hear what he has to say.

"Gabriel... would you please do the honors of showin' us your new gadget?" says Aaron, falling right into being host.

If it were another time, Gabriel would have slapped Aaron along the side of his head for calling his creations... *gadgets*. Right now, other matters concern him, so he yells up, "The call fer that is reserved fer the mayor."

Many in the audience support his words.

"Gabe... on behalf of the council, let's git the show a rollin'... Marcus will be joining us directly," demands Aaron.

From the second Aaron took the mic, Gabriel had sensed something wrong... now he's sure. Now he knows why today's visitor was kept at the B&B instead of the stone cell. He also knows he needs to walk a fine line to stay out of the way of the boulder.

Gabriel steps over to Ethan and has a private word which, in turn, causes a hurt look of being left out wash over Daniel's face. But as soon as Ethan rushes over and shares his marching orders, all's right with the world again. They both take up positions around the tall flying saucer.

Once the boys are in position, Gabriel picks up a bullhorn and clears his throat. The bullhorn squeaks at first, then comes, "Ya'll... I give you the *Funnel of Blood*." He raises a hand in an arc and drops it.

Both Ethan and Daniel release counterweights at opposite sides of the arena. The weights snap taut the lines that extend up through pulleys and down to the parachute. The two giant cargo chutes magically fly away in opposite directions, waving through the air as they go.

At first this produces oohs and ahs from the crowd... and then a moment of silence as the townsfolk try to get a sense of what this massive toy might be. Whatever it is, the contraption has put its best foot forward in its bright red, white and blue veneer. It's almost too colorful to be a killing machine.

The origin of the structure in the pit seems to be an old carnival ride akin to the Centrifuge, in which folks are pinned against the circular wall by the momentum of its spinning velocity. In Gabriel's variation, instead of the mesh walls being vertical, they are angled in like an upside-down cone. The small circular center floor is made up of the sharpened tips of blades firmly attached to wheels.

While others are eying the *Funnel of Blood* and guessing grotesque task it performs, Ethan pulls the cover off an accessory... a set of rolling stairs rising to a diving board on top. With a little struggle and a hand from Daniel, Ethan pushes the stairs forward so the diving board stands directly over the top of the cone's walls.

After helping Ethan, Daniel pushes an empty cart near to what appears to be an exhaust port of the structure... or spaceship. He takes his time lining it up perfectly.

With all the elements in place, Gabriel steps over to his field control box. He rubs the palm of his hand over the controls, as if stroking his favorite hound dog.

A yell comes from the gallery, "Right pretty, Gabe... now let's see what she does!"

Gabriel flips a switch. He focuses on his creation and glances up to gauge reactions. The *Funnel of Blood* shudders to life. The cone of walls starts rotating, slowly at first. Once Gabriel turns a rheostat knob, the walls pick up speed to transform into the window of a rapidly turning kaleidoscope. At this speed, the mesh walls become fairly transparent, so as not to obstruct enjoyment of the game. He had taken ages to come up with the right size mesh to get just the right effect.

So far it's very colorful... but tame.

Gabriel flips another switch and the cone's teeth come alive. The floor's rows of grinder blades let out their roar... sparks fly as the blades sync up. This lethal touch brings cheers from all around the arena.

Everything is proceeding on schedule... admiration of Gabriel's handiwork comes first. Next come the introductions. All eyes are on the grandstand, eagerly awaiting this next step.

The grinding, clanking premiere of Gabriel's creation is a success. With all eyes either captivated by it or watching the grandstand to learn who will taste it, Gabriel is out of the limelight. He has a quick word with Ethan and saunters over to a small exit door.

Before going through the door, he peers up at Hope's perch. If anyone were to notice him leaving, it would be her. When he catches her eye, he makes a wide arm wave, hoping she'll get the idea and run... and then he disappears through the exit.

Hope stands there, looking down, knowing in her gut what Gabriel is saying and what is coming... but she has to play it out to be sure. Running will have to wait.

By now, all the members of the council have come up to the railing of the grandstand. They're there in part to admire Gabriel's creation, but more to show solidarity. Looking exceptionally self-righteous, Hanna, stands alone like a queen. A few steps behind, Pastor Cain is her shadow.

Aaron steps up to the mic. "We got a downright sartified special event fer ya'll today."

On cue, the main arch doors open into the arena. Marcus, a little worse for wear, is pushed out into the pit by Jake and his shotgun. Still grasping at control, Marcus snaps, "Jake... I'm the mayor and... "

The words are cut off by a poke of the shotgun. Marcus continues forward, glaring up at those he's more used to addressing.

There's a range of emotions in the calls from the audience. Marcus has been high on the hog for some time... that time has generated respect, envy... and resentments.

CHAPTER THIRTY-FOUR

Quietly standing near the edge, Hope looks down on her pa. She has known that his own monster would eventually eat him... but not how quickly it would come about. All the signs were telling her not to be surprised... from her mother's taunting glare to Gabriel's concerned gesture. On top of which... Marcus always leads the Fourth of July doin's. It crosses her mind that he still is, but all she says is, "Holy shit!"

Her words are loud enough to draw both Lisa and Tom from their bushes. Lisa, in a yelling whisper, "What did you say... do we have a problem?" Her words are laced with distrust.

Hope snaps out of her thoughts and glares over at her, "Nothin'... jes' git back to ya'll's show."

Tom looks at her with much more concern.

"You too... I'm fine," Hope says coldly.

Realizing she probably needs some space, Tom mutely squirms back into his viewing bush... And Hope heads down the trail towards the cabin, trying not to look too much in a rush.

As he gets near Gabriel's machine, Marcus peers up to see Hanna at the rail. Her look of having done her duty comes off more like a smirk. Pastor Cain abruptly backs away from Hanna as Aaron leans towards the mic. The audience quiets down, taken with the importance of the occasion... Having Marcus there only quadruples the value of the spectacle... even if they have no idea what he's accused of.

"OK... we need to git to the formals," announces Aaron.

Someone yells out, "Git on with it... barkeep."

Pastor Cain reaches forward with his notepad, but Aaron brushes it away. His reign will have its own style... if anyone lives long enough for it to be a reign.

"Marcus McCoy... we done found you guilty of takin' from the trough... that's embezzlin' fer you's that want to be uppity 'bouts it."

It gets the laugh he hoped for. Aaron can see Marcus about to speak so he waves his hand that he's not finished. Out of the side of his eye, Aaron can see Hanna's urgent stare.

"And... fer havin' a affair with our own sweet Prudence."

This gets a sadistic smile from Hanna.

Before eyes can strike her, Prudence bolts up and yells, "Don't go lookin' at me... I gave testimony."

Hanna white-knuckles the rail as she leans over and spits at her husband. As she recovers herself, two men walk up and take her by the arms.

Twisting around so he can look at her while still at the mic, Aaron pronounces, "Hanna McCoy... you's been found guilty of enjoying the spoils... and fer turnin' on your husband." Places a hand over the mic, he adds, "And fer bein' so uppity sanctimonious that you's become downright scary."

With this he nods to the men. They drag a screaming Hanna towards the back stairs. Pastor Cain steps out of reach as they pass. He's pragmatic enough to walk the religious line... without putting his head in a noose.

Down in the pit, Marcus has decided it is what it is. One satisfaction is that his loving wife will face the same ending. Knowing how useless it would be, he's not interested in banter with Aaron. Marcus has stood in his place through more redeemings than he can count... and he knows that once the game is in play, there's no stopping it.

He glances around for his old friend, hoping not to see him. Ethan is in hailing distance.

"Where's Gabe?" asks Marcus.

Appearing extremely self-conscious over the situation, Ethan stutters out, "I... I... "

"Settle down, boy," Marcus urges. "I got it."

"I think he only know'd at the last... I was told to say so long... if you done asked, mayor."

Knowing he has to operate the machine that will kill him, Ethan politely excuses himself. Marcus gives him a *thanks* nod.

The heavy arch doors into the arena open and Hanna is dragged in, screaming at everyone in her range.

Marcus yells, just to get through her blanket of noise, "Dear... all your squawkin' hain't gonna change a dang thing... so, fer once, shut up!"

She quiets only long enough to spit and kick dirt at him. Hanna's gone off the deep end... and she doesn't look like she's coming back real soon.

"Git on with it... I'm more than happy to go first," Marcus yells up to Aaron. He underestimates the potency of Hanna's screaming.

"I think we'ez all want to change that order," comes back from the speakers. The crowd's robust reaction says they agree... anything to quiet Hanna.

"Good... then git to it quick like," Marcus yells back. The audience cheers to enforce this.

"Very well," announces Aaron. He looks around for Gabriel, not having seen him leave, and then calls down, "Ethan, lad... where's Gabriel?"

Puffing up with the pride of running his first big redemption, Ethan shouts up, "Gabriel done told me I'm ready to run his machine... he had to go fetch somethin'."

All know the friendship between Gabriel and Marcus. Aaron figures it's reasonable for the old man not to want to take part... and that he's probably off tying one on.

With a friendly smile down to Ethan, "Well then, lad, it's yer show... so let's git to it, as Marcus might say."

Ethan is beaming. He steps over and brings the *Funnel of Blood* back to life. The walls pick up speed at the command of Ethan's dial. The two men pull Hanna toward the stairs.

Not trying to speak over Hanna's screams, Marcus says, "So long, old gal."

He turns away, either not to watch his own fate or, reaching back to when he cared, not wishing to witness hers. It's most likely a bit of both.

Gabriel's contraptions have few flaws. A flaw they discover now is that the stairs are too narrow... awkward to maneuver up with a tantrum-throwing woman. It takes great effort to push Hanna up the stairs... even more so when Ethan kicks on the blades.

While one man keeps shoving her up, Ethan yells over the machinery, "Just over the edge... not too far." He's determined to have everything on his first solo redemption shine.

With his hands full of Hanna, the man glares back at Ethan. He finally gets her to the edge of the short diving board. The louder Hanna screams above the equipment, the more the gallery urges the man on with yells like "Push her ass over the edge!" and "Please... shut her up!"

Right at the edge he gives her a last push, with little care about where she falls.

Hanna drops straight down and catches herself with her arms wrapping around the end of the plank. Her dangling feet skip along the rotating mesh walls. Somehow she manages to keep howling through it all.

Reluctantly, the man goes to the end of the plank on his knees. He attempts to pry her arms loose. At last they come free but, with a last desperate grab, Hanna latches onto the man's arm. Off balance, he topples over and past Hanna... into the center of the bladed mouth.

His scream is followed by a hideous sound of crunching and munching. Blood spits upward from the spinning blades and spatters Hanna, now plastered to the mesh wall by centrifugal force.

Daniel had lined the cart up with the exhaust port almost perfectly, but not quite closely enough. A clumpy red mixture spews out, half caught by the cart, half by the sand.

Not realizing the mic is still on, Aaron comments, "Damn... there goes Carl." Maybe this is the reason Marcus always taps the mic.

Townsfolk have worked themselves up into such a frenzy that they will cheer anything with blood, even the demise of someone un-accused. Then again, as of late, they don't care much about the guilt part.

Like a salamander, Hanna squirms her way up the slanted sidewalls, inching towards the top. Somewhere in her panicked craziness she thinks if she can reach the top edge, this will all go away.

Ethan dials the speed down a notch, knowing it will lessen her traction. In spite of this, Hanna continues to struggle upward with all her strength. When she gets close enough, she reaches up with her right hand and grasps the top edge.

ZAP!

Gabriel had installed a live wire along the top of the walls... just for this eventuality. The shock knocks Hanna's hand away. She loses traction and slides down into the blades waiting below.

Her tantrum ends. The crunching sound of the wheels brings discussion to many tongues... and cheers from all.

David has succeeded in getting the cart in just the right spot to catch most of Hanna... along with any remaining Carl.

Tom's the first to pull back out of his concealment... his face shows it was grosser than he expected. A second later, Rick emerges from his bush and immediately throws up.

Without words, Tom gestures about for Lisa. He gets a confused shrug from his friend. Apparently, Rick was unable to pull her away from the show. After a couple deep breaths to let what he saw sink in, Tom carefully gets up and creeps away from the edge.

"Where you going?" asks Rick, as he wipes his face.

"I've seen enough... I'm going to check on Hope... you best stay with Lisa, and make sure she doesn't fall in," Tom answers quietly. Then he heads up the trail.

A chant grows, "Marcus... Marcus... Marcus... "

It's a chant that is normally a welcome sound to a politician... if it were not fraught with such hunger for him to ride the blades.

As a politician, Marcus has always believed in the righteousness of redemptions... as Marcus, he never has. It's probably the reason he got along with Gabriel... both of them had clear reasons for the redemptions. For Gabriel, it was his creations... for Marcus, it kept the town together for generations, bizarre as the method was.

Now, standing in the pit, he thinks the redemptions might have gone a little overboard.

It's the seventh inning stretch. Marcus knows this from the tone of the gallery... a mixture of satisfaction and tickled anticipation. From his years at the podium, he had learned to read audiences by ear. That's entertainment.

Milking time as he should, Aaron is off schmoozing with the council. He knows nothing can proceed without his announcement and he is giving the crowd a few minutes more to build the proper tension.

When Marcus glances up at the grandstand he can't help thinking Aaron's not bad at it. If Marcus can't influence the outcome and Jake's shotgun says no, then he can damn well cut short their entertainment.

Jake appears confused when Marcus strides away from him towards the *Funnel of Blood*. It's not towards an exit so he's not sure what to do.

The walls of Gabriel's ride still rotate and they aren't that loud. The blades are silent.

As Marcus storms past Ethan, he snaps, "Kick it over, kid."

Now it's Ethan who's confused. He glances up at the grandstand, where no one is paying any attention.

About halfway up the stairs to the platform, Marcus turns his head, "Gabriel would do it fer me."

This does the trick... with little concern for the council's approval, Ethan flips the switch unleashing the blades. The audience is caught completely off guard. Some take notice, many don't, as Marcus steps on the diving board.

He holds up two birds with his fists and yells out, "Fuck the show!"

Without waiting for a reaction or the audience to build, Marcus dives off the plank head first into the center of the blades. Marcus is no longer the mayor of the bloody town of Redemption.

Also caught off guard, Daniel's cart misses all of Marcus.

There's pandemonium in the stands, the same on the grandstand. Most the townsfolk completely missed the redeeming or just caught the exhaust... Marcus had it his way.

Not a bloody moment was missed at Hope's perch. Rick has had to pull Lisa back twice from wanting too much of a view.

The gallery below gets over its disappointment quickly. After all, it was Marcus and he did have a style to him. A few even stand in his honor. Fascinated, Lisa watches the crowd with a spare pair of binoculars she found at Hope's... So fascinated, she doesn't notice at first that her view through the binoculars reveals a few people who seem to be looking up towards the perch. She moves her view back to see one pair of binoculars aimed right at her.

Lisa bolts up, not even bothering to back out of the bushes. If that's not enough, she drops the binoculars... they skittle down the ledge and fall into the arena. The only thing missing is the blare of trumpets announcing her existence to Redemption.

A woman in the stands screams, "That hain't Hope up thar!" Her scream shifts many other eyes upward. More than a few have been keeping at least one eye in that direction long before the binoculars fumbled.

Hope has been a thorn under an umbrella for a long time... too long for most. For many, she lost any illusion of being a friend when she stopped supplying them with visitors... Most now foresee her on the menu. And with Marcus now gone, she's fair game.

Another yells, "There's two of them!"

By now, Rick can be seen helping Lisa out of the bushes she fell in.

Others holler out in a growing pitch. Aaron gets a set of binoculars just in time to see the two above disappear.

Ethan pulls a walkie-talkie from behind the pit control box. He keys it a couple times, "Gabriel... think you wanna know this... "

CHAPTER THIRTY-FIVE

Gabriel rumbles along a rough road, kicking up a cloud of dust. He slams on the brakes and the cloud catches up, engulfing his red truck. Inside the cab, Gabriel waves the dust away while concentrating on his walkie.

"Like I said, jes' thought you'd wanna know... good luck," comes Ethan's adrenaline-filled voice. He adds, "Over."

"Thanks kid... over n' out."

Gabriel sets the walkie on the seat. He thinks on it a few seconds before slamming the palms of both hands on the wheel... twice, in anger and in frustration... once for each.

Having let off the steam, he shifts his truck in gear and spins around in the field next to the road.

It's not in Hope's nature to be rushed, but now seems a good time to ignore that. With her pa gone she knows it's not going to be long before the town turns towards her and, worse, shows up. She figures she has committed enough indiscretions to fill two of Pastor Cain's books, but Hope has no idea how fast the looking is taking place.

Not frantic, but focused, she gathers what she wants to take on the road. Hope comes back in from the bedroom with clothes under one arm and a metal ammo can under the other. A gravelly slide and a short high-pitched shriek of brakes come from outside. Hope knows those brakes for the ones Gabriel has been meaning to fix for ages.

Hope comes out on the porch just as Gabriel slams the truck door. He rushes towards her with a spryness Hope has rarely seen in him.

"Girl... we'ez gotta go... now!" snaps Gabriel.

Hope tries to calm him. "I know what happened to my pa and Hanna... I'm a gittin' ready to clear these parts... and don't worry, I'm gonna take my new friends." She's not sure if the last part was wise to mention.

"No... Now! Those down below done saw your friends up on the perch." While he speaks, Gabriel grabs Hope's arm and tries to pull her towards the truck.

This new revelation changes things. Gabriel's right... there is no time. Plans for her three friends... even Tom... have to take a backseat to common sense. As far as she knows, they're all a good fifteen or twenty minutes away at the perch.

She breaks free of his soft grip. "I got a couple quick things to take care of... git the truck turned." She disappears inside.

Gabriel kicks the truck over and spins it around, and then gets out, prepared to go get Hope if she's not out right quick... even if he has to carry her. Just as he takes a step towards the stairs, Hope bursts out the door, taking the time to close it behind her. Instead of the traveling backpack she had been pulling together, she has two daypacks slung over her shoulder.

"Watch out, old man ... folks is gonna think you like me."

She drops one of the daypacks on the step and tosses the other in the truck.

"Quit your blathering and git in the truck," grumbles Gabriel as he jumps in his red beauty.

"A speck longer," says Hope.

She goes back to the porch... after rummaging through a box of tools she emerges with a hatchet. Using it, she nails a large folded slip of paper to the post by the stairs. Before Gabriel gets out again, Hope runs around and jumps in the truck.

"'Bouts time!" snaps Gabriel and he stomps on the gas.

As Gabriel's truck disappears around a bend in a cloud of dust, Tom stumbles off the trail from the perch. His ankle is healed enough for hiking, but not enough for running. In truth, he's not sure he'd be wise catching it if he could... Hope doesn't own a truck.

With quick steps, Tom heads for the cabin... but before he rushes through the door, he sees the note nailed to the post.

It doesn't take that long for Rick and Lisa to catch up with Tom, considering they were running as if townsfolk were chasing them with pitchforks and torches. Their panic is clear when they enter the opening and see Tom sitting on the porch. Lisa bolts towards the cabin and it takes all of Tom's effort to hold her back.

She screams, "They saw us... where's that hillbilly girlfriend of yours?"

Now Tom knows why Hope was in such a rush... That must have been Gabriel's truck. They had talked about him a few times and, from what she told him, Gabriel seemed the kindred type who would come to Hope's defense.

Lisa is still trying to pass, but Rick can tell Tom has his reasons for stopping her... disregarding her wrath, he lends a hand. When Lisa stops squirming, Tom shoves the slip of paper in her hands. It reads, 'RUN! DON'T GO INSIDE! TRUST ME!'

It gets scrunched up and tossed to the ground. "I'm not going anywhere without my things," declares Lisa.

Tom strains to hold her back. "Think we should trust her... and stay out," he insists. He waves at the daypack Hope left out, "She left us a few things to get by with."

Lisa is steaming, "What's to trust? She ran out on us!"

While this is going on, Rick eyes the shut front door, which is rarely closed.

"What I think we should trust is that she likes to blow shit up."

Well off in the distance there's the faint honking of a horn. With the way hills play with sound, the horn could be a fair distance away, or almost upon them... problem is, for outsiders, this is hard to know.

Rick and Tom drag a reluctant Lisa towards the woods. All they have is the jackets on their backs and whatever Hope put in that small pack... and it's getting dark.

"Now ya'll settle a piece while we'ez git organized... Hain't nobody runnin' off till we do," announces Aaron over the stadium speakers.

The crowd hasn't broken up yet, but it's on the verge, and few appear to be listening to him. Everyone is either cackling about Hope and her time being over... or about the strangers and speculation on how many there are to be caught.

It's drifting towards darkness and this has to break up soon. Aaron doesn't want to launch a night hunt but, looking at the hunger of the gallery, he may not have much of a choice. After a frantic tap on his shoulder, Aaron turns to find Daniel bent over, out of breath.

"What is it?" Aaron snaps.

Daniel straightens up, still a bit winded. "The Cole brothers done already let out after Hope. I tried to stop 'em... but you know how they's can git."

Aaron had wondered why they hadn't had problems with the Coles so far. The Coles... Jeb, John and Jerry... have somewhat of a reputation of doing damn well what they please. They live a fair piece out of town, and occasionally get out of the hills to raise hell and sell shine down below.

Like Gabriel, they have a good size still, but a bloody feud settled ages ago has them selling their shine anywhere but in town proper. To honor the tradition of redemptions, Jeb had to agree to keep a muzzle on his two brothers anywhere near town. What's changed? ... They were locked in the same pool as the town when the roads were taken out.

"Daniel... you, Ethan and Jake get up to Hope's before the Coles have their own personal redemption." Daniel nods, but before he leaves, Aaron places a hand on his shoulder and adds, "Best take more than jes' Jake and his one gun."

Frustrated, Lisa takes a long stick and smashes it against trees. She stomps around the clearing, screaming and kicking at every stone safe to kick at in her rage. Tom and Rick hang well back.

When she starts to whine down, Tom braves a comment, "You want to send up flares, too?"

She throws the stick at him. "It's all her fault!"

"Doesn't matter... we're the ones on the run," Rick says, trying to refocus to getting back on the move.

Lisa plops down on a rock, her jaw locked tighter than her temperament... and feet.

Strolling over to a tree near her, Tom asks, "I wonder which we'll get to do... ride the *Funnel of Blood* or play gladiators?"

In a feeble, but saving face argument, Lisa waves a flashlight in the air. "And what did your hillbilly girlfriend give us for our great escape? ... A damn flashlight!"

The Coles rumble up to Hope's in their stake bed truck, horn honking, with no attempt at stealth. Jeb knows Hope only by reputation... he stops the truck far enough away to go on defense, if necessary. Probably a little drunk by this time of day, they are whooping and hollering, as though driving their prey instead of sneaking up on them.

The three get out, armed to the teeth. If there were a militia up here in the hills, the Coles would be it... worn camos, assault weapons and all. While Jeb, the oldest, and John head for the cabin, Jerry, the youngest, reads the ground.

He looks up, "Hey... someone let out this way right recent... and by the look of the tracks, it weren't hill folk."

"Shit, who cares 'bouts them kids... I hear'd the mayor's daughter done hoarded a whole passel o' stuff from those she fed to the town," yells back Jeb.

This whets Jerry's appetite, "Like what?"

"Money... jewelry... shit, I don't know. But I hain't goin' anywhere without searchin' that shack of her'n," answers Jeb.

"Sounds like a right fine idee," adds brother John.

They all converge on the cabin.

Clanking, rattling and puffing, Gabriel's truck rumbles down a gravel road. Hope watches the hills in her side mirror, biding time, seemingly waiting for something.

BOOM! A massive explosion goes off on the distant hill, followed by a series of secondary explosions. A plume of black smoke rises from the trees. Hope looks away from the mirror.

"That your friends?" asks Gabriel, as he glances in his mirror.

"Naw... don't think so," answers Hope. She's pretty sure... by what Gabriel told her, the kids would have gotten back to the cabin earlier. And... if they trusted her note, the timing's wrong. She does know that someone disrespecting her privacy won't do it again.

The giant black cloud looms much closer to Tom and his friends. Lisa's still well keyed up, and the explosion doesn't help. "Was that...?"

"I reckon so... as Hope would say," answers Tom.

"Damn... that was a lot of dynamite!" exclaims Rick. Being from down in the flats he has no actual experience with dynamite... any large explosion would seem to be a lot.

If anyone were most clearly affected by Hope's Pandora's box of horrors, it would be Rick. Lisa got meaner, but that was under her smile anyway. Tom was about to dive into Hope's sanity, but he's prone to crazy things.

But in Rick's case, that Type-A jock side has faded... he's more indecisive. That civil war, sparked by wanting to stay, still rages in his head.

Lisa glares at Tom, "That's a lot of dynamite that bitch of yours was willing to let us walk into," she growls.

"If you want to get out of these hills alive, you don't call her that again." Tom doesn't get hard-faced often, so it's easy to see when he does. Even Lisa knows to hold her usual come back.

Rick breaks it up, "You know that was close... we better get moving."

With a casual wave of her hand towards the smoke, Lisa says, "I don't think they're even in one piece."

"There'll be others coming soon," says Tom. He's willing to forgo the argument for the sake of getting back on the move.

Hope's being abnormally quiet as she watches the high chimney of smoke in her side mirror. Gabriel is leaving her to her peace as they rattle along.

"Stop!" Hope blurts out.

Still driving, Gabriel responds, "Girl... what kind o' teched idee you gittin' in your head?"

"Gabe... Stop the truck!" snaps Hope. "Thought I could leave 'em, but a voice is tellin' me not to. Somethin' is still to be played out."

Gabriel slams on the brakes and the truck squeaks to a gravelly halt.

"You know you're in season back there," Gabriel says as he turns to face Hope. "It's jes' part of the art, as you would say, girl. They couldn't be left standin' anyway."

Set in her mind, Hope cinches up her daypack.

"If the explosion didn't take 'em... hell, the town will have afore you can git back." Gabriel can see he's losing the argument, without Hope saying a thing. "You have a head plum' harder than rock... So, what's you gonna do with 'em if you do find 'em?"

"Hain't quite ciphered that part out yet," Hope says as she opens the truck door.

Gabriel leans over... with a slam of his hand, he opens the glove compartment. He pulls out a .38 revolver and offers it to Hope. "You might be needin' this more than me."

Smiling, Hope leans in, kisses his cheek and says, "You is gonna have folks talkin' 'bouts us... And thanks, I got my own." She pats her pack, and then gets out.

After she slams the door, the way old trucks often need, she sticks her head in, "Don't worry, old man, I'll take care."

"I'll be waitin' up near my still till tomorrow." Then Gabriel puts his hands back on the wheel and stares straightforward. He's signaling that he needs to go, before a tear he would find embarrassing shows up. She lovingly taps the truck as it drives away.

Gabriel yells out the window, "Head fer the still."

Shouldering her pack, Hope turns towards the smoke and chaos.

CHAPTER THIRTY-SIX

What little that's left of Hope's cabin is on fire when Ethan, Daniel and Jake drive up. Not knowing what to expect from the Coles, Jake rides in the bed, shotgun at the ready. The massive explosion they saw on the way up has them on edge. They jump out quickly, all armed, and flank the Coles' truck. Anyone crazy enough to blow up Hope is best to be on guard against.

Daniel moves a little closer and picks up a pair of red sneakers. He waves them in the air, "I think we jes' found the Coles."

Relieved, Jake yells, "Dang right... Jeb was plum' partial to them red sneakers."

"Best keep it down... there's three of them Coles," warns Daniel. Both take more care to glance around further.

Not appearing to be on guard, Ethan trots up. "Fresh tracks headin' out over there."

"Coles?" asks Jake, though it wouldn't make much sense.

"Hain't Coles... or Hope... it's stomped out all over," responds Ethan.

In the meantime, Daniel walks a bit further around the crater of what was Hope's cabin. Staring at a pile of rubble, he stops and calls out, "Ethan's right... got more Coles over here, or at least pieces of 'em... think it might add up to three."

They hear other trucks approaching. Apparently Aaron wasn't able to hold back the tide. Three, now four trucks show up with more people than they can hold.

Ethan grumbles, "FUBAR." He smiles. Whenever Gabriel felt things went really south, he'd grumble FUBAR. Gabriel only told him what it meant once, but it stuck... *Fucked Up Beyond All Recognition.*

It was something his pa picked up in the war. Not all spend their entire life up here... just most. Ethan looks at all the folks piling out of trucks, and repeats, "FUBAR."

One more truck arrives with Aaron in the passenger seat. He reckons that if you can't control them, best to look like you're leading. He's taking well to the idea of being the new mayor, even if it's over a town going mad. He rushes to the largest gathering of folk, "OK... We gotta git this organized."

Few pay him much attention. Most are busy yammering about this and that... ranging from how many visitors they might find, to how great Hope's cabin blew up... speculations are always more colorful than the truth of things.

Ethan walks up hoping someone with some authority would say something... the trail's getting cold. But he knows the trail isn't getting that cold considering the prey... he's impatient. All that's going on is an overabundance of yammering.

After peering back and forth between do-nothing folks, Ethan clears his throat and speaks up, "If ya'll don't mind... could I suggest... "

A few glance up and pay attention, and his neck muscles ease. "Looks like three went into the woods yonder... They's leavin' a right good trail so followin' hain't gonna be a problem... that's if we'ez don't have too many folks in the woods."

He's proud he got it all out, and glad he restrained from adding, *and ya'll would be in the way.*

"What you sayin' to do, kid?" comes from back of the group.

"I'll take four guys and... " he glances near the trucks, "...and Paul with his hounds. That's plenty enough to bag 'em."

Still trying to sound pertinent, Aaron says, "The kid's prit' near as fine as his pa with night hunting."

Everyone that's come with an appetite reluctantly nods his or her agreement to the logic. Ethan puffs up. Probably the most he's said, all at one time, to a crowd larger than two in ages.

A few minutes later, his hunting party organized, Ethan heads into the woods. Night has arrived. Beams from flash-lights and glows from lanterns flicker away as the small group delves deeper into the trees. All that's left is the echo of hounds baying.

The remaining townsfolk are antsy, having been left out of the hunter's pack. After about ten minutes on simmer, the group is pretty worked up. So much for logic... one, then two, and then all grab flashlights and lanterns. Some folk jerry-rig torches out of the smoldering remains of Hope's cabin.

Not to be left out of the game, all head into the woods... yammering, armed and dangerous... to everyone.

The kids have stumbled into a densely wooded area, with nothing that resembles a trail. Tom has been trying to keep a direction by the stars, but with his limited view of the sky he may be leading them in a wide circle. Flashlights lead their way, though they're unaware of that way. The focused white beam of their flashlights makes the moonlit night around them pitch black.

In the hard light and shadows, Tom catches his foot on a downed limb. He's OK, but his healing ankle is showing its wear. The single crutch he brought along is awkward to use in this denser brush, so he asks for yet another break.

Rick, and especially Lisa, reluctantly agree to take a breather. Because of Tom's ankle, Rick has pack duty. He pulls out the canteen Hope packed for them and tosses it to Tom.

Looking a little hurt over not being offered it first, Lisa shakes it off... she has bigger fish to fry. She pulls Rick off to the side and quietly says, "He's holding us up... I know you were friends, but this is our lives at stake."

Rick says nothing, so she inches forward, "You and I could move twice as fast on our own... We were planning to split off anyway." She leans in, hoping she is swaying him.

"No," says Rick, and he gets up and walks away. Lisa's bubble pops.

Maybe Rick knows they're fighting against a lost cause since he can hear the bays of hound dogs in the distance... getting closer by the minute. They all can hear them.

Hope also hears the dogs baying... she can tell they're a good holler off, and they're moving away... Hope suspects too far off for her to do much good. To get a better perspective, she climbs a tall tree. She's made for the hills.

On the upper shelf of the forest, it's a crystal clear night. The moon plays up here like a blanket, while down below it's more like shadowy ghosts.

From her new perch, Hope can spy the distant hillside. Beams of flashlights break the canopy now and then. It amazes her how far the beams carry in the night air. Hope's attention shifts to a patch of woods where many more beams escape the canopy... way too many if they were using them with a speck of common sense.

Hope's unaware that this is the town's mob following the true hunters... who are busy following the prey. But it's not far from her imagination.

The baying of the hound dogs grows... first in volume and then in frenzy. And Hope knows it's over.

CHAPTER THIRTY-SEVEN

Rick and Lisa lie curled up on one metal bunk... Tom lies on the other. No one is really asleep.

It's been a long night of speculating until they are all guessed out. They're now quiet. None of the three are much the worse for wear, considering having been captured in the woods. Townsfolk have made a point of keeping them in fairly good shape so they can put on a good show in the arena.

No one tries to test the doors... their fists are sore from trying throughout the long night. All the fight in them is worn out... now there's only waiting for what comes next.

Speakers break the silence with a feedback screech. It's not that loud, but enough to startle all three. Rick and Tom stare at the doors, Lisa stares at the offending speakers.

It screeches again and then Aaron's voice comes over them, "Mornin', ya'll... You done wanted to see our arena, and now you's gonna git a right close look-see."

Lisa screams at the speakers, "What do you want from us! Anything... just let us go!" She doesn't realize how often those words have been yelled at those speakers.

"You do git right het up, don't ya, missy? What we want of ya'll is to be entertainin'," responds the speaker.

She pulls off a shoe and throws it at the box on the wall. At the same time Rick goes and kicks the metal door. Neither of which will do any good other than to release steam. Tom remains sitting on his metal bunk and lets out a laugh. He knows

Hope would find something artsy about it all... and despite their predicament, he can't help being glad she got away.

At the moment, Lisa is not sure whom she hates the most... the voice behind the mic, the hillbilly slut who introduced them to her dark side, or Tom, whom she blames for their staying. She's quick to forget her complicity in it all.

"We do have a speck of a problem," continues the faceless raspy voice.

"Who the hell cares?" yells Lisa.

Paying little attention, Aaron continues, "We need to be spreadin' things out a piece... and that's where ya'll come in."

Not addressing the speaker, Tom quietly says, "And you want us to choose."

"Yer boy there wins the blue ribbon... We do rightly want ya'll to decide who comes to see us first," is the response.

One of Tom's eyes catches Lisa as both of hers glare at him. He snaps his head towards her... she looks away just as quickly.

"Afore my boys show up with the big guns, ya'll have to make a choice."

"And what if we don't?" yells Rick.

A blast of flames erupts from a segment of the grated floor. It's far enough away not to harm but close enough to get the point across.

"If ya'll don't choose, we will... and the two left over will be downright uncomfortable waitin' yer turn."

The whole process of making them choose wasn't Aaron's idea. It came from the sadistic side of Pastor Cain. Aaron walks on eggshells as it is, trying to fill Marcus' shoes, and isn't about to challenge the Pastor... not for now.

The three look all about the room... grating is under everything. There's no place to retreat or take a stand.

"Ya'll gots an hour to be makin' up your minds."

There's an audible click off of the mic and the speakers are silent. The three stare at them for a few seconds, but hear no more.

This is different for Hope... she's more used to being very visible when she visits town. Often it's simply for the fun of rubbing salt in old wounds, but this morning she stays in the shadows and moves with caution.

Townsfolk are out and heading towards the arena, making her progress slow. She suspects the kids are being held in the arena cell but, from what Gabriel has told her, it might have been changed to the B&B where they held her pa. One thing she knows... with the townsfolk gathering, she's racing against the clock.

Psychological warfare is not limited to the outer world. In the stone cellblock, it comes in the form of hillbilly Muzak playing over raspy speakers. Besides the irritating hill music, it allows for private conversations in the small space. Aaron knows this.

Taking advantage of the cover noise, Lisa gets busy and pulls Rick off to the side of the room to lobby for her choice.

Rick has heard most of it before, but now they're in a different pickle and he's more willing to hear her out. He's caught between a rock and a hard place... between a waning friendship and what is now a borderline relationship.

Rick's fascination and revulsion over what they have chosen to witness has him wondering if he wants to keep contact with either Tom or Lisa if they were to get out. At the moment, it seems academic.

Lisa's scheming has not escaped Tom's awareness. There's not much he feels like doing about it... but he's not about to volunteer either.

Beaten down by her persistence, Rick reluctantly agrees with Lisa's campaign to have Tom take the lead. She's aware it's a fragile agreement. In spite of her objections, Rick goes to tell Tom the bad news.

Tom's calculated his odds of being voted in. As Rick approaches, Tom speaks first, "So, am I to be fed to them?"

Standing in front of his friend, Rick can't make it a demand. "No, it has to be voluntary... or we fight."

Tom glances at Lisa, suspecting she's not in on this decision. Then both he and Rick start surveying the sparse room for anything that might be usable as defense. Lisa realizes her plans have been abandoned. She joins them reluctantly, giving Rick a nasty glare and avoiding eye contact with Tom.

It doesn't matter because the guys are focused on their search for weapons. They check for any loose pipes attached to the wall, but nothing budges. Slowly walking the room, Tom peers down at the grated floor. At one point he stops.

"Rick, help me get this floor panel up."

Between the two of them they manage to lift the one panel. The flame jets below appear solidly built in, but Tom grins as he reaches down under one row and pulls out a loose steel pipe. It was probably left there during some maintenance.

He slaps the end of the pipe in his hand, testing its heft and hardness. Resigned to the boys' new tack, Lisa joins Rick in looking through other grates for additional loose pipes... no luck. At least they have one weapon... a three foot piece of pipe against shotguns.

Now they wait.

"You guys are tougher... I should wield the pipe," suggests Lisa.

Rick looks to Tom, who nods his OK. Considering she lost her battle to sacrifice him and has rejoined the team, it's a small concession. Neither of them figure they have much of a chance... just the idea of going down fighting is the appeal. With a smile, Rick hands the pipe to Lisa.

Just in time... there's the harsh sound of a bolt being un-latched outside the door. The three kids take a defensive stance. Holding the pipe like a baseball bat, Lisa appears to be up to the task.

The door squeaks open. First to enter are the barrels of two shotguns, followed by their handlers, Jake and Daniel. Aaron is behind them.

WHACK! Lisa hits Rick in the back of the head with her pipe and he crumples to the floor, unconscious. Pointing at Tom, she quickly blurts out, "He's your first volunteer!"

CHAPTER THIRTY-EIGHT

Slipping from one shadowed alcove to the next, Hope makes her way towards Gabriel's workshop. She suspects most folk are in the arena by now, but remains on the cautious side. She hears the announcing system in the arena but can't make out what's being said from outside.

Hope pulls a handgun from her pack and slips it into her waistband near the crook of her back. Then she stashes her pack between a couple of trashcans in the alley.

Arriving at Gabriel's door, she finds the padlocks are unlatched. Seeing this, she picks up a metal pipe leaning against the barn wall and cautiously tries the door. Much to her surprise, the interior locks are also undone. Hope slips in as quietly as possible.

Lisa's happy the pipe she laid to Rick's head didn't do more than knock him out... Rick's not happy at all. But he has too much of a headache to say much about it right now.

It's only been about a half hour since Tom was taken. They can hear applause and loud activity from the arena, but are not sure where Tom is in the redemption process.

Lisa is smart enough to keep her mouth shut, even if she finds nothing wrong with what she did. In her head, Rick was too weak to do what was necessary. They both sit quietly, listening.

The sudden unlatching of the door's bolt startles them... it's too soon. Though still dizzy, Rick gets up and moves to right beside the door, intent on giving fighting a second chance. Unfortunately their only weapon, the pipe, was taken.

When Lisa starts to join him, he waves her to stay seated. She's not sure if it's to distract whomever comes through the door... or he simply doesn't trust her by his side.

As the door creeps open, Rick is poised to attack. He's hoping that the barrel of a long gun comes through first, as before, so he can wrestle it away.

Instead of a shotgun, Hope's voice comes from the opening, "Tom?"

Rick backs away, allowing Hope to come in carefully.

"Thank God... you've come to save us," blurts Lisa.

Hope doesn't pay any attention to her... she scans the cell looking for Tom. Not seeing him tells her part of the story.

She asks, "Where's Tom?"

Not meaning to, Rick gives Lisa a quick, guilty glance... enough to tell Hope a little more of the story. A sudden loud mixture of applause and blood-hungry cheers tell her the end of the story.

Defensively, Lisa is quick to say, "Don't look at us that way... someone had to go first."

"And you pointed the finger," Hope states.

With no comeback, Lisa's eyes drift to the floor.

Tom is dead... or dying. The motivation for rescue drains from Hope. She steps backwards towards the door.

"I'm sorry about Tom... he did say you promised to get us out of these hills," says Rick.

Something about the way he says this tells Hope he wouldn't blame her if she walks away. This is the only reason she doesn't.

Lisa is Lisa, and only a fool would expect her to be something else. Rick has been conflicted ever since the first redemption. But he's right; she promised Tom she'd get his friends out of town. She doesn't owe them a thing, but she owes Tom... if it's not too much trouble.

With little enthusiasm, Hope finally says, "If we'ez gonna git... then let's git." She turns and walks out.

The first to rush the door is Lisa, but Rick grabs her arm, "Bring in your claws... now's not the time to piss her off."

She jerks her arm away, but realizes he's probably right.

As they come out of the room and into the hall leading to Gabriel's shop, Hope is waiting. Daniel lies on the floor with a nasty cut on his forehead. The pipe Hope took from the alley rests beside him. The two kids glance at the body and cut a wide berth around Hope.

She leans down and pats the unconscious Daniel on the head. "Danny... plum' sorry 'bouts the headache you's gonna have." Then she follows the kids.

Hope comes out of the hall to find Rick and Lisa frozen in their tracks. Ethan sits on a stool at Gabriel's workbench with a shotgun leveled at the kids. When he sees Hope, he gives her a smile and asks, "Got any idee where Gabriel might be?"

Without appearing concerned, Hope returns his smile. "My pa was his best friend... right sure he's out tying one on."

"You's probably right... or he's done let outta these parts fer good," says Ethan. He's more aware of Gabriel's feelings than he lets on.

With Ethan's shotgun aimed at the two kids, Hope fingers the automatic nestled in the back of her belt. She doesn't pull it... it's a last resort move and she has no desire to hurt him.

Lisa starts to say something... cutting her off, Hope snaps, "Shut up!"

Her demand for silence is reinforced by Rick stealthily grabbing and squeezing Lisa's wrist.

Stepping away from the line of fire, Hope says, "Ethan... it be your move."

He thinks on it a second and then lowers the shotgun's barrel, just slightly.

"Gabriel's always been right fond of you... even when he tried to hide it." He pauses a few seconds more, making up his mind.

Hope keeps her hand behind her, ready to do what's needed.

Finally, Ethan says, "You got two hours."

She eases her hand off the pistol, grateful not to have to use it. "And my friends?" she asks.

He glances back and forth between the two strangers... then, "Take 'em with you... they'll jes' slow you down. And, Hope, my favor to Gabriel has now done been paid... don't expect anything when we next meet."

"Don't fret... two hours is a fair lead. Reckon we won't be seein' each other again," Hope says with a grin and a wink, pushing Rick and Lisa forward before he changes his mind.

As the three head for the exit, Ethan calls out, "Hell... the hunt's prit' near most of the fun."

Leading the kids through the woods, Hope is a relentless taskmaster... Rick and Lisa struggle to keep up. At first, when not told to shut up, Lisa has been grateful for being rescued, but now she complains over the pace. Hope doesn't let up. She figures getting herself out of the hills would be a piece of cake... she's not as sure about her company.

Driving them is the distant sound of barking dogs.

They come over a ridge leading down into a large gully. About ten years back in heavy rains, a landslide, without Hope's assistance, toppled dozens of mature trees. Many bridge the ravine. They lie crisscrossing each other in all directions, like a pile of pick up sticks.

As Hope comes to one of the fallen trees, she sets down her pack and pulls a large tin of black pepper out. She opens it and spreads it about.

Rick and Lisa see it as an opportunity to take a break.

"What's that for?" asks Rick.

It's a question anyone from the hills would know the answer to and Hope ignores him, staying to her task.

"He asked you what that was for," says Lisa, in a tone no longer filled with gratitude.

"Got my reasons," is Hope's short answer, her mind on the hunt, not trivial questions. When she's finished, Hope re-slings her pack and starts climbing one of the downed tree trunks resting at about a thirty-degree angle. It's like walking a wide uphill tightrope. There are more level, less precarious logs that Hope chooses to pass by.

Lisa stops at the foot of the log Hope's on, "I'm not climbing this one... it's too steep."

Hope pauses halfway up and partially turns. She points off to the south, "OK... then run that way."

"Where will that take us?" asks Lisa.

"Beats me... but it'll git the dogs off my trail," Hope replies and continues to climb.

Rick shakes his head and urges Lisa onto the log. Their fate is in Hope's hands and he wishes Lisa would stop poking her.

About two-thirds of the way up, Hope transfers to another downed tree trunk that crosses over the first. Thus begins a zigzag procession of jumping from log to log down the ravine. Rick and Lisa do their best to keep up.

The kids are surprised that the last log Hope traverses in this maze ends on the same side of the ravine they started on, about a hundred yards down the canyon. The logic escapes Lisa, but Rick finds it very clever.

The baying dogs keep them moving.

Paul and his two hounds lead the hunting party. Ethan, Jake and a head-bandaged Daniel follow close behind. Ethan made a good guess to where Hope would go to trail... between being able to truck there and having the dogs, they've closed the gap substantially.

The dogs bound over the ridge leading down to the ravine of logs. When they get close, the dogs go into frenzy... shaking their heads and scratching frantically at their noses. Their baying is replaced by whimpering as they roll around on the ground. The pepper has, at least for the moment, neutralized them.

Paul runs to his hounds, more upset by their predicament than losing Hope's scent. He screams out, "God damn, girl... look what you did to my dogs!"

Atop the ridge, Ethan looks down at the canine chaos and says, "Well played, Hope."

Trying to calm his dogs, Paul yells again, "Damn you!" It echoes through the hills.

A good half hour ahead of the hunting party, and knowing the dogs have lost the trail, Hope laughs at the echoes. She knows the hounds will be fine after a while... redeemings are one thing, harming dogs is something entirely different.

She glances at the two kids and knows they are beat from having to keep up with her, so she offers a break.

Winded, Rick sits down next to a tree, "Nice little trick back there," he says.

"I got a few hidden out here and there... jes' in case," says Hope, with a grin.

"In case of what?" asks Lisa.

Both Rick and Hope shake their heads at such a dumb question, considering the circumstances.

"OK... I was just asking," says Lisa, with a pout.

"Maybe it's better if you jes' be quiet... fer a good long piece," warns Hope. "Ya'll best to rest up... we've got a ways to go." She tosses a water bottle to Rick.

Rick asks, "Won't they pick up our trail again?"

Hope doesn't seem concerned. "I suspect it's Ethan back there. He does rightly know these hills... but I know 'em a speck better."

"Are we anywhere close to getting clear?" he asks. His tone is more relaxed... just conversation during a break.

The casualness of Rick and Hope's conversing irritates Lisa... plus, she can't stand being marginalized by being ignored.

"Those nuts back there... your townsfolk... are the ones that truly need redeeming."

"Let's jes' worry 'bouts gittin' clear of 'em afore you git all fired up righteous," Hope tells her, tiring of Lisa's snippety ways.

"They killed Tom," Lisa snaps.

"And you done the pointin'... Anyway, it's merely brush strokes," Hope says. If she plans to mourn Tom, it won't be in front of Lisa.

Lisa doesn't understand the concept of backing off. "Screw your brush strokes... We should have left the day we met you."

"Now's not the time," warns Rick, though he knows Lisa can't help poking the bear... regardless of how stupid it is to do so.

Hope closes her eyes and leans back against the tree. It's clear she has no interest in continuing this prattle. She says, "Ya'll best rest up... we'll be movin' soon."

CHAPTER THIRTY-NINE

The three move more casually now that Hope's not driving them so hard... also, perhaps because they're all worn out from hours of hiking uneven terrain. Even Hope can get tired. Now they traverse easier ground.

The ease at which they travel gives Rick a sense of relief, or worry, he's not sure which. Trying not to signal one or the other, he asks, "After our last break seems we changed directions from east to north, didn't we?"

"You got yourself a right fine nose fer direction," answers Hope. To rest his mind, she adds, "These hills are always fluid... jes' like my art. And neither runs in a straight line."

He'll have to have to be satisfied with this as an explanation for now. But as they hike along, he tries to get a sense of direction to carry on if Hope disappears... something that may be necessary in the long run. Lisa tags along, trying to keep her mouth shut... a harder task than the trail presents.

They break out of the woods near Gabriel's still. Lisa's the first to react, in her typical tone of mistrust, "And what's that run down shack supposed to be?"

"Careful... that shack belongs to the best dang moonshiner in these hills... Gabriel Barnes."

"You mean the guy who created those horrible games?" Lisa says with self-righteous arrogance.

Hope spins to her, "That you found right entertaining."

Rick nudges Lisa to back off yet again.

Easing her look back to a smile, Hope adds, "It's also the shack with supplies fer gittin' out of these hills." Continuing on into the clearing, she says "Before we move on, let's rest our heels a piece."

Rick pauses and scans the woods surrounding the clearing. "What about the guys chasing us?"

"I suspect we got four, maybe five, out lookin' fer us... and they hain't on our trail... fer now." Hope is pretty sure it's a lot more, but no use getting her companions more on edge than they are.

They'll keep up the pace she sets, so she's the only one that needs to know the true threat. Further attempting to ease them, Hope steps over to a wooden bench and sets her pack down. Taking a seat, she pulls a baggie out.

Both Rick and Lisa look at her like... *doesn't she know we're on the run?* The glares don't faze Hope. She takes a joint from the baggie and lights it. After taking a drag, she offers it to them.

At first, both hesitate. Rick's the first to break. He takes the joint and sits down on a facing log. Sour-faced, Lisa shakes her head and plops down near Rick. Having gotten them settled, Hope gets up.

"Relax a piece... I'm gonna grab a poke of supplies from the cabin." Cabin is a term that over-honors Gabriel's shack.

An ever-mistrusting Lisa pops up, "I'll give you a hand."

"Sorry, darlin'... Gabe is a right private fella." Without wanting any more argument, Hope heads for the shack.

Still pushing, Lisa asks, "Are there guns in there?"

Hope stops and turns. After scrutinizing her for a couple seconds, "Gabe's only got one, and that's prit' near always with him." To settle it, she adds, "If ya'll would be set at ease, there's one in my pack there." Not interested in any more discussion, she climbs the stairs and vanishes inside.

Lisa scopes the pack... while Rick scopes her. He says, "We don't need a gun."

Reaching for the pack, Lisa gives a nod back at the shack, "You sure?" It's not meant as a real question since she proceeds to open the top flap.

As she pulls out the automatic, Rick is quick to take hold of the barrel. "You ever fire one... I have. I think I should hold onto it."

He doesn't have much experience with them either, but Lisa is a little too volatile for him to be comfortable with her having a weapon... he also remembers Tom.

At first she tightens her grip on the pistol... then she relents, "As long as she doesn't have it."

Rick pulls the slide to be sure the pistol's loaded and slips it in his belt, making sure to drape it with his shirt.

She takes a seat on the log, scooting in like a comic spy, and lowers her voice, "We can't trust her."

"She's weird... but she's also our best bet of getting clear of these hills." In a tone attempting to reassure her, he adds, "If she wanted to hurt us, she would have left us there."

Continuing in her lower voice, "She's crazy, you know it... They're all crazy." She drops the volume to a whisper, "And I'm going to make sure people know."

"About what... our being a willing audience to killings... a bunch of killings?" Rick quietly returns.

Hope takes a jute bag of coffee beans from a rickety wall shelf. Into a smaller cloth bag, she transfers one handful of beans and reaches for another, while watching out a window. Window is a generous term... it's more like a few planks missing in a square shape, looking out towards the kids. From the opposite direction, the shadows leave her less seen. She smiles and returns the second handful to its bag. Hope's not sure of Gabriel's plans... wouldn't want to help herself to too much.

The small porch creaks when Hope comes out. Rick and Lisa snap up straight, wearing a bit of guilt.

Hope is carrying a gunnysack for the road. Hanging on her shoulder is a wine bladder of shine... on a fine summer night, warmer than a sleeping bag. As she comes up to them, she sees the open flap on her pack. She casually closes it.

Despite his urging to trust Hope, Rick's right hand unconsciously slides closer to the pistol, now resting in his belt. When he realizes it, he pulls his hand away.

Hope is not unaware of the instinctual movement, but it doesn't concern her. She unslings her shine bladder and hands it to Rick.

"Ya'll take a right good swig each... then we're gonna hit the trail."

She drops the gunnysack. "One of ya'll needs to hump that." For the moment, it seems their fates are intertwined.

"How far do we have to go before we're safe?" asks Rick as he stands, signaling he's ready.

Lisa joins him, with less perk in her movement. She's slightly more at ease, seeing Hope didn't come out of the shack with a weapon... at least, not one she can see.

"Wait here a second," says Hope and walks to the edge of the woods. She looks around. Seeing what she's after, Hope picks up a bushy, broken tree branch. Satisfied, she comes back to them.

"Ya'll go up there and wait off the trail, by that big rock." Hope points at a large granite boulder protruding from the ground about thirty feet away. "I'll brush out our tracks."

Rick turns to do so, but Lisa still watches Hope. He has to tug on her arm to get her to move. The two walk up the trail to wait where Hope said.

After a prolonged swig of shine, Hope starts brushing out their tracks around the bench and log, working her way backwards towards the kids... all along, erasing their existence, dust kicks up.

Lisa watches her like a hawk. Quietly, she says, "Between the weed and liquor, I'm surprised she knows where the path is."

Rick nudges her, "We're not out of the woods yet."

As she sweeps the ground, Hope speaks up so the kids can hear her. "Girl, you hain't quite got that whisperin' thing down right well."

Lisa starts, "I... "

Rick cuts her off, "That's just Lisa being Lisa." All that concerns him is an end to their constantly going at each other... there's an escape to get done.

Hope continues brushing, speaking in the other direction. "A piece back, you was askin' how the redemptions grew from their humble beginnin's."

"That's not important now," says Rick, still trying to keep the focus on getting away. Lisa, on the other hand, nods towards the gun in his belt. He shakes his head no.

"It's important to me... it's my finest piece of art... so far," Hope declares in a definitive tone.

"Your piece of art... you keep going on about your damn piece of art... just watching people kill each other," snarls Lisa, against Rick's tightening grip.

Not sounding upset, Hope responds, "Sometimes art is the absurd fringe of life... and you gotta admit, we are on the fringe. And you done become part of it." She has yet to turn around, as her path clearing nears them.

"You have an interesting way of seeing it all." There's a patronizing sound to Rick's words, as though he's trying to talk someone from the edge of a precipice.

Lisa's body language reeks of fear. She reaches for the pistol at Rick's waist. He pushes her hand away again, but keeps his near the handle, still unsure of where this is going.

Hope finishes her clearing task and abruptly spins. "Not jes' seein' it... but orchestratin' it. It's plum' amazing how a whisper in the right few ears, at jes' the right times, can git the ball rollin' this way or that."

"You mean... you started all this killing?" asks Rick, a touch caught up in it now. At the same time, almost without being aware of it, his hand has gone to grasping the pistol's grip. Seeing this, Lisa hopes he'll pull the weapon.

"Naw... I done told ya'll, they's been goin' on fer ages... I jes' elevated it all." There's a coldness now slipping over Hope. "It were right easy to grow their appetites... luring folks up here fer skiing or backpacking... feedin' them to the town at a right pace... and then cuttin' back to play with their hunger."

She goes on like they're not actually there. "And then when the piece got growin' pains, it was time fer another brush stroke."

Without Lisa's urging, Rick softly pulls the pistol... but leaves it hanging at his side. "So you did take out the road?"

As though there would be no other answer, Hope says, "Of course... everythin' has its time."

Hope's eyes are now that of a hunter... and Rick sees it. He raises the pistol and holds it in two shaking hands. He cocks the hammer. The move doesn't startle Hope. She smiles and, with a gesture of surrender, tosses away the limb she used for brushing the path.

It hits a trip wire that releases a spiked log floating in the trees. The stretching weight on the rope creaks as the log swings in a graceful arc towards their backs.

Without glancing back, Rick knows. In panic, he jerks the trigger. The hammer falls just as the spikes impale him and Lisa with a dull, moist thud. The swing of the log lifts them off their feet... The pistol, unfired, topples to the ground.

Hope steps back to let the log eventually settle. She walks up and, with a look of curiosity, peers at both their faces. Their eyes are filled with confusion... no one's actually prepared to die.

Answering their query, "And... now is your time."

She backs away a few inches, flippantly adding, "And that's jes' me bein' me. You jes' didn't git it... you don't fuck with per-formance art... 'specially not mine."

Rick and Lisa's eyes fade... their bodies go limp.

CHAPTER FORTY

Minutes pass as Hope stands there staring at the bodies of Rick and Lisa. With their heads drooped, she no longer can see their eyes. It's the first time she's killed someone... by her own hands. She's calm.

Gabriel clears his throat as he comes out of the woods, back near the shack. "I take it neither of 'em are the one you had a hankerin' fer."

Hope breaks from her fascination with the bodies and turns with an angelic smile. "Naw... he was the last brush stroke in the arena... fer me." Casually she reaches down and picks up the fallen pistol.

"Don't seem right... almost fittin' your pa be the last to see the official pit... I mean, afore the craziness in town plays out... fer certain there'll be more blood."

Hope laughs, "Might be it plays down to the last two... but that's someone else's show." She pats his shoulder as she passes, "What's you still doin' here, old man?"

Hope continues on down the path.

Following along, Gabriel says. "Done told you I'd be stickin' around a day to git you outta trouble."

They both take a seat, one on the log, the other on the bench facing.

Hope puts the gun back in her pack. "I rightly appreciate it... but you know me, I'm right good at it... cause I git a right fair bit of practice."

Gabriel waves his hand towards the hanging kids. "Yeah, I can see... I was too far off to git a shot with my twelve... not without catchin' you." He chuckles, "You didn't look to be frettin' it."

She pulls a small length of steel from her pocket and holds it up.

He smiles, "Ah... firing pin." Gabriel pulls a jug out of his knapsack.

"Everything's a brush... it can be used in right different ways... if you can read folk, and sense what they might do next," she says.

She knows Gabriel's obliging when it comes to her art terms, but they say a lot of the same things, just with different words.

Gabriel perks up, "Since we'ez both here, might as well share a nip with a friend to toast our gittin' out... the dogs must still be a far holler off."

"They's got sidetracked... and, I'd be plum' delighted to share a drop." She reaches out and accepts the jug. Holding it up, she says, "A last drop before we part ways."

"Girl, I hung out here to git you out with me... at least, clear of these parts." Concern is uncomfortable for Gabriel to show... he's doing his best.

She understands, but she sees it's not a time to be wasted on arguments.

"Gabe... where you off to?" she asks.

Gabriel already knows he's lost the argument, but he doesn't let on. "I thought long and hard last night... and done come up with the derndess idee."

Hope leans in.

"I got the skills to make my contraptions... I reckon they's the same skills they use in makin' them horror movies... so, I think I'm bound fer Hollywood," he says with a big grin.

This absurdity makes perfect sense to Hope. She slaps him on the knee. "Sounds like a prime idee to me."

"You could always tag along... you got a right dark imagination," says Gabriel, not expecting much to change.

"I got a few brush strokes to still git done. And it's all settin' the way I planned. They're lookin' fer me... and those two over there... "

"All the more reason... " Gabriel tries to interject.

"That truck of your'n gits maybe fifty on a fine road... you're gonna be goin' over the old fire road. They know I'm not drivin' so they'll drop the search up that way... if they have a trail to be followin'. Right now they think you's out tyin' one on over my pa... if someone came across you, I'm sure you could talk your way out, but... with me in the truck... " Hope's look finishes that sentence.

Gabriel takes a swig from the jug, sets it down and slides it with his foot towards Hope. He can tell she's got the story in her head, whatever she calls it, and suspects she has a final stroke... it eludes him what that is, except that she's set in her path.

"I'll tell you what it is." She sees that her uncanny sense of reading his mind sets him back. She grins, "The male folk in town hain't gonna admit not bein' able to catch a girl... unless some superstitious crap gits thrown in."

Gabriel's face says he gets the point, but not the particulars.

"I'll become some kind of a legend... reported sightin's will pop up long past when I should die... the old witch, livin' in the hills... and the likes."

Hope says this as if it's a done deal. And she's probably right... these hills are filled with bizarre, superstitious stories that last generations.

She digs in her pack and pulls out a larger plastic bag of weed and tosses it to him. "That's to keep you relaxed... I hear'd those Holly-weird types are a might wound up."

She sees Gabriel is still struggling with it, so she puts a hand on his knee and reassures him, "Let's play it my way... who knows, might jes' show up on your porch after you git right famous out thar."

Goodbyes are lousy for many. Gabriel pulls another small jug from his sack and places it next to Hope. Standing there, he makes the Indian sign for fair trade with a swipe of his hand... and he leans down and kisses her forehead.

Blushing, he says, "You take care... and I'll be waitin' fer that visit."

With nothing more to be said, he grabs his stuff and heads into the woods in the direction of his stashed truck.

Hope wipes a tear from her eye... and then perks up. She has one last scene to play out.

It's become late afternoon and the shadows are long.

Hope rests near a waterfall's segment, as it deflects the falling stream from above and cascades further down into the deep ravine far below. It's one of her favorite spots. This is not part of the plan she chose to reveal to Gabriel... and even she's not sure it will work out in her favor.

There's a distant baying of the hounds that have reacquired her trail from Gabriel's still. They're getting closer.

Hope yawns at the warmth of the remaining sun. Then she sees the hunting party trickle out of the tree line... more than she expected, the fever must be growing. The tree line is a good meadow away, so she has time. She can see Ethan in the lead. He's a good kid, she thinks.

As they get about halfway across the meadow, Hope moves over near a ledge. She cinches down an extra piece of rope on her small backpack.

Now that her hunters are in the range of seeing her face, she gives them her best theatrical smile, since words would be a waste... and she bows. Having said all, Hope McCoy spins and jumps from the ledge into the winding river far below.

After Paul's dogs, Ethan is the first to reach the ledge. He leans over and sees nothing but a river's pool. Ethan's fished that pool over the years... he smiles.

The group catches up with him. They all have to have their gander over the edge.

Since Ethan was leading the hunting party before more from the town joined in, he says, "Looks like she most likely done drowned and floated on down the river."

"Damn... that's all three of 'em now," says one of the men.

Jake, who rarely says anything, speaks up, "She sure did go out her own way."

This is the first seed of a legend.

Not to let the official word come from a gofer, Pastor Cain cautiously peeks over the side and says, "That's a right long way down... prit' near sure she done drowned."

A hollow feeling is shared by most, not for Hope, but from having come on a hunt, only to lose their prey... times three.

Amid the grumbling of the small gathering, another man speaks up, "We'ez still got that tellin' box plum' full of sinners, don't we."

Pastor Cain is determined to hold the lead. He booms as if from the pulpit, "You have a right good point, brother. Let us head back to town and take another tally."

EPILOGUE

The sun has set, but there's plenty of moonlight in the open canyon. Hope pulls herself out of the river, well worn, but intact. She's dealt with the river before and gave herself fair odds of living. Her daypack even survived.

Canyons and small towns run through the hills like small capillaries, and the river runs free amongst them, crossing boundaries as it chooses. It doesn't take that much to get out of the shadow of Redemption... especially when she chooses the course.

Once most of the water has dripped away, Hope rummages through her handy sack and pulls out yet another large baggie. She opens it and extracts a sundress. She slaps it up in the breeze a couple times to shake out the wrinkles.

A half hour later, Hope comes over a ridge of the hill that looms over the river below. Carved into the hillside, she finds a two-lane country road.

Hope stands and brushes off the dirt from the climb. She's wearing the sundress and hiking boots. As she pats her pocket, she gets a nice surprise... a forgotten joint. She lights it up and, with a glint in her eye, starts walking down the road.

As Hope rounds a bend, she smiles at a sign in the distance... *'ATONEMENT – 15 MILES'*... and she knows there's a whole wide world out there... and maybe another painting.

THE END